T H E
WRATH
O F   A
SHIPLESS PIRATE

THE GODLANDERS WAR
BOOK TWO

By Aaron Pogue

The Godlanders War
The Dreams of a Dying God
The Wrath of a Shipless Pirate
The Crown of a Common King

The Dragonprince's Legacy
Taming Fire
The Dragonswarm
The Dragonprince's Heir
"Remnant" (short story)
"From Embers" (short story)

The Dragonprince's Arrows
A Darkness in the East

Ghost Targets
Surveillance
Expectation
Restraint
Camouflage

THE
WRATH
OF A
SHIPLESS PIRATE

THE GODLANDERS WAR
BOOK TWO

AARON POGUE

47NORTH

Text copyright © 2014 Aaron Pogue
All rights reserved.

Published by 47North, Seattle

www.apub.com

Amazon, the Amazon logo, and 47North are trademarks of Amazon.com, Inc., or its affiliates.

ISBN-13: 9781612184531
ISBN-10: 1612184537

Cover design by Kerrie Roberston
Illustrated by Chris McGrath

Library of Congress Control Number: 2013947617

Printed in the United States of America

THE
WRATH
OF A
SHIPLESS PIRATE

THE GODLANDERS WAR
BOOK TWO

The bustling city of Khera crowded close to the mighty river Nel, but even at the docks the air sweltered with the vicious heat that rolled forever in from the Endless Desert. The locals didn't seem to mind. In the marketplace, on the streets, or even bustling up and down the gangplanks loading goods for sale in the Godlands, they dressed in long white robes and wrapped their heads in turbans.

The foreigner stood out like a beacon among them. His sun-darkened skin might have matched theirs for tone, but he wore only loose pantaloons and cheap thong sandals. His bare chest prickled with sweat despite the dry air, and his ragged hair clung wetly to his forehead. He fanned himself ineffectually and repositioned his chair every hour or so to steal what little shade the wine shop's awning offered.

He drank without ceasing and cursed almost as often, but he never left his post. For days at least, he held this place, staring out across all the docks, and watched the comings and goings of every passenger, sailor, or slave to board a ship. The man was clearly waiting for someone.

And then, between one heartbeat and the next, someone stepped out of the shadows behind him. This newcomer was a foreigner as well, a Godlander by the looks of him, but this one seemed unaffected by the heat. He was dressed in black from top to toe and wore a long, cowled cloak of the same color. He held a sword of blue steel with a golden grip in his right hand and an ancient book with cracking leather in his left. He leaned down beside the watcher's ear and grinned.

"Looking for me?"

"Gods' blood!" the watcher screamed, diving to the earth in fear before he tried to scramble off. The newcomer stopped him with a boot planted firmly on the back of his scrabbling knee. The man on the ground yelped, then fell still, panting.

"In truth," the other said, still grinning, "I did not expect such a strong reaction."

"Corin Hugh! You're dead!"

"You threaten me? I've seen the way you fight, Charlie Claire. I suspect you have that backwards."

"No! No. It's not a threat. But … but I was there. Blake fed you to the fires. He closed the cavern's mouth with the cannons. How could you have escaped?"

"Consider me a ghost, come back for revenge."

The prisoner wept against the packed-earth street. Passers-by were watching now, but the man in black dismissed them with a cutting glare and a meaningful gesture with the beautiful blade.

When they'd turned away, Corin fell into a crouch beside his former crewmate. He turned the blade back and forth across his knees, considering how the sunlight played along its edge, and spoke with feigned disinterest. "We have business to attend to. Every man who stood against me is going to pay."

"But why here? Why now? After all this time?"

Corin cocked his head at that, confused. *All this time?* But he had more pressing questions to pursue. He ran a quick eye along the ships docked in the port. "Where's the *Diavahl*?"

"What? The *Diavahl*? She's gone, Captain. Long gone."

Corin frowned, confused again. He'd left his ship in trusted hands. Had that scurvy dog already taken the ship and left Khera behind? That would certainly complicate Corin's plans. Even without Corin's ship and crew, Ethan Blake had all the resources he would need to slip away and hide in safety. That wouldn't do. The traitor needed to die. But how was Corin to find him? He *ached* to have his vengeance, but how?

Before he found an answer, he sensed a new commotion beginning some way down the street to his left. Some local had clearly reported the altercation, because a contingent of the caliph's guards was fighting its way down the street in his direction. They were big men with huge swords, and Corin had no wish to tangle with them at all.

So he rolled his eyes and bounced to his feet. The sword went into a sheath too plain by far, and Corin slapped at the back of the deckhand's shoulder until Charlie rolled over and accepted help up.

"Come with me," Corin said. "We have much to discuss."

Charlie shook his head, oblivious to the approaching danger. "I can't. I can't. I'm sorry, Captain, but I can't leave my post."

"A wine shop's patio is no common post for a pirate."

"Is that what we are? I haven't felt a pirate since you dragged me from the sea, and if things go right today ..."

"Aye?"

"No, I ... Storm's favor, Captain! This is no place to talk. And you caused such a ruckus—"

Corin gave a rich laugh, covering the sound of shouts from the rapidly approaching guards. "You're not wrong there. We should talk somewhere private. For now, accept my apology for the rough treatment and accept my hand."

He thrust out his empty right hand, and for a moment Charlie Claire considered it with suspicion. Corin only waited, his face carefully blank, but he was silently counting the time before the guards arrived. He was one heartbeat away from leaving Charlie Claire on his own when the deckhand rolled his shoulders in a shrug and caught Corin's hand in a hearty shake.

"I make apologies as well. The way we treated you—"

Corin didn't listen to the explanation. He closed his grip tight on Charlie Claire's, then shut his eyes and concentrated. *All the world's a dream*, he thought. The creator-king himself had said so, and he'd taught Corin how to navigate it. Corin focused hard on a rented room elsewhere in the busy city, and when he opened his eyes, he was there.

Charlie screamed again.

Corin looked around and shrugged. "You protest too much. I wouldn't call it luxurious, but what's so fearsome here?"

"What is this place? What happened to the docks?"

"It is a room I sometimes rent when I must pass through Khera. And the docks should be just fine, though I suspect the caliph's guards will be quite confused."

Charlie tore his hand from Corin's grasp and darted to the window. Halfway there he faltered and fell to his knees with a wretched groan. "Oh, what have you done?"

"I've brought you somewhere private to complete our conversation."

"You've cost me everything!"

"Not yet. Not yet."

"But don't you see? The stars!"

Corin growled, irritated. "What of them?"

"The stars are out! The sun has set. Whatever spell you used to bring us here has brought the night down on us!"

Corin stalked back toward Charlie. "I am not a child to fear the dark. I intend to learn a thing or two from you."

"I swear I have no answers, Captain. But if you will just take me back to the docks—"

"So you can summon Blake back to betray me?" Corin snapped, an unexpected anger flaring in his breast. "I know why they would post a man to watch for me."

"To watch for you? Stormy seas, who'd watch for you? We all knew you were dead."

"And yet you staked a perfect sentry spot." Corin chuckled, but his hand clenched hard around the fine sword's hilt. "Where is Ethan hiding?"

"I can't tell you, Captain!"

"You will. In time. I've no ill will for you, Charlie, but I've a mission I won't soon abandon, and you stand in my way."

The frightened deckhand backed away until his shoulders bumped the wall. He held his empty palms toward Corin. "Easy, Captain. Careful, there. I think you are confused."

Corin slashed the sword. It whistled as it sliced the air and passed within a breath of Charlie's nose. "There is nothing easy about me! I have faced Ephitel in person and seen the death of legends. I sacrificed what might have been to save a girl who I let down. And there is blood to pay for all of it. Will you pay with yours, or will you point me after Ethan Blake?"

Charlie Claire whimpered weakly and sank down on his heels. "I'm not the man you want! I swear, I'm not the man you want. It's Blake. And Dave Taker, right? They're the ones who wronged you."

Corin lowered the blade. "Every man who went along became my enemy."

"No! No, no—never! I would never call you enemy! But what was I to do? I couldn't stop an inferno! I couldn't drag you out!

Blake said you had fed the fires, and even Sleepy Jim gave you up for lost."

Corin blinked, remembering. "At least Jim stood for me. At least he tried to fight."

"So he did, and that cost him dear. Almost as bad as you've cost me! They put him off at Aljira and left him with the fishermen."

"Aljira? Impossible! That's two weeks' worth of sailing even under favorable winds."

"Hah! It is. It took us nearly three in wicked storms, but Blake had his heart set on making for the open ocean lanes."

"There hasn't been time enough for any of this!" Corin snapped, and a vicious déjà vu nearly dazed him. Something like panic came in its wake, scrabbling at the back of Corin's breastbone. Time. Time had bent for him once; it had melted like wax and dumped him into a memory of the distant past. But not again. Not here. He was supposed to be back, home in the real world he'd left behind.

He needed to find Blake. To rescue Iryana. Or avenge her. He couldn't do any of that if time were still such a fickle thing. He clenched a fist and fought to keep his voice level. "How much time has passed, Charlie Claire? How long since you left me in that cave?"

Charlie narrowed his eyes. "That is no ordinary question."

The blade whipped back around, almost of its own accord, until the very tip made a dimple in the pirate's nose. "Answer it all the same."

"Aye, aye, Captain! Aye, aye. It's been a hundred days since we entered that cursed tomb. Time enough to leave the desert and regain our ships. Time enough to sail west and sink the ships and scatter half the crew. Time enough to find my own way back to Khera, to unravel my own plans."

"A hundred days? In truth?"

Charlie nodded. "There's nothing more of the life you left behind, Captain. Everything has changed."

"Is Ethan Blake alive?"

"I think he is."

The next question was already on his lips, but his throat felt suddenly dry. He swallowed hard and forced it out. "And . . . and Iryana?"

"What, the slave girl?"

"Aye!"

"She was, last I saw her."

Some of the tension left Corin's shoulders. "She escaped?"

"I wish she had. I wish all of us had before the man went mad. But no. She was still with Blake and Taker when I left."

"Left?" Corin frowned, and for the first time it truly hit him what the old deckhand had said. "*A hundred days*? Three months on open water? He could be anywhere by now!"

"Gods grant it's nowhere near here," Charlie said. "He was no stable captain. He was wicked. Cruel. I breathed easier a'shipwreck than I did in his crew."

"But why . . . ?" Corin trailed off, more confused than ever. Charlie waited patiently, but Corin couldn't find the track of his thoughts.

At last his prisoner spoke up. "Beg pardon, Captain, but if I may be so bold as to ask . . . how many days did *you* think it was?"

Corin met the sailor's eyes. "Two. Or three at most. I closed my eyes and stepped across the sands, but in an instant I lost weeks and weeks."

Charlie's mouth hung open. He clearly had no answer. Corin laughed and put his sword away. He stepped past the frightened sailor and stood for a moment, staring out the window. Charlie wasn't wrong. Night had fallen, dark and deep, and by the position of the huge silver moon hanging over the desert, morning was not far off.

It had been midafternoon down by the docks, but a blink of the eye had cost him twelve hours. *At least* twelve hours. For one long moment Corin just stood staring at the night, trying hard to understand. It had to be something to do with the magic he had used. Fairy magic. Wild, dangerous stuff.

Corin gave a weary sigh. "It dearly messes with your head to wander 'round in a dead god's dreams. Perhaps I need more answers from you than I thought."

(2)

Corin shed his cloak, careful not to disturb the contents of its many pockets as he stretched it out across his bed. He tucked his book beneath it—the precious artifact bound up in cracked leather—and then unbuckled the sword *Godslayer* and laid it on top. He rolled his shoulders, shut his eyes, and caught a long, slow breath.

"I haven't rested," he told Charlie. "Not since you left me in the cavern. I have done war with ancient gods. I have pursued my enemies across a trackless desert and abducted you from just beneath the caliph's guards." He sank down on the floor and leaned his head back against the bare wall. "I'm tired, Charlie."

Charlie answered with a stammer in his voice. "Are ... are you gonna kill me, Captain?"

Corin smiled without opening his eyes. "I am afraid the moment's passed. Unless you do something new to earn it—"

"*Never*, Captain!"

"Then no. I will not kill you. But I will thank you for some information."

"You picked the worst of men for that. You should know better."

"You're all I've got."

"Then I'll tell you what I know. We left the cavern full of books—"

"Empty-handed," Corin growled.

Charlie surprised him. "Umm…mostly. Mostly empty-handed."

Corin cracked an eye. "Only 'mostly'?"

"There were some among us heard the sense in what you said. You have to know that. When you was screaming that these books were worth a ransom, some of us thought to grab one here or there. To tuck one in a pocket, say, or down our breeches."

"Clever," Corin said. Then, after a moment, "And you were one of them?"

Charlie snickered. "I'm hardly clever, Captain. No. But some of the men came away with books. That's all I'm saying."

"Is it an important point?"

"It likely is. I'll let you decide it soon enough."

"Ah. Then carry on."

"Y'see, the captain—"

Corin arched an eyebrow, and Charlie stammered to a stop. "Beg pardon, Captain, but you was gone. So Ethan Blake said he was captain now, and Dave Taker backed him up, and who were we to challenge him?"

"Your loyalty commends you."

"Thank ye, Captain."

"Go on."

"Well, the captain caught wind somehow that there were those who'd stowed some books away, so halfway back to Khera he called 'em out. There was an argument on the topic, and Dave Taker stuck old Carter in the back. Bled 'im out right there on the sand, just to take some dusty book from him."

"Some dusty book?"

"Aye, well, the captain said it'd be safe enough, now we were clear of the cavern. But these books were booty, right, and there're rules. So he gathered them all up—"

"Every one?"

"Every one, and he stowed 'em in a strongbox saying he'd divide the ransom once he'd found a buyer."

Corin nodded. "I begin to see where this is heading."

"Well, not everyone was happy with this turn."

"It was Blake who set all the *other* books on fire, after all."

"Exactly! So some of the men who'd been clever enough to save them thought that *they* deserved the loot."

"And they mutinied? Before he ever got to Khera?"

Charlie shook his head. "They never got the chance. Captain Blake discovered their intentions, and Dave Taker slit their throats while they was sleeping."

"Gods' blood!" Corin spat.

"Nope. Just nameless pirates'."

Corin ground his teeth. "This is the man you chose to back instead of me."

"You don't have to point out my mistake. Oh, now I know it well. I know it well. And that's why I decided to get out of the pirating business altogether. That's why I was *here* when you came looking."

"Here in Khera?"

"Aye, aye! Y'see, I found myself in possession of one of these books."

"I thought you said you hadn't looted one."

"Oh, not from the cavern, no. I got mine later."

"From the strongbox?"

"Well, we couldn't take the strongbox with us when we sank the ships. That was where we stored the dwarven powder."

"You sank the ships? You sank them on purpose?"

"Not *me*. I couldn't have made up a plan like that. It was Taker. When the justicar had found us, Taker trapped him in the ship's hold and told the captain we would have to sink the ship, or we would all be answering to Ephitel."

"You sank the *Diavahl* to kill a justicar."

"Ooh." Charlie gave a little whistle. "Gods grant we killed him. He's a justicar. I wouldn't be surprised to learn he's still alive, still trapped inside our brig beneath the sea off Jebbra Point."

Corin closed his eyes again and groaned. "You raise more questions than you answer, Charlie Claire."

"Beg pardon, Captain."

"No. No pardon. Just save the tales for now and tell me *why* you stole a book."

"To get away. It's like I said. Ethan Blake was a miserable captain, and his first mate was a madman. When we moved the booty off the ship, I found a chance to slip away. I grabbed a book and slipped away in the confusion."

"That worked?"

"Oh, when the powder blew, there was a good confusion. They likely think I'm dead. I'd be surprised if all of them survived. It was not a careful blast."

Corin had his doubts that someone like Blake would miss such a detail, but he kept that to himself. He rubbed his brow, still trying to understand how all the pieces fit together. "Again. You stole the book and brought it here to Khera ..."

"Not straight to Khera. I stopped in Aljira, where I found Sleepy Jim."

Corin perked up. "Is he here? Did you bring him with you?"

"Nah. Jim gave up the sea. Found a pretty brown girl and an olive press and made himself a proper man."

Corin grinned despite himself. "Good for Sleepy Jim."

Charlie spat. "What kind of life is there on land?"

"The kind you're looking for, unless I lost track of your story."

"True enough. It's true enough. I found Sleepy Jim and told him what I had, what I wanted, and he found me a buyer."

"Here in Jepta?"

"No. Ithale. Some scholar who was interested in ancient things. I don't know how Jim knew him."

"Jim knows everyone. It's one of the advantages of becoming an old pirate."

"Well. There you go. He sent a messenger to Nicia and got one back, and we arranged a meet. The scholar didn't trust a trip to Aljira, but he was willing to come to Khera."

"It's a shorter trip."

"And the caliph's guards do not like pirates much."

Corin chuckled. "No. Less and less, it seems."

"Well. That's it. That's my whole tale."

Corin sat up straight and tossed a glare at his old deck-hand. "What? That can't be all. What became of Iryana? And Ethan Blake?"

"Storms take 'em, but I don't know. That's why I ran away."

"And you've heard nothing?"

"I've done everything to keep right out of sight. I don't know a thing."

"Then…" Corin sighed. "You were right, Charlie Claire. You're useless to me. But tell me the rest."

"The rest?"

"What became of your transaction?"

"You're not listening!" Charlie wailed, gesturing wildly toward the open window. "It was today. *That's* who I was waiting for down at the docks. He was coming in this afternoon, but you abducted me!"

"Then I begin to understand your earlier frustration."

Charlie grumbled under his breath a moment, then raised his voice in something close to despair. "What am I to do, Captain? I had one shot—"

"You do still have the book?"

"Oh, of course I do, but how often will you find a man who'd pay two thousand livres for a book?"

"Show me. Where is it stashed?"

Corin had expected Charlie Claire to name a place, but instead the pirate blushed a bit and turned away. He rummaged in his breeches a moment, muttering, then dragged out a battered volume. Corin accepted the manuscript only reluctantly, but he could not have refused. He had to see it. He had to know.

But there was nothing special here. Its cover was of ordinary leather, supple, and its pages silk-soft paper. Nothing like the artifact that Corin carried. The pirate captain opened to an interior page and read a line or two, but it was dry and dull. Corin had rescued from the fire the final memory of Oberon himself, scratched out on the flesh of the city's dying biographer, and in its epilogue it told of Corin's future.

But this? This was the biography of some meticulous hotelier who once had lived in Jezeeli. It would be worth a fortune at the University, but it was no treasure trove for Corin. Still, he riffled the pages and listened to their gentle whisper.

A fortune indeed. And as it happened, Corin was in need of some funds. Perhaps Charlie Claire would be some use to him after all. Corin kept that thought to himself, but he offered

Charlie Claire a genuine grin. "A book like this will find a buyer on its own. Let's get back down to the docks."

They didn't travel by the dream this time. Powerful as Oberon's magic had proven, Corin had no desire to lose any more time. Instead, they walked the city's empty streets. Once or twice Charlie spoke up to tell him of some event that had transpired in the hundred days he'd lost, but mostly they were quiet. Silence lay across the city in the early hours, and it seemed wrong somehow to break it.

But the docks were far less reverent. Sailors woke and slept according to the hours of the tides, not sun or moon, so even now the piers were bustling as ships were loaded and bleary-eyed passengers climbed unsteadily up narrow gangplanks. Charlie's gaze kept drifting toward them, searching for the man he'd hoped to meet.

Corin never even looked in that direction. Instead, he caught Charlie's sleeve and dragged him hard toward the wine shop where the two had planned to meet. "Come on! Forget the ships. The man you're looking for is over here."

Charlie sighed, defeated. "I'm telling you, he won't be there. Chances are, he left at sunset. We're near enough ten hours late. What kind of posh would wait that long?"

Corin arched an eyebrow. "The same kind who'd travel all the way from Nicia to meet with you. The same who'd pay two thousand livres for a book." Corin hesitated, weighing the book in his hand. "Four thousand. I would swear to it."

Charlie shook his head. "It was Sleepy Jim negotiated two. You can't do better than Jim."

"I can. I have. Why do you think they made me captain?"

Charlie stared at him a moment. Then he ducked his head, looking almost bashful. "Captain ... would you ... I mean, if you would be kind enough ... will you do the deal for me? Four thousand livres'd get a man much further than two."

Corin couldn't hide his grin. He'd been thinking the same thing and wondering how to get Charlie to trust him. "I'll see what I can do. Just peek inside and find the man and point him out to me."

"I still find it hard to—"

"He's there. Have faith. Just take a peek."

Charlie shrugged aside his doubts and complied with Corin's orders. He crept close to the tavern's open door and peeked around the corner. His search had barely started when he gave a startled gasp and turned back to Corin. "How did you ... how could you have known?"

"He's there?"

"He's just about asleep in his own cups, but he is there."

"Which table?" Corin straightened his tunic and adjusted the sword belt on his hip. "What's he wearing? What age?"

"Fourth table down the far wall. He's dressed in robes like these dirty locals wear, but you can tell him by his golden rings and pale skin. And er ..." Charlie's lips moved silently as he reviewed all the questions; then he nodded once. "Oh! Twenty summers. Maybe twenty-one."

"Twenty? He's a boy!"

Charlie laughed. "And you're a doddering old man?"

Corin shrugged. He was not yet twenty himself. "I am a pirate. That is a young man's trade. But scholars, academics ..."

"Jim said he was no ordinary buyer, but he is rich and anxious to be ... less so."

Corin shared a grin with Charlie Claire. "You have a way of making things clear. You're right. Now step aside, and let us see if I can gain a double share."

The pirate captain adjusted his shirt, accepted the book from Charlie, and strode through the tavern door with all the pomp and confidence of an Ithalian lord.

He barely made three paces before he spotted the buyer at his table. Then Corin stumbled in his shock. He caught himself, just short of falling, with a hand on another patron's table. The rattle and clatter of dishes there raised the dozing buyer, the youthful scholar, and Corin almost slipped away through dream. He hesitated, desperate not to lose any more time, and that moment was long enough.

The buyer blinked the sleep from his eyes, searching for the source of the disturbance. When he saw Corin, recognition flared into a blazing fury.

The scholar lunged to his feet and stabbed an accusing finger toward Corin. Then he shouted with a sonorous voice that overwhelmed the tavern's chatter, "Guards! Guards! Someone call the caliph's guards! This man's a pirate and a villain and a thief! Someone capture him!"

The scholar scrabbled at his belt for a modest work knife, but Corin felt far more concerned about the caliph's guards. The pirate captain dashed forward, caught the scholar's extended hand in his, and growled a curse even as he closed his eyes. He stepped through dream and brought the buyer with him, back to that same rented room.

(3)

How much had that cost him? Hours or weeks? Foolish! He should have sent Charlie to make the sale and pilfered a share of the money after the deal was done. But here he was, and almost too late he remembered the work knife on the scholar's belt. Corin struck the scholar one sharp backhand to keep him disoriented, then chopped down hard to knock the knife from his grip. As long as he was at close quarters, he seized the chance to snatch the heavy purse at Tesyn's belt. Corin slapped him openhanded to keep him distracted, tucked the purse inside his own cloak, and withdrew two paces in a bound.

Then he caught his breath and heaved a weary sigh. "What have you done, Tesyn?"

"What have *I* done?" The scholar raised his voice to shout through the thin walls. "Scoundrel! Thief! Release me!"

Corin didn't strike him again. He didn't touch the sword on his hip. He merely raised one eyebrow, and the young nobleman shut up tight as a Medgerrad clam. Corin took a slow step back and sighed. "So. It would appear that you remember me."

"Remember you? You sank my father's fastest merchant ship! You held me captive seven weeks and cost my family an enormous ransom!"

Corin shrugged. "But that was years ago."

"That isn't all! You ransomed me my books at twice the price you asked for me."

Corin couldn't quite hide his grin. "My crew would not believe it."

"It isn't funny! You cost me my destiny."

"I'd hardly think—"

"No! No, you never would. You're just a stinking pirate. You're just a dirty brute. I doubt you even read, so how could you guess what secrets those books held?"

Corin bit his lip, considering his response. He knew those secrets quite well. It had been young Tesyn's map that led Corin and his crew to the buried city of Jezeeli—the same tomb of a forgotten god where his men had found the book he now hoped to sell.

But how much should he share? By the weight of Tesyn's purse—assuming the thing held good Ithalian gold—Corin already had enough in coin to fund his plans for revenge. But now that he knew whom he was dealing with, Corin wanted something more. The scholar could give him information.

So the pirate let the insults pass unanswered and instead asked a question of his own. "What was it, then? What was this destiny I stole?"

"I am not here to lecture history with my very nemesis! Now step aside or draw your sword, because I have no reason left to tarry here."

Corin raised the eyebrow again. It didn't work this time. The scholar shook his head. "If your accomplice lured me here in hope of another great ransom, resign yourself to disappointment now. My father has disowned me."

"And yet you promised quite a fortune for a book …"

"My own funds. And that was everything I owned, but I won't share a sou of it with you. I'd rather go home empty-handed."

Corin considered all the threats that he might use, but in the end he chose another path. He produced the ancient manuscript and tossed it almost casually to the scholar.

Tesyn nearly dropped it. Even after he'd secured the book, he didn't understand. "What's this? Your ridiculous demands? You had them bound?"

"It is the promised book. The one you came here for."

"Impossible! That manuscript should be at least six hundred years in age."

"Nearly twice that."

The scholar shook his head. "No, no. I've seen the Khera Codex too, but I suspect its timeline—"

"You are wrong," Corin said, unyielding. "Jezeeli fell twelve hundred years ago, and in your hands you hold a perfect artifact, untouched by time."

The scholar's eyes strained wide. He shrank away from the book in his own hands, gripping it delicately with just thumb and forefinger. He shook his head slowly back and forth. "It can't … It's not … How could …" Something clicked behind his eyes, and he fixed Corin with a piercing glare. "How can you know these things?"

Corin spread his hands. "As it happens, I *can* read."

"You … you read my notes?" The nobleman went pale and in a voice just above a whisper, asked, "You deciphered my map?"

Relishing this reversal, Corin held his gaze. "I? A stinking pirate? A stupid brute?"

The scholar frowned, considering, then he unleashed a booming laugh. "Hah! No. No, how could I have thought it?"

"I did!" Corin shouted. "It took three years, but I uncovered all Jezeeli's secrets."

"Three years? Your story crumbles with every word. My family has been searching for this place for decades."

"Your family searched libraries and ancient records. I searched in the world. That's the key. It's not enough to read the books; you have to risk your neck. You have to go adventuring to find anything worth having."

Tesyn snorted. "You sound like Lorenzo. But there, you see? The Vestossis are hunting for Jezeeli too, with ships and expeditions. And for all their vast resources, they can't find it."

"But I did! You hold the proof within your hand."

The scholar glanced down at the book, then heaved a weary sigh. "Oh, more the fool am I. I wanted so much to believe, but I should have known." He cast the book aside. Corin winced as it struck the stone floor, but the scholar had already forgotten it. "I say again: Draw your sword or step aside. I'm finished here."

Before Corin could find an answer, the door slammed open. Charlie Claire came bustling in, all out of breath. "Oh, praise the thunder! You're here."

"I am," Corin said. "And how many days have I lost this time?"

"Days?" the scholar asked.

"Not half an hour," Charlie answered. "But you near lost me. The caliph's guards came faster this time."

"Half an hour," Corin mused. "But over the same distance that cost us half a day. It makes no sense."

"What makes no sense?" the scholar asked, suddenly interested.

Corin met his gaze. Perhaps this shipwreck could be salvaged yet. He showed his teeth. "The magic of Jezeeli. How did you think I brought you here? King Oberon himself taught me a trick or two."

"King Oberon," the scholar breathed, almost reverent. "You are a monster *and* a madman, but I'd give much to hear your story."

"Aye, you will. Two thousand livres, as agreed, and you will tell me everything you know about this place. About its lore and its strange magics."

"As easily done as asked," the scholar said. "And alas, as quickly done. What can I say you don't already know? The legends tell of Jezeeli or Jesalich or—"

"Gesoelig," Corin told him. "But Jezeeli's really close enough."

The scholar sighed. "You see? It cost me years of study to learn the things you already seem to know."

"But there are gaps in what I know. Who are the druids? What was their pact with Oberon? Why did they leave yesterworld to come here? What was the purpose of the strictures?"

Both men stared at Corin, the scholar every bit as baffled as the deckhand. Corin's stomach sank. "Forget the druids, then. Tell me about the elves who remained loyal after the city fell. Where did they flee? What became of them? Surely they didn't all join Ephitel."

The scholar took a sharp step closer. "The elves? The ghosts who haunt the Isle of Mists? Are you telling me that *they* came from Jezeeli?"

"That's all you know?" Corin sagged, suddenly very tired. "You truly *don't* know more than me."

The scholar bristled. "I know the grammar of a dozen living languages and half a dozen dead. I know the economy and culture and military disposition of every nation in Hurope. I know—"

"Too much by half," Corin interrupted. "And yet none of it of any use to me." Corin felt a sickness in his stomach, exhaustion in his bones. "If you don't want the book, take your money and go."

"But ... but ... you must tell me what *you* know!"

"I know a place not far from here that serves a proper glass of rum."

"But—"

"You've already cost me more than I could ever claim in ransom for your sorry bones. Be glad that you convinced me on that point, and gladder still that I choose to set you free. In my line of business, that counts as a lucky break."

The scholar scoffed. "What would you really have to gain from hurting me?"

"Your two thousand livres, for one," Corin answered, casual. "And I'd still have Charlie's book to sell to some other sad scholar somewhere."

Corin turned away from the ashen scholar. Suddenly he did not feel at all friendly. Charlie came to meet him, but Corin spoke beneath his breath. "I'm going for a drink. Don't you worry. Tesyn will not really pass up the book, although he may pretend he's lost his purse. Press him, take your time, and you'll get all your gold."

"But what about your share? You done your part. I can't keep all the money."

With Tesyn's fortune already tucked inside his cloak, Corin felt a pang of guilt at Charlie's concern. But he had important business to do. And after all, Charlie had left him to burn in the fires of Jezeeli. He could afford to lose an easy score.

"Whatever you can get from Tesyn," Corin said, "consider it your own. I don't need anything more than I already have."

"Aye, aye, Captain."

"Stow that talk. I'm not your captain anymore. You're your own man now, Charlie Claire. Revel in it."

"But ... surely you still need a crew."

Corin stopped, one foot already out the door. He didn't turn back, but he did consider the matter for a moment. Then he shook his head. "I am alone in this, Charlie Claire. The path I plan to walk ... who could possibly walk it with me?"

Charlie's hand closed warm and strong on Corin's shoulder. "I'll go with you, Captain."

Corin shared his sad smile with the empty night and spoke over his shoulder. "I know you will, Charlie. I believe it. But ..."

In the end, he shook his head, shook off the sailor's hand, and headed down the narrow lane. As he went, he finished the thought silently, for himself alone. *You couldn't follow where I'm going. You aren't bad enough.*

(4)

Night was always quiet over Khera. Back home in Aepoli, the cruel investigators fought hard to enforce their lord's curfew, but the caliph faced no such challenge here. The bitter cold of desert nights did far more than thumbscrews and burning coals could accomplish in civilized lands.

So Corin stalked through empty streets as he left his inn behind. The silence suited him well. For as much as that was worth, the cold suited too. He wrapped his long black cloak more tightly around him and strode through shadow and silence and gloom.

He should not have been so disappointed. He knew that, but the knowledge didn't help. An hour ago he'd only hoped to score a handsome bounty, but for a moment there in the room—for one brief instant—he had thought he'd found an ally. He had thought he'd found someone who'd understand.

Charlie couldn't understand. The man was true enough and brave to a fault, but he had been the third dumbest of all the men in Corin's crew. No, Charlie Claire could never really help him in his quest. But Corin had hoped that perhaps the scholar, the same man who had pointed him to Jezeeli, who had spent his lifetime scouring the world for clues, could at least share an understanding of the things Corin had seen.

And with that thought, Corin understood why he felt so sour to discover the scholar's inadequacy: He needed help. His quest ... gods' blood, it made his knees quake to consider it. What was his quest? Revenge, but it would be no easy blow. He still hoped to save the girl, but she could yet become one of the many scores he aimed to settle with the traitor Blake.

Not Blake. Not Ethan Blake, as he had called himself, but some blasted Vestossi's son or cousin. For all he hated them ... for all the secrets he had learned, how could Corin hope to cut down a Vestossi and survive? And if he *did* survive, he had another promise to fulfill. He had a god to kill.

Unconsciously, he closed his hand around the hilt of the sword on his hip. *Godslayer.* There was one answer, anyway. He had the means. But how was he to *find* Ephitel? How was he to face him?

Corin laughed despite himself. It scarcely mattered. He had no way of settling with Blake, so plans for Ephitel could wait. In all likelihood, some unseen knife from the Vestossis' thugs would settle Corin before he ever came close to his first goal.

He was so thoroughly lost in these thoughts that he nearly missed the sound of footsteps trailing him. How had Charlie uncovered his deception so quickly? He'd expected it to take at least half an hour before the two men realized that Corin had stolen Tesyn's purse. Still, he felt confident he could sort things out. He put on his most innocent expression and spun around. "Listen, Charlie, I can explain everyth—"

But it wasn't Charlie Claire. It was a woman, judging by her frame, but Corin spotted little else to know her by. She was draped in miles of the light white fabric that the natives wore, her face concealed behind a veil and obscured by the dark.

She froze in place for half a heartbeat, but Corin found himself just as shocked. The woman recovered first. She raised one arm toward him like a marksman aiming a flintlock pistol. She might even have concealed one in the voluminous folds of her sleeves. But she made no threat. She asked no questions. She backed slowly to the nearest crossing alley, then darted off with a slipper-soft step.

Instinct drove Corin after her, but he only went two paces before he caught himself. Concealed though she was, something in the woman's stance had felt alluringly familiar. But who could he know in Khera? This one had been too small of frame for Iryana, and he could scarcely believe the fierce slave girl would have run. But who else? His life left little room for female entanglements.

No. His desire for *some* companion had fooled him into seeing what wasn't there. Surely. Far more likely she was some local lady on an errand, frightened to encounter an outlander alone on these dark streets. Aye. He nodded to himself. Far more likely, she was just a stranger.

And not the only stranger in the night. Before Corin could turn back to his path, he spotted a pair of shadows approaching down another side street. Cautious now, Corin concealed himself within a narrow alcove and watched them approach. These men too carried a familiar aura, but this time it was one Corin placed easily enough.

They were pirates. He knew it at first by their rolling gait, and then by their dress, and then by the stink of them. A sinking suspicion settled over him as he remembered some of the things Charlie Claire had said before. He and Tesyn had chosen Khera because it was not a safe place for pirates anymore. That meant these two men wouldn't be here without some pressing business.

And they were not just in Khera. They were *here*, in this neighborhood that Old Grim had so much preferred. They were rounding the corner and heading back up the street Corin had just come down. They were heading toward Charlie Claire.

An angry snarl tugged at Corin's lips. These were no strangers at all. These were Ethan Blake's men, come to punish Charlie Claire for daring to leave their ranks. It wasn't enough that Corin had robbed him; now the poor sod was going to get his throat cut.

Run, Corin thought, shouting the order in his own head. *Get clear of this place. It's their business now; let them sort it out. You're supposed to be hunting Ethan Blake.*

And yet he didn't move. He stood frozen in place, staring down the dark street after the retreating figures and thinking of poor Charlie Claire sobbing in a corner. The man didn't deserve to die like this.

You're nobody's hero, Corin Hugh. He licked his lips and clenched his fists and fought to restrain an angry growl. He wasn't a hero. He had more important business to do. And yet he couldn't make himself move.

Then a thought struck him. Charlie wouldn't just die. Charlie would talk. Charlie would tell them everything, and then Ethan Blake's thugs would go rushing back to him with news that Corin Hugh was still alive. That Corin Hugh was hunting him. That Corin Hugh had strange new magic powers.

Somehow, that realization eased the weight on Corin's chest. He was no hero—that was sure. But he wasn't about to lose his only advantage over Ethan Blake. He had no choice but to stop those men. He checked his sword within its scabbard and the dagger on his belt. Then he ducked his head and, silent as a shadow, crept down the road behind the stalking pirates.

He'd lingered too long in his hiding place and couldn't catch the men before they reached the inn. Still, he was not more than a hundred heartbeats behind them when he slipped into the inn and up its narrow stairs. The door to his old rooms stood open just a crack, and Corin stood a moment on the landing, motionless, listening for some clue as to what was happening in there.

For a moment there was nothing, and Corin began to wonder if the pirates he had seen were truly Ethan Blake's at all. Then Charlie cried out in surprise, and a moment later a violent blow landed with a wet *crack* against the sailor's skull. Corin cursed and moved like lightning. He burst into a sprint even as familiar voices carried out into the hall. "Oh, Charlie, you never shoulda run on us."

"Never shoulda stole the captain's rightful booty," another answered.

"Never shoulda showed your face. Never shoulda come back for more."

"It's all ours now! Search 'im, Billy!"

Billy Bo. Corin's grip tightened on the hilt of his sword. One of Ethan Blake's favorite cronies. And that would make the other—

"Slit 'is throat, Tommy?"

Tommy Day. Dave Taker's half-brother. Two of the cruelest men Corin had ever known, and he'd been seven years a pirate.

An animal grin twisted Corin's mouth. He wasn't a pirate anymore; he was a vengeful spirit. And these two men had a reckoning to pay.

The sword escaped its sheath as Corin spun into the room. With his left hand he drew a heavy dagger too and put it almost immediately to use. Tommy stood two paces closer to the door than Corin had guessed, and the fiend reacted to his old captain's appearance without a moment's hesitation. He swung the same heavy cudgel that he'd used to club poor Charlie, but Corin caught it on the guard of his dagger and then plunged three feet of silvered steel into Tommy Day's abdomen. The old sailor didn't even scream, but he fell away.

Corin flung himself aside half a heartbeat before Billy Bo's hooked axe slashed through the air where he had been. Corin landed on his shoulders, looking back on his attackers, and he kicked out hard with both feet. Corin's boots found Billy's shins, and Billy *did* scream. Corin sprang right up, ducked a wild swing of the axe, and dropped Billy with a vicious backhand.

Still, old Tommy hadn't made a sound. Corin turned that way, curious, and found Tommy stretched out on the floor, his shoulders propped against the wall. The man's right arm was extended, and in his hand he held a flintlock pistol.

Something cold and crushing closed around Corin when he saw the weapon. He hated guns.

Tommy grinned, and his teeth were red with his own blood. "Give my regards to Ephitel."

Corin fought down the icy panic and grinned right back. "I'll add them to the list."

Tommy roared in anger, his hand clenching convulsively around the pistol's grip. Corin closed his eyes and stepped through dream. The pistol's crack was loud enough to drown out Tommy's roar, but it came too late to harm Corin. Faster than a man could blink, Corin sprang ten paces across the room. The gunshot flared and roared and faded, all more quickly than it should have, and Corin already knew it was a waste of effort when he hurled his dagger across the room.

The blade buried itself a hand's width deep in painted plaster. Full daylight flooded the room, blinding Corin for a moment, but there was no enemy left to take advantage of it. Everyone was gone. He'd stepped through dream again, and once again he'd lost hours or days.

"Gods' blood," Corin said, then stopped to catch his breath. "I've got to get a hold on that."

He strained his ears for a moment, but the house was strangely quiet. Midafternoon then, when all the locals retired from the searing sun for prayers and meditation. But Corin wasn't interested in locals.

A bloodstain marked the place where Charlie Claire had fallen. It was no sure sign that he was dead—scalp wounds always poured like summer storms—but Charlie had left a larger pool than even Tommy Day's.

Corin curled his lip at that. Tommy Day was gone, his debt yet unpaid. And Billy Bo as well. Corin had quite hoped to wring some news of Ethan Blake from them before he put them down. Worse still, they'd *seen* Corin alive, and seen his new magic firsthand. *Grays take them both*, Corin thought. *They'll tell it all to Blake.*

A groan from the far corner caught his attention. He took two hurried steps that way and half-drew his sword again before he saw the sad figure who'd been left there.

Corin heaved a weary sigh. "My lord."

The young scholar groaned the louder. "What more could you *ever* do to me?"

"I could tell you everything I know about Jezeeli," Corin said, and some mad joy bloomed in the scholar's blackened eyes.

Corin shook his head. "But I am not that unkind. You have suffered enough."

"But—"

Corin didn't stay to listen. If the scholar were still here, just waking, then Oberon's magic had not stolen days or weeks this time. Midafternoon suggested hours. Corin had a guess where he might find his former shipmates, but he had to hurry.

He went two steps toward the door and then stopped. In the wreckage from the struggle, beneath a broken side table, Corin spotted the corner of the book that Charlie Claire had stolen. He scooped it up, weighed it in his grasp, and flipped the priceless treasure underhand across the room to land in the scholar's lap.

"Keep better care of it this time," Corin said. "Next time we meet, I'll want a full report." Then he left the room, cloak flapping, and hit the empty streets at a full sprint.

Midafternoon in Khera was not much unlike midnight, although the daylight boiled where the night wind seared with chill. Still, the streets were strangely empty, the shops closed up, and Corin crossed the deserted city with an eerie sense of déjà vu. That sense was only heightened when he turned a corner and ran full-tilt into a woman—the only other living soul on Khera's streets. She was shorter than Corin, thin and light, but she barely gave a step when he hit her. Instead she pirouetted, graceful as a University swordsman, danced around his momentum, and sprang free.

Corin nearly lost his own balance, startled as he was by her agility. She fell back a pace and watched him through a smoky veil. Her head was covered, her garments plain, but once again he got the eerie feeling that he *knew* the stranger watching him.

Corin brushed the dust from his knees and elbows, unthreatening, and offered her his most disarming smile.

"Are you stalking me? A pretty little thing like you—"

Too late he remembered she was armed. Her right hand came up, lost within the folds of her robe, but he didn't doubt she held a pistol of her own.

"Age of Reason!" he screamed and turned on his heel. "Does everyone in Khera have a gun?"

He had no wish to lose more time to Oberon's dream travel, and the city streets gave him more room to maneuver than the crowded inner chamber had offered before. He vaulted an abandoned fruit cart, feinted to the left, then sprang and rolled to the right. He went half a block down the next street, then took another alley. Three quick jogs—left and right and left again—and half a mile separated him from that strange woman.

He slowed, but only to a trot. He *did* have somewhere to be, and time was precious. He had to catch Tommy and Billy before they left the city. But as he headed for their most likely point of exit, he thought back on that strange encounter. Who *was* this woman following him? It couldn't be coincidence that he had met two such figures under such circumstances. And yet, how could she have found him? Hours apart, the timing made more random by his strange magic movement. Yet twice she'd stumbled on him. She'd seemed surprised both times, but she'd been quick enough to draw her gun.

And yet, she hadn't fired. He had no doubts she had the skill—not after that martial display—but she clearly meant her arms to pacify him, not to injure. That was something, anyway.

For a moment he regretted leaving her. He glanced back to see if she had followed, but flight came as easy as breathing to a boy grown in the dark streets of Aepoli, and Corin had truly lost her.

It was likely for the best. The girl was some kind of mystery, but Corin had a purpose. Ethan Blake. And all his hopes for revenge were likely leaving with the tide. Corin ground his jaw and sprinted harder despite the searing sun. There was somewhere he had to be.

(5)

Khera had no Nimble Fingers; the elite network of thieves and fences kept themselves to more civilized climes. But Khera's next best thing was Ahmed the Fig. Ahmed ran a dirty little brothel outside the city. He was famous for it, though no one seemed much interested in hiring his women.

But ... perhaps it mattered that his fine establishment backed right up to the river. Perhaps his private jetty saw an inordinate amount of traffic—mostly by the sleek, fast ships so suited to smugglers and slavers. Perhaps the caliph's guards were well rewarded for overlooking Ahmed's business.

Every pirate on the Medgerrad knew of Ahmed the Fig, but Corin almost always kept away. Old Grim hadn't liked the man, and Corin knew better than to doubt his mentor's judgment. Still, Corin knew the way as well as anyone, and he was willing to bet everything that Billy Bo and Tommy Day would be at the Fig's place now—if they were not already gone.

The sun was sinking low when Corin reached the brothel. A hard-packed footpath curled past wild dunes in an empty stretch of desert. As he approached the run-down clay building, Corin searched the horizon carefully, but he could spot no other signs of life. The river's floods never touched this high spit of rocky land, but it was likely Ahmed's reputation, more than the challenging agriculture, that kept him short on neighbors.

The only other structure in sight was Ahmed's camel pen. In busier times it served as much as a horse stable as a proper camel pen, but it seemed poorly suited to the task. The thin, cracked wooden slats that made up the pen's walls were sun bleached and sand blasted, and fully half of them hung loose or slapped against their posts. Yet somehow no one had ever heard of Ahmed losing one of his patrons' charges.

As Corin approached the pen, a shape that he'd mistaken for another of the loose fence posts peeled away and revealed itself to be a child. He'd have made a fine street urchin in Aepoli—thin as a post, hip-high to Corin, and missing all but a handful of teeth. His eyes were sharp, though, and he carried himself with a bobbing reticence that probably passed for respect. Corin recognized it as prudent caution. This was a child after his own heart.

"Take your horse, Effendi?" the urchin called, hand extended.

Corin chuckled. "As you can see, I have neither horse nor camel."

"No, but you can see I *would* have served you well if you had. That must be worth a coin or two."

Corin barked a laugh. "Here's my offer: Tell me who has come by here today, and when, and *that* will earn a handful of silver."

The child spat. "That would cost you good king's gold, and me my hand. Effendi."

Corin took a knee to face him on a level. He pressed a heavy silver coin into the boy's hand and met his eyes. "That's yours regardless. But all I need to know is if my shipmates passed this way. If they're still here. Three Godlanders like me. Likely wounded. It would have been this afternoon."

The boy spent a moment idly prodding one of his remaining teeth with the tip of his tongue while he considered how he'd answer. At last he shrugged and looked down at his feet. "I guess they wouldn't have horses, either."

Corin frowned. "I don't—"

But it hadn't been a question. The boy went right on. "Just two men walking through the dunes, one carrying another on his shoulder like a bag of grain." He shrugged again. "If they had no horses, they were no concern of mine, so I couldn't tell you anything."

Corin grinned, but kept his voice solemn. "I can hardly fault you for that. Keep your coin all the same."

The boy ducked his head and turned to resume his place in the shade, but Corin caught his shoulder. Voice cast low, he asked, "Are they still here?"

The boy tore free of Corin's grasp. "I told you I can't answer questions like that." He went three paces, plopped down by the fencepost, and closed his eyes against the sunset glare. Almost idly, he said, "But I can say the tide has not yet changed. That's no one's secret, right?"

"Exactly right," Corin said. He flipped the boy another coin, loosened his sword in its sheath, and pushed through into Ahmed the Fig's Fine Brothel for Weary Desert Travelers.

It looked considerably more impressive on the inside. The same high, rocky soil that made this spot so bad for farming had allowed Ahmed to dig down and build a stable structure below the sun-seared earth. From the outer door, Corin descended a dozen steps into a wide, dark pit of a common room. Low tables stood here and there in an apparently random arrangement. Cushions surrounded the tables, but at the moment they were all unoccupied. One glance was enough to show Corin his old crewmates weren't in the common room.

That didn't rule out the private rooms around the edges of this one, hidden behind heavy curtains, but Corin had his doubts that Tommy Day would spend that kind of coin. No, far more likely they were waiting on the jetty out back or already aboard some smuggler's ship and simply waiting for the tide to turn.

That last possibility seemed like the greatest risk, so Corin headed straight toward the storeroom and the jetty. But he'd barely taken a step before Ahmed appeared to intercept him. The seedy little man barely came up to Corin's chin. He was thin and greasy, with a fringe of tight, graying curls and deep-set eyes that never stopped moving. They barely touched on Corin, but the Fig effortlessly interposed himself on Corin's path and corralled him.

"Isn't this that Corin Hugh, once captain of the *Diavahl*? Some call you Old Grim's heir—don't bother to deny. You do me great honor!"

"You do me too much. I'm just a humble sailor looking for safe passage."

"But first you will enjoy my hospitality! Stay a night. No charge for you, and I'll see you have no cause for complaint."

Stay a night at the Fig's brothel? He'd be lucky if he woke to find that only his possessions had been stolen. He'd be lucky if he woke at all.

He was careful to keep such thoughts from his expression, though. It was dangerous business offending someone like the Fig. Shadows shaped like men lurked around the edges of the room. Large men. Corin had no wish to tangle with them. So he bowed his head and offered his regrets.

"I hate that I must pass up such a generous offer, but my business calls me urgently away."

"Surely you can spare one night!"

"Alas, but there are affairs more pressing than the comforts of one poor sailor. I cannot spare a minute. I must catch the very next ship that passes your jetty."

So saying, Corin tried to push past Ahmed, but the little man slapped a firm hand on Corin's chest, and two of those menacing shadows solidified as quickly. Hulking guards came forward, and they wore long, curved knives the way a courtesan might wear strings of pearls.

Corin swallowed hard and fell back a step. He moved his hand slowly toward the purse on his belt and spoke plainly. "I've no quarrel with you, Fig. We are both businessmen. Name your price, but I *must* be on the next ship sailing for the sea."

Ahmed grinned, gregarious as ever. "The tide won't change for an hour yet, and I am a host before I am a businessman. Come and have a drink with me—"

"Ahmed," Corin interrupted, begging, but he cut short when the hulking guards started forward, fury in their eyes.

The Fig clapped his hands lightly, and the guards fell back. Then he caught Corin's elbow and guided him toward a private room on the back wall. "Show honor, Corin Hugh, and we will return every favor. But please show honor. Godlanders' blood leaves such a cruel stain."

Corin smiled, lips tight, and went meekly along. He strained for a glimpse through the jetty door as he went, but it was all smoke and shadow. Distracted as he was, Corin misplaced a step. His foot landed in some slick spill on the hard stone floor, and he went to one knee before he caught himself. The hand that caught him landed in the same spill that had tripped him—something thick and sticky and warm. The stink of it was a metallic tang.

"Ah, you see?" Ahmed cried. "Just as I was saying? What kind of host am I?"

He clapped his hands again and barked, "Fetch Corin Hugh a rag to clean his hands. Godlanders' blood!" He spat, every bit disgusted with himself, but his gaze never left Corin's face, and there was immense satisfaction in his eyes.

Corin fought to hold his grin. The blood was drying on his hand, congealing into a too-tight glove. It was warm, but not warm enough, and it had lain thick in that pool.

Whose was it? That was the question. Corin would shed no tears to learn that Tommy Day's belly wound had bled out on the floor here. Especially if he could compel Billy Bo to point him toward Ethan Blake.

But if it had been Charlie Claire, if Tommy Day had murdered him here while this greasy Fig stood witness . . . well, Corin had a list of men who needed killing. It would be no extra effort to add one more name.

But first he had to learn the truth. Corin fought down his anger and disgust to answer with a quiet calm. "Godlanders' blood is no strange thing for me. Perhaps I could share a trick or two."

Ahmed gave a grin. "I would be forever grateful. But come! Our drinks will lose their chill. This way! We have been waiting."

Ahmed strolled ahead, chatting amiably about local politics and weather. Corin followed after, bracketed by the hulking guards. They hadn't asked him to surrender either of his visible weapons. That thought didn't comfort him at all. It only meant they knew that they were faster.

Ahmed was first to reach the outer wall. He caught the curtain's edge in one hand but, like a true showman, waited until Corin stepped up close before pulling it aside. Corin tensed himself against the surprise. He clenched one hand tight around his sword's grip, the other on his dagger's, and braced himself to spring out of the guards' reach. Then he took the final step, so close that his nose nearly brushed the heavy textiles, and rolled his eyes toward Ahmed. "Well?"

Ahmed frowned, grumbled something, and whisked the curtains back. They revealed a private room like others Corin had seen—a low dining table and cushions, a pile of heavy blankets in one corner—but this one held a liquor cabinet too, and a great mahogany writing desk. There was a chair as well, out of place here, though it matched the desk nicely. It looked to be master-crafted woodwork and fine Ithalian leather.

And bound and gagged in the chair was Charlie Claire.

Poor Charlie looked ghastly, his face and chest caked with mostly-dried blood from the scalp wound. He had new bruises too, on his face and hands and forearms. There'd clearly been some struggle, but he was subdued now. His hands and feet were all tied tightly to the heavy chair—so tightly the cords were cutting deep into his wrists and ankles. His face was pale, from the pain or from the loss of blood, but his eyes were open and alert. They widened as they fixed on Corin, and some new terror gripped the man. He struggled anew despite his bonds, despite the hulking guard who stood behind him, and he received a brand new blunt trauma to his skull as punishment.

His head snapped violently forward at the blow, then lolled limply, though his eyes still fluttered with some trace of consciousness. The sight of him so unsettled Corin that it froze him in place. Ahmed said something that Corin didn't catch, and again louder; then he clapped his hands, and one of the hulking guards shoved Corin between the shoulder blades hard enough to send him staggering into the room.

At the motion, Corin's mind started working once again. He caught his balance on the second step but took a third anyway, with thoughts of flinging himself on Charlie's warden. The slithering whisper of steel on steel stopped him, and he turned to find more guards in the room. Three on Charlie, two for Corin's escort, and Ahmed himself was said to be a ruthless killer with a bit of cord. Corin's heroism flared up hot and bright when he saw what they'd done to a battered member of his old crew, but overwhelming odds rushed in and doused it like an ocean swell.

So Corin drew up short. He buried any indication that he'd ever meant to fight, and with a wholly disinterested expression, he turned to Ahmed. "It seems this room is already in use. I'd hate to interrupt these men before they're done. Perhaps another?"

Ahmed laughed. It was a grating cackle. "You do nothing to deceive me, Corin Hugh. You try and try and try and try again, but I can see beneath your skin. I can peer into your coward's heart. I know that you know this man. I know that you were once his captain and that you would not much like to see him dead."

Corin raised an eyebrow, feigning unconcern. "He played his part in a mutiny against me. Kill him and I'll thank you for it."

Ahmed called his bluff. The Fig clapped his hands once, and the guard standing close behind Charlie Claire knotted a fist in the sailor's blood-soaked hair. He hauled back hard, jerking Charlie's chin up and eliciting a groan despite the knotted gag. With his other hand, the guard whipped out his heavy dagger in a wide arc and brought it slashing back toward Charlie's throat.

Corin screamed, an animal protest, and flung himself forward to intervene. But two hands fell like blacksmith's hammers on his shoulders and clamped tight, dragging him back into his place. Still, his reaction seemed to be enough. The guard stopped the dagger just before it tore the deckhand's throat open, though it came close enough to draw a thin new flow of blood. It looked to be a graze, but bright, fresh blood washed down to damp the drying clot on Charlie's shirt.

Corin rolled his head to glare back at Ahmed. "Let him go! What has he ever done to you? He's just a stupid deckhand. Let him go!"

"Ah, but he has *value* to me in this current state."

"What could he mean to you?" Corin snarled, but he saw the answer even before Ahmed said it.

"He gives me power over you. Power over the legendary Corin Hugh. And that is worth something."

Corin caught a deep breath and then forced it out slowly. He calmed his hammering heart and wrestled his emotions into order. They were doing nothing to serve him now. He took another calming breath, then rolled his shoulders. "Have your thugs release me, so we can talk like gentlemen."

"Oh, no. You struck a truer note before. We are not gentlemen, but *businessmen*. Still ..." He clapped his hands, and those iron clamps on Corin's shoulders relented. Corin stretched, wincing, then turned back to face Ahmed.

"You've always shown a ... flexible nature," Corin said. "And a shrewd sense for seizing an opportunity. I can respect that. But this time you're mistaken. I'm worth nothing to you."

Ahmed raised his eyebrows, doubtful, but he said nothing.

Corin pressed his case. "I was a famous pirate captain once, it's true. But I have been marooned. I'm nothing now. I have no crew, no ship, no more treasure than the purse on my belt. I do understand a smart businessman seizing a chance that falls into his lap, but I am not the prize you think I am. I'm worth almost nothing to you. Same as Charlie here."

As he said it, Corin turned to gesture back to Charlie Claire, and with the gesture shifted half a pace closer to him.

The Fig didn't seem to notice. "Can it truly be? Corin Hugh has fallen so low?"

"I am afraid it is."

Ahmed clucked his tongue, disappointment clear in his expression. "Ah, such a shame. And here I thought I had some better use for you than the one Tommy Day has already paid me for."

Corin swallowed hard. "Tommy … what?" He stifled a curse. He'd taken this all for an act of Ahmed's own initiative, but if Tommy had already placed on offer on the table, then Corin had misplayed his hand.

Ahmed nodded earnestly. "Oh, yes. He was here an hour gone. Paid a handsome fee for safe passage to Marzelle; then he paid me double that to lay a trap for you and see you dead."

"And … and Charlie?"

"Half a livre to make him disappear. It would be insulting at four times the price, but I had my own reasons to take Charlie off their hands."

Corin gaped. "So you could *kill* me?" He still had an ace up his sleeve. He took a confused step toward Ahmed and then two steps back toward Charlie. Six hostile gazes followed him, but no one yet moved to intervene.

Ahmed did come a step closer, overflowing with his victory. "Aren't you listening? I never planned to kill you. I planned to *use* you. But now you say you are no use …"

Corin laughed and forced an uneven hiccup into it. "Wait! Wait! That's not what I said." Both hands rose defensively, and he backed slowly away from Ahmed. Two paces, three, until he bumped into the guard standing over Charlie Claire.

Ahmed showed his teeth in a predatory grin. "Are you prepared to change your story now? You might still have one last little bit of value?"

Corin sighed. "I suppose I do at that. You said Tommy Day took passage to Marzelle?"

Ahmed blinked, surprised by the sudden change in topic. "What? I ... yes, but—"

"And he's already gone?"

"Yes! But *you* are here! And I have Charlie Claire."

"Had," Corin corrected. He dropped his hand on Charlie's shoulder and stepped through dream again.

It was a perfect exit. Except, somehow, it all went wrong. Something in the magic faltered, and Charlie Claire began to scream.

(6)

The world went soft and gray around Corin, but it didn't instantly transform this time. Instead, everything went still. Ahmed the Fig, mid-clap. The guard behind Charlie Claire, slashing with his dagger. Four others starting forward, frozen on their first step.

The room receded, dwindling to a point in Corin's vision, while everything else was thick gray fog. Then he began to move, soaring northward above the nothing, while the Fig's establishment rolled to the horizon. But Corin had barely gone far enough to cross Khera before he slammed to an abrupt stop. And there in the air before him, surprised as ever, was the woman he'd met twice in the city streets. She cried out in shock, and perhaps Corin did as well, but the sound was gone a moment later. The vision was gone, and that strange woman with it.

Corin was back in Ahmed's private room. The others still stood frozen, but perhaps they had begun to thaw. Perhaps Ahmed's hands came closer together. Perhaps the guard's dagger shifted downward. Corin ground his teeth and focused his will on a bolthole he knew in Marzelle, and tried to step through dream again.

Again the gray world rolled away, and Corin felt himself rushing down the same path he'd taken before. With an effort of will he heaved himself off course, veering sharply out around the city's edge. Some touch of color lit the world below, just shadows and hard edges, but it was enough to show Corin the coastline flashing by, the stormy Medgerrad he knew so well, and moments later he saw the distant shape of rich Ithale.

No sooner had he passed over the land than another figure sprang into the air before him. This one Corin knew all too well. Ephitel himself, the tyrant king of gods. Shock and outrage washed across his face in the fraction of a heartbeat that passed before Corin reached him.

For his part, Corin felt nothing but animal rage. Before he could even think, the sword was in his hand. Corin swung with all his might, slashing at the monster's throat—

And he was back in Ahmed's office. Corin roared his fury, closed his hand more tightly on Charlie's shoulder, and leaped away again. He went west this time, not east, but somewhere in the desert he encountered a new figure—a total stranger who had the grace and bearing Corin had learned to associate with the ancient elves. Again, as quickly as they met, Corin was thrown back. He closed his eyes and fixed his will and jumped. Another path, another interloper over Meloan. Another path, and an elf on the high seas near Jebbra Point.

A furious panic now clawed at Corin's heart, as every time he returned to Ahmed's lair, he saw the flashing dagger, saw the closing trap. This *had* to work! If it didn't, Charlie was a dead man, and Corin likely was too. He caught a heavy breath and leaped again.

Yet another path, and Corin steered a wild course between the points he'd learned to avoid, like deadly rocks off the Spinola coast. Somehow this time he dodged them all. He crashed home in Marzelle—blackest port in all of Raentz—rushing down toward the cellar he'd imagined. That room exploded in his mind just as Ahmed's had receded, until Corin saw himself standing there in gray-fog darkness, Charlie Claire beside him, still tied to that expensive chair. Corin blinked his eyes, gasped for breath, and shook the spell away.

It took a moment more, but at last the eerie gray faded to black, and time returned.

Charlie never once stopped screaming in his ear.

"Steady on, sailor," Corin said. "We are safer now."

"What was that? What happened? Where are we?"

"Marzelle."

"Raentz? You bring me to Raentz? We may as well have stayed to die at the Fig's brothel!"

"Be still!" Corin hissed again. "Marzelle is not so bad as that."

"For us it is! Storming seas, Captain, this is Dave Taker's home port!"

Corin turned slowly to face his loyal follower. His voice came out a dangerous growl. "You knew this and you didn't tell me?"

"You asked about the girl and Blake—"

"But Taker's his first mate!"

"I've told you more than once. The ship is sunk. The crew's split up. And Ethan Blake is gone!"

Corin closed his eyes. "This changes things."

"Yes! Take us away from here!"

"No! Be still." Corin turned away, pacing. "So Taker finally rose to first mate, then lost it within weeks. That might serve me well."

"On a spit, perhaps. Can't you guess how angry that has made him?"

"Oh, aye. But that anger belongs to Ethan Blake."

"Perhaps it should, but he directs it at the crew. At the men who rejected Blake's command."

"Fascinating," Corin said.

"Terrifying. You know this man! You saw how his cronies treated me."

Corin hesitated. Blake's men had found Charlie just after Corin betrayed him and abandoned him, but Charlie hadn't thrown any accusations yet. Perhaps he didn't know. Corin tried to argue in his own defense. "It's just a shame you weren't able to see how I punished them for that."

Charlie offered Corin a grateful smile, without any sign of accusation. "Oh, I saw Tommy Day bleeding from his gut. Pale as a ghost and wailing almost as bad as one. Billy had to hold him up. I just wish you'd done the same to that sneaking scholar. He tried to rob me, just like you said he would."

Corin shook his head in mock outrage. "The knave! Well, you'll be glad to know I settled all our debts with him. And now we'll settle up with Taker and his cronies."

Charlie swallowed hard and looked away. "Why ... why now? If you're so anxious to do battle, why'd you leave me to 'em back in Khera?"

Corin shook his head. "Tommy had a pistol, and I had to step quick."

"Ah. You worked your magic?"

"Aye, and it lost me hours."

"Well ... you came for me anyway. And for that I thank you. But I'll beg you now—take me somewhere else!"

"Steady on, sailor. Steady on. We have our tasks to do, but there is glory in it."

Charlie shook his head, then had to reach up to steady himself. "I can't do it. I'm sorry, Captain, but I can't face Dave Taker. I stole from him. Don't you understand? And if he finds me here..."

Corin heaved a weary sigh. In Khera, he'd tried to leave Charlie Claire, and Charlie had avowed his faithfulness. But faced with Dave Taker—no, faced with the very city Dave Taker was staying in—Charlie quailed.

And that made Charlie into a risk. Corin didn't dare turn him loose, and unless he could calm some of the deckhand's fears, Charlie was going to bolt. Chances were all too good he'd dash right into the hands of their enemies.

So Corin caught Charlie's shoulder and gave it a strong squeeze. "You've convinced me, Charlie. I owe you better. I'll find you passage."

"Us! This place is no safer for you."

Corin hesitated; then for Charlie's sake, he lied. "Aye. I'll find us passage. Where'd you like to go?"

"I hear good things about far-off Ellena."

"Good man! Far indeed, but the architecture's lovely there. I'll see it done. You just get some rest."

Charlie looked around and patted the cool earth wall. "What is this place?"

"A safe house. Aren't you in the Nimble Fingers?"

"Sorry, Captain. Never been a cutpurse. Honest sailor all my life."

"You're missing out. The Nimble Fingers is a powerful brotherhood."

Charlie rubbed his recently split scalp. "Better brothers than a pirate crew?"

"Oh, quite! If it had been the Nimble Fingers, you never would have felt a thing."

For a long time, Charlie said nothing. Then he crossed the room to kick at a straw-stuffed mattress on the floor. "This is all for us?"

"For anyone who needs it. This isn't the nicest house in town, but it's usually pretty empty. You get some sleep. Heal your hairline. I'll leave our marking at the door and then go see what ships are sailing soon and what they'd cost us."

Charlie dropped down on his back, staring blankly up at the dirt ceiling. "I'll work. Don't have to pay ... I'll earn my way."

"Nonsense. I've ... got a bit of coin. I'll be glad to pay your way."

A smile touched the sailor's lips. "Sounds ... sounds good."

Corin watched his old crewman for a moment, then turned and headed for the stairs. He'd find Charlie passage and get him safe aboard his ship. But first, he had to find some old friends.

The cellar room had its own exit to the alley behind its house. Corin's senses strained as soon as he closed the door behind him. A warm night lay over Marzelle, and the city provided a strong contrast to desert Khera. Lamps glowed on every street corner, showing the reserved locals, who went quietly about their business in modest working clothes. Here and there among them were the swarthy sailors who made the port town so wealthy.

Corin spent little attention on the locals, though he blended easily among them in his plain black clothes and long, rich cloak.

No, his attention focused on those who moved with the easy, rolling lope of seafarers on city streets.

He saw no sign of Dave Taker or his vicious cronies, but there were certainly familiar faces here and there. Corin saw old crewmates—none from his command, but more than one who should have recognized him from his days aboard the *Chariot* under Old Grim.

But Corin had been more than a pirate. Even without touching Oberon's strange magic, he had his tricks. He drifted down Marzelle's city streets like a dim reflection over still waters. He adjusted course and hugged the shadows and turned his face before any old compatriot might recognize him. And he did it all without ever breaking pace. It was almost as good as coming home, to walk the shady streets of a port town in the proper Godlands once again.

He drifted absently, guessing at which ships might be in port, which crews might be broken up, by nothing more than the occasional familiar face. And all the while he made his way toward the east, toward a Nimble Fingers tavern that might offer him more precise information.

Halfway there, he slipped around a corner into what should have been an empty alley and, for all his grace, he crashed into a woman moving fast the other way.

Both figures spilled apart, down to the cobblestones, but even as the woman fell—even as she spat a vile curse—she raised her right arm to keep her weapon trained on Corin.

"Gods' blood!" he shouted, as astonished as he was angry. "It can't be you again!"

But even as he said it, he registered what he was seeing. She no longer wore the long white robes of Jepta, but a tailored cotton dress that left her arms bare and revealed quite clearly the outlandish weapon she carried.

It was something like a flintlock pistol, but smaller, with a glossy casing of glass and precious metals. Seemingly too delicate, too light, too small to be any serious threat, but Corin knew better. He'd seen this thing in action—twelve hundred years ago, but less than a week to him.

An instant after he set eyes on the druids' poison pistol, he saw her face. And then he understood why she had felt so familiar. He knew her. He had met her in the streets of Jezeeli just before it burned, but he would never forget that face. This was the woman who had rescued him, who had defied the tyrant Ephitel to stop a war, and who had clung to Oberon's rules even after he relinquished them.

This was Aemilia, a one-time moneychanger in the city of the gods. And here, at last, he'd found a friend who might truly understand him.

"I don't know what you are," she said, "but if you so much as move, I will make your body a prison for your mind. Do you understand?"

"I don't," he said, but he was not so stupid as to move. He had watched one of the tiny darts from that strange weapon incapacitate an elven soldier in a fleeting heartbeat. But still he was confused. Why would she threaten him at all? Why pretend she didn't know him?

Ah! But it had been more than a thousand years since she last saw him. How many other dashing pirate captains had she met in all that time? How many other grand adventures had she enjoyed? Any answer just raised questions of its own.

He frowned at her. "How can it be that you are still alive?"

She flashed her teeth, though it was not a friendly smile. "I am careful and I'm smart and I overuse my ammo."

Corin took a risk. Slowly, unthreateningly, he shifted. She twitched the dartgun, but she didn't fire it, so he rolled up into a more comfortable position. A moment later, almost reluctantly, she did too. On their knees now, two paces distant, they faced each other.

Would a thousand years be time enough to forget a face like that? It lacked the fine, sharp lines of Raentz's noble ladies or the snowy pale so praised in Princess Sera. Her hair was short, held back with combs, her eyes a boring brown. She was not beautiful, but there was something in her bearing, in her every expression, that was absolutely *her*. Intelligence and strength and fear in equal measure. He smiled, despite himself, to look on her again and wondered aloud, "Where did you get a thousand years? How did you get here?"

"I will ask the questions!"

"Why?" Corin asked. "Why have you been stalking me?"

"To find out what you are. To understand the threat you pose."

Corin spread his hands. "You could more easily have asked. I will tell you. I am Corin Hugh, an enterprising manling who has seen much of the world."

"Manling?" she asked, shock in her tone. "Where did you learn that word?"

"In the same place I learned the tricks that so alarm you. It's also where I learned that *I* am not the threat you fear. That honor is reserved for Ephitel."

Her eyes went wide. She forgot the weapon in her hand and bent toward him. "Do not say such things on open streets."

"It is also where I met you, Aemilia. A druid in a moneychanger's shop. Or should I call you Emily?"

The druid's eyes narrowed. She said, "Everything about you is wrong." And then she shot him.

Corin saw her pull the trigger. He saw the glass-and-silver dart exit the barrel, flashing distant torchlight. The dart bit into his neck just above the shoulder, sharp and hot like a scorpion's sting, and the poison went straight to work. Corin's world turned gray and fuzzy, soft around the edges, much like it had done when he tried to leap away from Ahmed's place.

And again, he watched time unwind. He felt himself slam back down into the alley. The pain in his neck faded, and color washed back in.

Corin stared, stunned but clearheaded, while Aemilia still covered him with her weapon. Her eyes narrowed. She said, "Everything about you is wrong." And she shot him. Again.

He had a chance to curse this time, but nothing more before the dart struck home. The tranquilizer seemed to burn worse this time, but the effect was the same. Gray fog enveloped him, pulling him away, but he lashed out against it. *No*, he thought, furious. *I have no time to rest.* And back he went. The memory of pain remained, but history unwound itself so Corin found Aemelia once more narrowing her eyes.

"Wait!" he shouted, trying desperately to twist away, but there was no time. She shot him in the back of the shoulder, and that worked just as well.

And once again he clawed his way back. This time he didn't hesitate. While she was still deciding, he sprang forward, closing the narrow distance between them, and knocked the dartgun from her grip with a full-arm backhand.

She dove after it, but he rolled once and tripped her up with a scissor kick. Then he leaped like a frog and flung himself to cover up the weapon with his body. He curled around it, fighting for his breath, and tensed himself against whatever violence would come next. Surely this toy was not the druid's only magic.

But before he felt anything, he heard the sound of running footsteps. He shoved then, taking the weapon with him as he rolled to his feet, but Aemilia was already halfway down the alley and moving fast. "Stop!" he shouted after her. He raised the dartgun. "I'll shoot!" But the woman didn't slow, and Corin didn't fire. By the time he reached the alley's mouth, she was lost to sight.

(7)

Corin didn't dare give serious chase. There had been too many familiar faces in the crowd. Frustrating though it was, he let her go. For now, anyway. He would have to track her down eventually because he needed answers only she could give.

How *had* she survived a thousand years? She certainly looked no worse for wear. Was that some druid secret, or had she stepped through time the same as Corin?

For that matter, how had she been able to find him? The woman seemed as close as his shadow, popping up every time he turned a blind corner. The thought was an alarming one because Corin needed his anonymity. He had dangerous work to do, and a persistent tail might get him killed.

At least he had her weapon. He looked down at the contraption in his hands and remembered the stabbing fire of its bite. It only had one shot, but it was a strong one. He remembered what had happened all too well: four different chains of events, all of them mutually exclusive. What had happened in that weird gray fog? Was this more of Oberon's power, or something new at play?

He cursed quietly to himself while he watched the slow tides of sailors and villagers flowing past the alley's mouth. Only one person in this city could answer his questions, and he had let her slip away.

Again, he felt some small victory at capturing her weapon. If he tracked her down before she found another one, he'd have the upper hand. In the meantime, he had other business to attend to. As Corin slipped back into the flow of traffic, he stashed the druid's gun beneath his cloak, in a pocket near another pistol that wasn't his. The dwarven revolver was a piece of mastercraft, but still it made Corin's skin crawl.

Another memory torn from the past. He had promised to deliver it to its rightful inheritor, the dwarf known as Ben Strunk, but that would have to wait. Aemilia would have to wait. Even Ephitel would wait. There was so much to do, but Ethan Blake came first.

Corin ground his teeth as he remembered the traitor. So much to do, and all of it required information. At least he knew where to find it. Cautious as he was being, the journey took twice as long as it should have, but at long last Corin found the shady tavern used as headquarters by the local chapter of the Nimble Fingers.

Corin watched the door for half an hour, assuring himself that nothing was amiss, but in the end impatience won him over. He slipped across the empty street, announced himself with a patterned knock, and flowed through the narrow doorway.

The room beyond was barely more than a cellar, with unfinished walls and a low ceiling. Choking smoke hung heavy in the air and almost overpowered the stink of stale beer. At half a dozen little tables around the room, tired-looking men drank beer or wine, but no one seemed much interested in conversation.

Half a pace inside the room, Corin's eyes burned and his shoulders sagged. He breathed deep of the noxious air and grinned despite himself. At long, long last, he had come home.

Then someone hit him. The blow came in from the side—from the doorman he'd just passed—and it nearly unhinged Corin's jaw. Light burst behind Corin's eyes, red and orange, and he stumbled two paces into the smoky room.

His attacker was talking, something puffed up and obnoxious in a deeply slurred Raentz dialect that Corin didn't bother trying to unravel. He was just waiting for the gray fog to take over, for the chance to unwind time and catch this villain unprepared.

It didn't happen. Still mouthing off, the villain closed with Corin and slammed a kick right into his gut. Corin folded over, gasping, and rolled away a moment before the brute's foot came stomping down hard. Still no gray fog. Still no help from Oberon.

If you can't count on a dead god these days, who can you count on? The thought flashed through Corin's mind, and the answer was an easy one. He'd never been able to count on anyone—not even Old Grim, once push came to shove—but Corin could always count on himself. And he wasn't about to lose a fight to some stinking Raentzman!

Corin rolled again, curled up tight, and sprang to his feet. His hand went instinctively for the dagger on his belt, but the Nimble Fingers had its rules. He left the blade alone, ducked a vicious haymaker, then stepped in close and threw all his weight into an uppercut. The villain's head snapped back with a *crack* that drew a groan from someone else in the room, and Corin's opponent staggered back a pace, but he didn't go down.

His heart pounding now with unspent anger, Corin pursued the bigger man. He feinted high then threw a quick, sharp kick that snapped something in the villain's ankle. The Raentzman started to fall then, and as he passed, Corin smashed an elbow against the back of his neck. That drew another groan—as well as some approving grunts—from his audience. It also left the Raentzman out cold on the floor.

Now Corin drew a weapon. He went for the sword *Godslayer* too, instead of the little dagger. Bar fights were not uncommon in a Nimble Fingers tavern, but the rules said to keep them one-on-one. If anyone felt an urge to avenge the big man on the floor, the rules went out the window.

One slow glance told him he was safe. For now, at least. There were perhaps a dozen patrons in the bar, dressed like locals and none of them with the look of a sailor. If any had thought to spring on him, the sword had instantly dissuaded them. Now it held all their eyes transfixed, and that gave Corin time enough to catch his breath and formulate a question in his uneasy Raentzian. He found the inn's proprietor among the watchers, marked as clearly by the scars across his face as by the tarnished tin ring on his right hand. Corin nodded his direction. "What was his problem?"

The innkeeper answered in easy Ithalian. "Josef has no love for your countrymen."

Corin frowned. "My countrymen?"

"That was an Ithalian knock if ever I've heard one. Josef's something of a connoisseur."

"Of *knocks*?"

"All manner of secret signs." The innkeeper jerked his head toward the bar, then pulled Corin a flagon of beer. As he passed it over, he went on. "Josef is our records keeper."

Corin gaped at that. He spun on his heel to stare at the man he'd dropped, and took in details he'd missed during the frenzy of the fight. He was old, for one—nearly thirty—and the fringe around his big bald head was dusty red. Corin shook his head. "Josef of Marzelle? I know him! I studied under him."

"Oh, many have."

"But I don't understand. He bore me no ill will then."

The innkeeper shrugged. "Times have changed. Some of your countrymen have staked a claim on Marzelle, and they play by no rules but their own. Josef thought you had the look of one of them."

"Aye," Corin said, staring sadly at the unconscious form of Josef. "He's got a good eye. These countrymen of mine. They would be pirates?"

The innkeeper nodded. Corin took a long drink, then nodded back. "I know them right enough. Dave Taker and his boys. I only just learned that they call Marzelle home. In fact, I came to your tavern tonight to ask for aid in finding them."

The innkeeper pursed his lips, clearly worrying he'd said too much. "You...you struck me as a man who knows the rules."

Corin grinned back. "Friend, I've shaken hands with Avery himself. I mean you no trouble. I have a score to settle with Dave Taker and his crew."

The innkeeper breathed a heavy sigh, "Then we are friends indeed. Even Josef may clasp your hand when he recovers. He always did respect a worthy foe." He stepped aside to call out orders in his native tongue to the other patrons, who still stood watching Corin in utter fascination.

At the innkeeper's command, the others finally began to move. They lifted Josef from the floor and found him a more comfortable position on one of the long benches against the outer wall. Someone ran to fetch a physician too, and that reminded Corin that he had other pressing questions.

"If you would call me friend," he said, "I could dearly use some information."

"We get but little news since the pirates settled in, but I will tell you what I can."

"What do you know of druids in Marzelle?"

"Druids?" He laughed. "There are none here. If you need druids, head out west to the Dividing Line. They keep to their circles and rarely trouble us at all."

"But I just met a woman in the streets. She dressed like a local, but she carried a druid artifact."

"No doubt stolen."

"No. I know her to be a druid."

The innkeeper shrugged. "Then you know more than I. But I can tell you they do not find favor with our ruling houses or our gods, so if she is still in town at all, she'll do everything within her power to stay hidden."

"And that's a problem?" Corin asked. "Is there no one in your Nimble Fingers who excels at finding just such people?"

"There may be one or two. Are you prepared to ask this favor of them?"

Corin didn't answer right away. Favors carried heavy weight within the Nimble Fingers, and Corin had no surplus to share. He could scarce afford the extra burden, with all the work he already had to do. So he sighed and shook his head. "No. Forget the druid. I'll find her on my own. But I will ask their help in tracking down two of my enemies."

"Are these the pirates?"

"Aye. Dave Taker's cousin Tommy and Tommy's loyal sidekick, Billy Bo."

The innkeeper shook his head. "Such silly names you pirates wear."

Corin shrugged. "They are a kind of armor. And at times, a kind of weapon too."

"And you mean to do battle with these names?"

Corin showed his teeth. "They dared to mutiny against me. They have harmed a loyal friend. I mean to war with them."

"Then these charges will not cost you any favors. I suspect when you provide an adequate description, we will already know where to find them. We are watching, after all."

"Ah, but I don't even know if they've arrived yet. I may have beaten these two to Marzelle, so it may require a careful watch."

"When did you expect them?"

Corin paused, calculating in his head. They'd spent the winter in the Endless Desert. It had been about the end of February when they found Jezeeli. By Charlie's estimation, Corin had lost more than three months in his short step across the desert, and some couple days with Charlie there in Khera. If Tommy and Billy both went straight to Raentz from Ahmed's place, it would still take them weeks. Corin plotted the most likely course, double-checked it, and nodded to himself. "No sooner than the first of June," he said. "No later than July."

The innkeeper blinked, surprised. "Then they arrived two months ago."

Corin groaned.

The innkeeper went on. "Or it will be most of a year. Do you mean to wait so long?"

Corin buried his face in his hands. "When is this?" The innkeeper didn't answer right away, so Corin clarified. "What month and year? How much time have I lost now?"

"It is the fourth of August in the twenty-third year of the reign of Francis."

"Two months!" Corin groaned again. "Two more months lost while Dave Taker plays the tyrant here. While Ethan Blake slips through my fingers! While Iryana..."

Corin fell silent. He remembered all too clearly the fiery anger that had fueled him during his fight with Josef. Already the fire was stoking forge-hot again. No matter what he did, his enemies slipped further and further away. And the only ones he managed to hurt at all were his friends. He thought of Charlie Claire, his scalp split open in the scholar's rooms. He thought of the poor young scholar Tesyn. And of the terrified look in the druid woman's eyes when he confronted her. Even old Josef had been a friend once.

He'd spent too long silent. The innkeeper cleared his throat and, with a nervous edge to his voice, asked, "Is there something troubling you?"

"I have been blown about by stormwinds," Corin said. "And it has gained me nothing. It is time I took the tiller."

"Oh?"

Corin laughed darkly. "Aye. I have much work to do, and I will ask a thousand favors if I must. You say Marzelle is starved for news?"

"The Captain's men are hanging Nimble Fingers in the streets. No one comes this way."

"But you can leave? Even Raentz has roads, hasn't it?"

The innkeeper puffed up behind the bar. "We have the finest post in all Hurope."

"Then choose your finest sneak and send him down the road. If news won't come to you, then go and fetch it."

"But the Captain—"

"Will be busy soon. Too busy by far to catch your slinking messenger."

"You truly mean to go to war with him?"

Corin shook his head. "No. He is no mighty foe. He and his crew alike are wretched vermin, and I mean to exterminate them."

"It will be no easy task."

Corin clapped the innkeeper on the shoulder. "I am no normal thief."

"Then ask anything you need of me, and it is yours. I speak for this chapter of the Nimble Fingers, and I will guarantee you anything Marzelle can hope to offer."

"But all I ask is news. There is a nobleman's son of the house Vestossi who, for some time, sailed under the pirate name of Ethan Blake. Some months ago, he gained and lost his first command."

"You called him Ethan Blake?"

"Aye, just so. Find out what has become of him. And he had with him a desert girl named Iryana. I must know her fate as well."

"Iryana. His ... mistress?"

"Perhaps. Perhaps his slave. Perhaps his victim. I do not know."

"We will do our best to discover it."

"Good. And find Ben Strunk for me. He's most likely to be—"

The innkeeper interrupted to clarify. "Another pirate?"

Corin gaped. "You don't know Ben Strunk? Well, there's another favor you will owe me. He is no pirate. He does not belong to the Nimble Fingers either, but he loves to patronize our taverns."

"Is he a spy? A justicar?"

"Gods' blood, your heart is grim. He's no kind of foe. He is just a dwarf who loves to drink and lose at cards. And he's a close friend of mine."

"Then we will find him for you."

"I'll be grateful for it. And last, when I have made Marzelle safe for you once more, I will ask your aid in finding me this druid. She too is a friend. Or ... I hope for her to be."

The innkeeper paused, clearly reviewing Corin's requests, and after a moment he nodded. "All these things can be done. And if you but rid us of the Captain, they all together will not be reward enough."

"Then I will also let you find some easy retirement for a friend of mine. A former pirate who goes by Charlie Claire."

"It seems a fair exchange."

Corin fetched a tiny silver ring out from his purse. It was a thing of no great value, but it was sufficient for a pledge. The rules insisted coin could not be used, so Corin always carried something of the sort.

He slapped it down on the bar. "You have my pledge according to the rules. I will free this town from Dave Taker and his men."

The innkeeper produced an empty leather sheath, something fitting for a lady's tiny poniard, but decorated in gemstone flakes and delicate gold leaf. "You have my pledge as well. Let it be done."

Corin finished off his beer, glad to have a plan at last, then settled in to sort out the fine details.

(8)

The surgeon who came for Josef was no druid, but he seemed a quality physician. Once old Josef was on his feet, the two of them shared a friendly pint, and then Corin asked someone to show the doctor across town to look in on Charlie Claire. It felt a small price after all of Charlie's loyalty.

But mostly Corin focused on the traitors. He learned everything he could from the locals, and everything pointed back to Dave Taker. All their troubles had started back in April, shortly after Corin disappeared. For a while, there had been an uneasy peace, brokered by an unseen pirate who called himself "the Captain." That *had* to be Ethan Blake. Corin was sure of it.

He'd come to town with a small fortune to spare, and he'd spent it buying out the local watchmen and justices. Those few who wouldn't tender to Ithalian silver disappeared. For a while, the Nimble Fingers had considered it a luxury.

But then, some weeks back, the Captain had disappeared. He left an authority in his place, and that one went by "the First Mate." He was the man so fiercely despised by Marzelle's citizens, for he had ruled through violence and force. He'd crushed the Nimble Fingers and anyone else who had threatened either his authority or wealth.

Discussing all this with the innkeeper, Corin had tried to offer help. "That must be Dave Taker, though I've never known him to think so big."

The innkeeper shrugged. "It might well be. He's never used an honest name."

"How can that be?"

"He never needed one. The Captain came with silver enough to justify his quirks, and the First Mate has operated under the authority that silver purchased."

"Then I'll describe Dave Taker to you."

"No better. We have never seen the First Mate at all."

Corin rocked back. "Absurd! How can he run this town without someone in your organization encountering him? There should at least be rumors."

"Of course, but the rumors paint him ten feet tall with pointy teeth and claws for hands."

"And none of you has gone in person to find out?"

"That's what I'm telling you! There is no 'in person' with this man. He reigns by proxy. In all his time here, he has never shown his face."

Corin's shoulders sagged. "Well, this I can believe. The Vestossis have always loved their paranoia. But it's an opportunity too."

"What opportunity?"

"If he reigns by proxy, and if I can remove him, someone else can step into his place. Someone like you or Josef. And simply use his proxies to your own ends."

The innkeeper whistled in stunned admiration. "You are a devious creature. But no."

"What? Why not?"

"You do not understand how cruel this man has been. Who of us could bear to step into his role? Even as a farce. No. We won't."

Corin licked his lips. "That's fine. That's fine. I will remove him all the same."

"But how?"

"Where does he hide? Can you at least tell me that much?"

"He lives aboard his ship, the *Espinola*. As far as we can tell, he never leaves. Magistrates and justices and even local lords will sometimes come and go, but they speak only with his concierge."

"Then how can they even know they're truly dealing with the Captain's man?"

"Those who defy the orders they receive invariably ... suffer. Lord Béthané's manor burned to the ground, his wife and child still inside it. The Marquis's prize thoroughbreds were butchered to the last and left to rot in their own paddocks.

Corin shuddered. "This sounds like Dave Taker and his men."

"And those who obey their orders are handsomely rewarded. But it is fear, not love, that grants the Captain and his First Mate such authority."

Corin spent a moment thinking. "What has been tried already?"

"The Marquis did send a plea to the court at Pri for aid."

Corin scoffed. "And I suspect they answered that this was a local matter."

"To be resolved by local authorities. Exactly so. Lord Béthané roused his own armed militia to take the ship or sink it."

Corin sighed. "And his militia was cut down. Did they even make it to the piers?"

"Only a handful. Most of them died in the streets while crossing town."

Corin nodded. "Aye. I'd have done the same. But what has the Nimble Fingers done?"

Surprise and incomprehension reigned in the innkeeper's expression. "The Nimble Fingers? We have done everything within our power to keep concealed and keep alive."

"You haven't fought him? When he's been hanging your people in the streets?"

"We're thieves. We aren't soldiers."

Corin stopped himself short of shouting. Would *he* have done anything, before he rose to captain of a pirate ship? Likely not. Even then, it might have been the visit to Jezeeli that finally forged him into a man of action.

But now he had seen too clearly the cost of inaction in the face of tyranny. Such monsters knew no bounds, and any price was a fair one if it could strip them of their power.

Corin closed his hand around the grip of the sword *Godslayer* and caught the innkeeper's eye. "This darkness is nearly at an end. But first, I ask you to prepare me something warm and rich to eat, and pick out a room for me."

"You will rest? Now?"

"It has been two months since I last had something real to eat, longer since I slept. Besides, it will take some time for my plan to be set in motion."

"Then you *have* devised a plan?"

"I have."

"Will you tell it?"

Corin thought a moment and shrugged. "It is very much like Béthané's except that I will go alone. And I will do what he could not."

"How?"

Corin grinned. "In much the same way I defeated Josef here. I am one of them, and I am worse than them. They will never see me coming."

⬧

Corin set out at dawn, with encouragement from the inn-keeper and a hearty breakfast warming his belly. He had to cross half the town again to reach the port, but this time he didn't skulk. He went boldly by the light of day, and his long black cloak flared around him. He pretended not to notice when a deckhand from Bad Brandon's crew recognized him. Carl? Cane? Something of the sort. From the corner of his eye, Corin watched the man's burst of recognition shift to surprise, and surprise to dark ambition. After all, there would be some reward to the man who informed the First Mate that Corin Hugh was in town.

So Corin marched on, apparently oblivious, as Carl or Cane or Connor—whoever he was—sprinted off toward the docks. Corin allowed himself a fraction of a smile as he went on.

Three more old acquaintances repeated Carl's performance, and then a fourth surprised Corin. It was Lucky Lou, a gray-haired, stringy old veteran who had served with Corin on Old Grim's crew years ago.

Lucky Lou didn't run for the docks; he ran to intercept Corin. He didn't pretend any ignorance either. He'd always been a straight talker. "It's a fool move, son. I don't care what you've heard, it don't apply to you. Get out of town."

Corin answered in the same low tone. "I appreciate the warning, old man. More than you can know. But nothing's changing my resolve, and they might make you regret stopping to talk with me."

"Regret is a young man's vice, Corin. The only people in the world with that power over me are Old Grim and Ephitel himself." He went two paces in silence, then sighed. "And right this moment, you. I don't want to see you dead over some blasted ship."

"It's not the ship."

"Fine. Some blasted mutiny. Not much difference in my books. Listen to an old man's experience: Count yourself lucky that you survived, and find some new endeavor."

Corin shared a smile. "I've found one. I'm doing a favor for the good people of Marzelle."

"Pfft! Not much reward in public service. Would you really spill a drop of blood for a few stinking Raentzmen?"

"I'd spill all of Dave Taker's."

"You mean Tommy Day's?"

"I mean every rat left of that crew, if I get the chance. Ethan Blake too."

Something in that name snapped Lou's patient resolve. He stopped in his tracks, knotted a fist in Corin's shirt, and pulled him close. Eyes flashing and voice cast low, he said, "Hear me, son, because wherever you've been lately, you've lost your bearings good. Ethan Blake is a Vestossi, Dave Taker owns a port in Raentz, and Tommy Day kills off regiments for sport. These are the men you want to tangle with."

Every bit as serious, Corin answered him. "I don't much care what his father's name is. I plan to put an end to Ethan Blake."

Lucky Lou snorted. "As well say you plan to pick a fight with Ephitel. You can't tangle with a Vestossi."

Corin weighed his answer. It served him naught to tip his hand, but he couldn't stop himself. He shrugged. "One thing at a time."

Lou shook him like a child's doll. "I'm not joking. I'll tell you one more time: Leave town."

"I will. Tomorrow."

"Stormy seas, Corin! I never thought you a fool."

"Have a little faith. I keep some secrets of my own."

"I *had* some faith. Right up until you defied me."

"You never were my captain, Lou."

"No. No. But I used to be your friend."

"You still are."

"If that's a fact—if you feel any kindness to me at all—abandon this whole enterprise. I have rooms in a country inn an hour outside town. These blackguards don't reach that far. Come share a drink with me, and I will change your mind."

When Corin hesitated, Lou leaned closer still and begged him. "Please."

But even as he stood there wrestling with the choice, Corin caught sight of Doug the Gar across the way. One of his old hands, and almost as loyal to Taker as Tommy was. Doug didn't try for stealth at all. He cried out in alarm and then ran all-out for the docks.

And that was why Corin couldn't yield to Lou's pleas. No matter what he owed the man, Corin's plans were already in motion. Already word of his presence had reached Dave Taker's ship. If Corin arrived within the hour, he'd find chaos waiting for him there. If he waited any longer, the First Mate would have time to restore order, lay a trap for him, or send someone to kill him in the streets as he'd done to Béthané's militiamen.

Corin dropped his gaze. "I'm sorry, Lou. I can't afford to wait. I would love to share a drink with you. I'm sure there's much I need to know. But after—"

Lou spat. "There won't be any 'after.' I won't hang around to watch those dogs tear out your guts. I'm leaving this town and glad to be done of it. Are you coming with me or no?"

"I *can't*."

Lou showed no understanding. He sneered at Corin, disappointed, then turned and stomped off up the street. Away from the docks and everything that waited there. Corin watched him go. Perhaps with the Nimble Fingers' help he could track down the old man once this mess was settled, but right now he had urgent business.

And just as he was turning to continue on his way, he spotted another familiar face in the crowd. Not an old crewmate this time, but the blasted druid woman. She was hugging a busy street corner twenty paces distant, watching him with interest and scarcely trying to conceal herself.

"Gods' blood!" Corin shouted. "Not now!" Then he turned his back on her and ran.

He went two miles to the docks, without slowing. He leaped the harbormaster's wall at full sprint. It only took a glance to pick out the *Espinola*—the only ship in port with the gall to fly the black flag—and Corin covered half the pier before he remembered his dignity enough to slow to a more stately walk. That was far too late. Already the end of the pier was crowded with curious spectators. The decks of the other ships he passed were packed as well, all work forgotten as everyone in port watched the man in black march bravely to his doom.

Corin was not too concerned. There were more familiar faces on the deck of the *Espinola*, not just old acquaintances, but his own crew. Certainly there were some like Dave Taker and Tommy Day among them—vicious hearts who'd been glad to slip free of Corin's restraining hand—but there were others who were merely followers, who had gone along with the prevailing winds in their mutiny, but who bore Corin no genuine ill will. Likely they had seen hard times since Corin disappeared. Likely they felt pangs of guilt and regret as much as their companions felt amusement watching Corin's approach.

Corin sought the guilty expressions as he passed below. He caught those men's eyes and offered each one a penetrating stare. By the time he reached the gangplank, more than a few up there had slipped quietly away.

But at the foot of the gangplank, he found a hulking brute who was no acquaintance of his. The man didn't even look to be a sailor. This was likely one of the local watchmen whose loyalty had been purchased with Blake's silver. The man did not yield as Corin approached, but drew a heavy sword, notched and scarred with much hard use. "Halt. What is your business here?"

Corin looked him up and down, trying for dismissive, and gave a weary sigh. "I am Corin Hugh, captain of these men, recently returned from the dead and ready to reclaim my post."

The watchman shook his head. "I know the Captain. You ain't him."

"Soldier," Corin said, packing his voice with contempt, "I am a problem above and beyond what the Captain pays you for. Surely you have heard the rumors." He waved expansively. "You see the crowds who came when they heard whispers of my name. I am here to speak with your employer—"

"The First Mate said no visitors!"

"And I am the exception. If you don't tell him that I called, after all these good people came to see us talk ... why, they may spread rumors that the First Mate was too *afraid* to face the ghost of Corin Hugh."

"Let them say what they will. It's not my problem."

"Oh? And you are sure your master will see things this way? You are sure he won't blame *you* for this slur against his reputation, when you were too stubborn, too arrogant to simply *ask* if he would like to speak with me?"

The watchman glared at Corin. Corin just gave another sigh. "Oh, very well. You can take me before the First Mate, and if he doesn't wish to see me, just stab me there. What do you say?"

"He'll probably stab you himself."

"You see? This whole plan saves you work."

The watchman hesitated, his lips moving as he worked through Corin's argument, but his eyes glazed over too. Corin breathed a silent thanks to Fortune for stupid watchmen everywhere.

"You know," Corin said, "I can save you even that much trouble. I'll go and settle this and tell you what he said." He brushed lightly past the watchman and made it halfway up the gangplank before he heard an angry cry from the man below. Corin didn't tarry any longer. He dashed straight to the top.

Another watchman waited there, but Corin was no stranger to close fighting on ships. He sprang from near the top of the gangplank, grabbed the ship's railing off to one side, and swung himself up into the crowd of watching crewmen. That drew a cheer from the pier below, but Taker's men all shrank away, leaving a clear path for the soldier.

Corin found a plan. He backed slowly away, luring the watchman all the way to the stern railing. All out of deck, Corin crouched there, waiting, and the hired guard came forward with a glint of anger in his eyes. "Got you now!"

He lunged.

"Not yet," Corin said. He ducked beneath the soldier's grab, swept his legs from under him, and planted both his shoulders in the big man's gut. Corin heaved upward, redirecting the watchman's momentum, guiding him up and over the low railing. The watchman gave a little yelp before he hit the harbor's water two stories down with a mighty splash. Another raucous cheer rose up from below.

Corin gave the watching crowd a wave, and then he moved before anyone else could come to stop him.

(**9**)

Corin dashed across the deck and down a ladder to the door that led into the captain's cabin. He wrenched it open, darted through, and slammed it shut behind him.

The captain's rooms were dark, shutters sealed against the morning light, and spacious even for a ship this size. Corin could not immediately pick out his target in the gloom, but an exasperated voice rasped from across the room. "Storm and fury, Billy Bo, you're back already? Are you sure you've done it right?"

Corin held his tongue and eased forward into the room. As he went, he drew his sword and, for good measure, the dwarven pistol too. His firearm wasn't loaded—gods preserve him, he was happier unarmed than carrying around a charge of dwarven powder—but it was an impressive sight all the same.

But for all his stealth, for all his success in getting this far, he felt a growing dread with every passing heartbeat.

"Well? Speak, man!" the voice cried again. "Are they ready? Is he here? What have you disturbed me for?"

Corin could contain himself no longer. As he passed one of the portholes, he kicked its shutters open to flood the room with light. Then he answered with an animal roar, "For vengeance!"

The First Mate wasn't at his desk. He wasn't backed against the wall, a cutlass in each hand. He lay half reclining in his bed, propped up with pillows and pale as a ghost.

And he was not Dave Taker. He was Tommy Day.

"Guards!" the First Mate shouted, but his voice was thin and weak. "Where are my guards?"

"They're likely coming," Corin said. "But not soon enough to save your sorry hide."

Tommy struggled to sit straighter, but Corin stomped forward and leveled the dwarven pistol at his face. "Don't move. Don't even twitch, or I will put you down."

Tommy licked his lips. "Well? Just what do you intend?"

Corin didn't have a ready answer to that question. He had never guessed he'd find an invalid Tommy Day here. Was this truly the notorious First Mate? Or had Corin come to the wrong rooms?

Dave Taker didn't seem the sort to share his cabin, even for someone as seriously ill as Tommy clearly was. Not even for his own cousin. But where *was* Dave Taker, then?

There were questions here, but there were answers too. Everything he'd heard about this First Mate—the brutality, the public displays of power—those fit Tommy Day much better than Dave Taker, who always had preferred the anonymity of shadows.

Meanwhile, Tommy's illness explained why he'd maintained his leadership by proxy. The man looked wretched, his limbs shrunken to sticks, his cheeks hollowed, his eyes bloodshot and bruised. Clearly two months had not been long enough to overcome the injury Corin had done him in Khera. But that was just another piece of unfinished business.

Corin held Tommy's dark gaze. "I've come to finish what I started. But I didn't guess you were so pitiful already. I'm prepared to make a deal."

"You will regret this day," Tommy rasped, "but not for very long."

Corin lowered the pistol until the end of the barrel rested over Tommy's heart. The tiny tremors that shook his feeble frame suggested he believed the empty threat. Corin nodded. "It's time for you to listen. I'll let you do your talking in a moment. But here's the deal I'll offer you: Leave Marzelle. Take nothing with you and no one from the crew. Run. Run fast and hard, and I won't bother to chase you."

Tommy considered Corin for a long time. Time was not on Corin's side, but he could not afford to appear concerned, so he counted seconds and left Tommy to stew.

But when Tommy spoke at last, it was just to say, "I paid the Fig good money to see you dead. I'd almost thought he managed it."

"Seems you've been paying lots of folks good money to let you down. Where'd you come by it?"

"Would you believe it was the books? The miserable scraps we stole from your stupid hole in the ground. They're worth a fortune!"

"Worth enough to chase down Charlie Claire in Khera?"

"We'd have chased him all the way across the Endless Desert. No one steals from the Captain and lives."

Corin narrowed his eyes. "The Captain. That'd be Ethan Blake?"

Tommy snorted in contempt. "Blake walked away to be some dandy of the court. Davey was the one was smart enough to see the value in the books. *He's* the captain now."

"And you're his First Mate."

Tommy showed his rotting teeth. "Important man like him needed someone strong and sharp to run the day-to-day."

Corin's grip went white-knuckled on his sword hilt. Dave Taker had inherited his crew? Ethan Blake was bad enough, but Taker? And the man had made a fortune off their backs. This ship was testament to that, even without the tales of his exploits here in Marzelle.

Corin growled. "Where is Davey now?"

Tommy paused again. Time slipped away. At last, the First Mate shrugged. "He's in the Wildlands on some errand of his own."

Shocked, Corin lowered his weapon and took a half step closer. "The Wildlands? What could take him there?"

"Some task for Ethan Blake, no doubt. Rumor has it he's a Vestossi lad, and now he's gone back home to the manor. But he has jobs for us from time to time, and stormy seas, the man pays well!"

"Where is he?" Corin demanded. "Where's Ethan Blake? What's his true name?"

"Ask the storms, but I don't know. He's somewhere in Ithale if I had to guess, but he and me were never chums."

"But Taker would know."

"If anyone, it's him. He has to get his orders somewhere."

The next question landed on Corin's lips before he could consider it. "And what of Iryana?" He wanted it back as soon as it was asked, and even more so when he saw the surprise in Tommy's eyes.

"What, that desert slave?" He paused to consider it, then shrugged. "Blake kept her as a pet."

Some sense of caution gave Corin pause—he could ill afford to show his vulnerability here—but he had to know. He'd all but handed her to Ethan Blake, and whatever became of her, it was Corin's debt to pay. He swallowed hard against his own restraint, and asked, "How … how did he treat her?"

Tommy curled his lip in amused contempt. "How would you treat a girl you owned?"

Corin clenched his jaw. "Somewhat better than Ethan Blake does, I suspect."

"True enough at that. But rest your gentle heart. The Vestossis didn't earn their place by letting their produce spoil. He keeps her clean enough. And not too badly bruised."

Corin snarled, raising his pistol again if only to smash the smirk from Tommy's face.

To his surprise, Tommy's smile only broadened. The First Mate shook his head. "You always were too soft."

There was some hint in Tommy's expression, perhaps some tiny sound somewhere in the room, but Corin felt a sudden, perfect clarity. Tommy had been buying time, stringing Corin right along.

What had he said when Corin first arrived? *"Billy Bo, you're back already? Are you sure you've done it right?"* And then a moment later, *"Are they ready?"* Corin hadn't really had the time to consider what that meant, but now he recalled the flintlock pistol Tommy had fired on him in Khera. The man must have sent Billy off to charge a pair as soon as he heard rumors Corin was coming to the ship. And now, in this frozen instant, Tommy's wicked grin suggested Billy had returned.

Corin didn't dare step through the dream as he had done before. He was too close now, and he couldn't let the time escape him. He had to hope that Billy was a lousy shot and trust in Fortune to preserve him one more time.

Corin didn't bother turning, didn't try to confirm his suspicion. He dropped to the ground like a sack of meal, and a heartbeat later came the explosion he'd been expecting. Fire and noise blasted from the direction of the door, and against all his instincts Corin scurried *toward* the gunman. Behind him, Tommy screamed in impotent rage, but Corin had little attention to spare for him. His eyes were full of Billy Bo, who stood big and dumb between Corin and the door, raising a second pistol to fire.

Corin had a pistol of his own. It wasn't loaded, but it was more than ten inches of forged bronze and that made a decent weapon of it, even empty. Corin flung it underhand at Billy, and as the pirate dodged away, Corin closed the gap and perforated Billy's heart with *Godslayer's* flawless point.

Billy fell back, surprise as much as anything else in his eyes. Corin sent him to the ground with one last kick, then climbed up to his knees, scanning the floor for the loaded pistol Billy had dropped. It was lost in the gloom.

An animal snarl was all the warning he got, but it was just enough. Corin forgot the gun and spun around in time to see Tommy Day leaping for him. Frail as Tommy was, Corin had overlooked the threat he posed, but Tommy was as much a street fighter as anyone Corin had ever known. He came charging now, and despite his stick-thin arms and scrawny legs, he brought a long, curved knife in each hand.

Corin tried to bring his sword to bear, but he was too late, the quarters too close. Tommy caught the clumsy swing on crossed blades, then planted a vicious kick in Corin's sternum. It drove Corin to the ground and stole his breath. Tommy followed him down, one knee pinning Corin's sword-arm to the floor and the other driving down at Corin's collarbone, threatening his air supply.

Corin bucked and heaved against the withered man, but he could not quite dislodge him. He fought to throw Tommy off his sword arm, but the arm wouldn't budge. He plunged his other hand beneath his cloak, grasping for the dagger on his belt, but Tommy's bulk blocked him.

A manic fever blazed in Tommy's eyes as he crouched over Corin, both knives held high and ready to strike.

"You dared to come against me. You *threatened* me on my own ship? Well, now you'll pay." He hesitated a moment more, savoring his victory, and just then Corin's searching hand found another weapon in the pockets of his cloak. The druid's dartgun. He tore it free, just as Tommy showed his teeth.

"I always said you were soft," Tommy sneered. "How did you ever survive this long?"

"I go well armed," Corin said. He stabbed the dartgun against Tommy's thigh and pulled the tiny trigger.

It pulled almost too easily. Corin had fired the dwarven pistol twice before, and he expected the strong metallic resistance, the fierce buck and snap of tamed explosion, but the druid artifact merely twitched and hissed. For one terrifying moment, Corin feared something had gone wrong. The blades came slashing down toward his face. ...

Then Tommy Day fell forward, limp as a sodden rag. One of the knives went finger-deep in the fine, smooth floorboards next to Corin's ear, and the other skittered out of Tommy's nerveless grip. The First Mate lay over Corin like a smothering blanket, a dead weight under the effects of the druids' poison.

(10)

For a moment Corin didn't move. He only lay there on his back, fighting for his breath. He'd killed Billy Bo. He'd defeated Tommy too. What now? He needed to retrieve the dwarven pistol—that was not his property to lose—but otherwise, he was finished here. He'd have to find some answer for the crew, but perhaps the Nimble Fingers could help with that. If not, Corin had some contacts. He could break them up, see them on a dozen different ships, and soon enough this business would all be forgotten.

While he was still scheming, someone coughed above him. Boots scuffed nervously on the planking. Corin closed his eyes and heard the quiet rustle of several anxious men crowded together and waiting to see what would happen next.

He was not alone. He jerked his left shoulder just enough to twitch Tommy's head aside, and found half a dozen crewmen standing over him, just inside the cabin's door. At least twice as many more jostled at them from behind. They must have arrived during the struggle—likely drawn as soon as Billy Bo fired his one shot—but none of them had rushed to Tommy's aid. Corin took some comfort in that. Still, there were unfamiliar faces in the crowd, and even those he knew had not left him on the best of terms.

In a blink, Corin made a plan. He palmed the tiny glass-and-silver dart that had disabled Tommy Day and concealed it with the dartgun beneath his cloak. Then he heaved with all his might and sent Tommy crashing back against the outer hull. Corin made no effort to conceal his exhaustion, but crawled clumsily to his feet, still panting, and stood a moment staring out at the half-circle of men around him.

Among them all, Corin found a friend. Big Jack Brown broke from the crowd and came within two paces of his old captain before he pulled up short. He shook his head in disbelief. "It's really you. They said it was, but I couldn't half believe them. You came back from the dead."

"Aye," Corin said, his voice as grim as he could make it. "I have unfinished business here."

"I can't doubt you do, but if it's worth a sou, I'll say I'm sorry, Captain. I wish I'd stayed to save you. I wish I had come back."

Corin didn't dare show the gratitude he felt for those words. Big Jack, like Charlie and Sleepy Jim, was least among the men who'd wronged him. But now he had his part to play.

"You may yet be forgiven," Corin said; then he passed his gaze on to the others in the room. "But there will be a price for those who owe it. Billy Bo and Tommy Day have paid already."

One of the strangers in the crowd spoke up. "What ... what'd you do to the First Mate? He had you dead to rights, and all you did was touch him."

Corin flashed his teeth. "Haven't you heard my tale? They left me to the ghosts of old Jezeeli. They marooned me in a dead god's tomb. They buried me beneath the desert sands, but I came back." He raised his empty hand and let it hang for a moment in the heavy silence. "All I had to do was touch him. Now Tommy

Day is with the ghosts I left behind. Dave Taker's next, unless one of you wants the honor."

One and all they shrank away, and Corin nodded at them. "Good. Then hear my words: Any man who serves Dave Taker is my enemy from this day on. Save that one promise, those of you who need my pardon, have it. Go your way. Find new work, and may you prosper in it. But if you remain in Taker's crew, I'll show you to your grave."

Nervous whispers danced like wildfire through the crowd, until someone brave enough stepped forward and asked, "But ... but what about the First Mate? What about our plans?"

"The First Mate's dead," Corin said. "The plans are done."

"But—"

Corin cut him off. "Do not make me regret my pardon! Marzelle is yours no more. Find some other port to ply your trade."

The unknown pirate wanted to argue more, but fear held him back. Corin held his gaze, imperious, until the man backed down and slunk away. Most of the others followed his example, though some few remained. Corin knew them at a glance—men from his old crew, and these were some of the best. Corin guessed what they intended, and he cut them off.

"You have your pardons. I know your faces all, and I will credit you for staying to the last, but now's the time to leave."

"Beg your grace," Big Jack stammered, "but there's a business left to do."

Corin arched an eyebrow. "Aye?"

Big Jack came forward gravely. "Aye, aye. I count two bodies on the plankings, and we've all seen enough of pirate ghosts, I hope you know."

Corin broke at that. He chuckled once, and it became a roaring laugh. "I suppose I do," he said.

"Then we'll consign them to the deep, and straightaway. You can count on me, Captain."

Corin hesitated. Big Jack would keep his word, and superstitious as these men had proven, he'd likely do it quick. The *Espinola* had to have a boat sufficient to the task, and these men could get out past the breakers before the sun was even high. Give it an hour, two at most, and every trace of Tommy Day and Billy Bo would be buried in the sea.

One thing only stayed Corin's hand: Tommy Day was not yet dead. He knew the druids' poison ought to keep him comatose for half a day at least, so that was no concern. But it seemed a dreadful thing to dump a sleeping man into the sea. Even a man like Tommy Day.

In the end, it wasn't Corin's own grievances that decided him. It was the memory of something the shady innkeeper had said. Tommy had punished Lord Béthané for his defiance by burning his manor to the ground—with his wife and child still inside.

"See that it's done quickly," Corin said.

"With a ball and chain around their ankles to keep 'em down," Jack said. "I don't ever hope to see the likes of this First Mate again."

Corin clapped him on his back, then stepped aside to yield the corpses to Jack and his assistants. While they set about their tasks, Corin finished his, snatching up the dwarven pistol from the floor. He caught up both of Billy's too and passed those to Big Jack. "For your trouble."

"You're too gracious," Jack said. "The standard fare's a silver coin."

"Find me at the Nimble Fingers tavern when you're done, and I'll see you get at least a handful. Fair?"

"More'n fair."

Corin nodded. "Clear skies 'til then."

"Just one more question, Captain."

"Aye?"

"What do you have planned for Dave Taker?"

Corin thought a moment, then shrugged. "I said before. He still has a price to pay."

"And if there was someone in his crew, someone who'd stood by while he did awful things, someone anxious to see that price paid..."

"Aye? Out with it, man."

Jack shrugged one shoulder. "I can point you after Taker. I know where his messengers meet him in the Wildlands. And when. I could get you there."

Corin held the sailor's gaze for a long moment. "You really want to see him dead, don't you?"

"I really wish I had done something sooner. You arriving here... you just reminded me that I am not the sort of man who does great things. But I have served that kind of man before. I'd be glad to do it once more."

Corin offered him a smile. "You're a good man, Jack. Hold onto that. As for Dave Taker... he'll pay his price in time. Right now, I'm angling after bigger fish."

"Blake. You know they say he's a Vestossi?"

Corin chuckled but said no more.

Jack just shrugged. "Well, I can't guess how I would help you there, but when you're ready to find Taker, I'll be here. And if you think of something else..."

"See to these corpses," Corin said. "That's all I ask."

"Aye, aye. Clear skies to you."

"And you as well."

They shook hands almost formally; then Corin turned his back and left the *Espinola* to the dead.

Taker's crew had melted away, so Corin found the deck abandoned, but the pier below was still crowded close with the curious. A hush fell over them as Corin reached the top of the gangplank, and he couldn't help but grin as he came down. They must have heard some rumors already from the *Espinola* crew, but shock and admiration still reigned on every face to see Corin emerge victorious.

He felt a little shock and admiration of his own. The sun was bright, the breeze was cool, and everything was well with the world. For a moment, anyway. He'd survived again. There was an old familiar thrill in that. He'd bested a brutal enemy and come away unscathed.

And more importantly, he realized with a start, he'd done it without tapping any of Oberon's strange powers. True, he'd used the druid's dartgun, but that was spoils of war. Fair and square. From the moment he'd arrived here on the pier, it had been pure Corin Hugh.

There was more to the victory too. He hadn't *just* put down a rabid tyrant. He'd also made real progress in his quest for vengeance. For the first time since he'd left Jezeeli, he had a lead on the men he wanted dead. Dave Taker was in the Wildlands on an errand for Ethan Blake. The Wildlands was no small place to search, but Big Jack could lead Corin right to the man. But he had also freed up his new friends in the local Nimble Fingers—new friends much indebted to him over this morning's work—and Corin felt some confidence that they could find Blake for him.

Corin's grin faded, but his resolve held strong. Iryana was alive and still in Ethan Blake's possession. "Only barely bruised," Tommy had said. Oh, yes. Ethan Blake would answer for his sins.

Lost in these thoughts, Corin reached the bottom of the gangplank and ran aground against a tall, familiar form. Most of the idly curious onlookers had pulled back to grant the hero space, but the watchman who'd confronted Corin earlier had never budged, and now he looked set to resume that conversation.

He dropped a heavy hand on Corin's shoulder and squeezed hard. "You think you get to walk away from this?"

"I do," Corin said. "I really do. You need to ask yourself if *you* will."

The watchman laughed. "I'm not afraid of you, little man."

"That suits me fine," Corin said. "I prefer when folks don't see me coming. But I am not the one you need to fear."

"Oh? Who've you got in mind?"

Corin rolled a casual gaze over the gathered crowd. There were pirates in the crowd and sailors who had left their work to watch the show, but there were locals too. There were villagers who'd lived under the First Mate's cruel reign. Corin nodded in their direction.

"Think about the people of Marzelle. Think about the men you've pushed around."

"The First Mate—"

"Is dead!" Corin interrupted, and he raised his voice enough to let the message carry. "Your master's gone. There's no more hand on the tiller, and no more money coming either. You have just become an orphan in a cruel, cruel world."

The watchman shook his head, but sweat already beaded on his brow. "There's more of us—"

"You mean the First Mate's crew? You saw them slinking past, didn't you? Defeated. Even as we speak, they're calling in favors and quietly booking passage on the first ship they can find to leave this town. So how many does that leave of your sort, the hired force? Half a dozen? Even if it's a score or more, I hear Lord Béthané has a grudge to bear against you. And the Marquis too.

I'm sure there are more, and all those greedy hearts who backed the Captain, everyone who bowed to his rich bribes ... they're going to forget you now the money's gone."

"But ... but ..."

Corin reached up to clap the big man on the shoulder. "The way I see it, you have one chance, here and now, to make things right. Play it right, and you could be a hero."

"How? Tell me!"

Corin didn't show a grin. He jerked his head toward the ship behind him. "The First Mate's dead and the Captain is long gone. The crew's dispersed too, but their ship is still in port."

The watchman frowned, perplexed. "What?"

Corin sighed and said it plainly. "Take the ship."

"Oh, I'm no sailor."

"No. You ... No. Claim the ship on behalf of some injured nobleman and you might make yourself a friend. Better still, loot the captain's cabins and the storage holds, and share whatever you find there with the common folk."

"That'll work?"

Corin held his gaze. "Move fast, act confident, and never look back. It always works for me."

The watchman dropped his grip on Corin's shoulder. He transferred his attention to the mighty ship towering over them, and while he was still mulling possibilities, Corin ducked his head and slipped quietly away. The crowd there welcomed him, and seconds later the watchman was lost to sight.

Some among the sailors came to clap him on the shoulder. Some villagers came forward to thank him or to ask if the rumors were all true. One was a familiar face, the same old Josef who'd attacked him just last night, but now he came to Corin with a warm embrace and clumsy Ithalian.

"Is true? The First Mate's end?"

Corin threw a glance over his shoulder and just caught sight of Big Jack Brown and his assistants in a little boat, pulling hard against the tide to leave the harbor. Corin nodded. "Aye, he's done."

"And this guard? He'll hero?"

Corin cocked his head, really considering the possibility for the first time. "That I couldn't say. He might. He might find a pardon. He might just as easily end up in stocks. It doesn't matter."

"Then why?"

Corin chuckled. "It's my final blow against Dave Taker. If he ever finds his way back here now, he'll come back without a crew, without a ship, and without the resources he'd invested."

"It is all conniving?"

"Truer words were never said, my friend. It is *all* conniving. Now come. I think I've earned a drink."

Half an hour later, the innkeeper met them at the door. "It can't be true! Is it true? Josef! They are saying—"

Josef answered. "Is true. This Ithalian is hero."

"But so soon! You only just arrived, while they have plagued our town for weeks. Now they say the First Mate is dead and his victims are picking at the bones of his old power."

"Did I not give my word? I did exactly as you asked of me."

"But so soon!" the host repeated.

Corin favored him with a smile. "There is one thing in this world I can't afford, and that is hesitation. That's *also* why I need the news I asked of you last night."

"Francois left town last night. He will post word to us if he learns anything in Brinole, but he intends to travel all the way to Aepoli if that's what it takes."

"You see," Corin said. "You are just as quick to do as you have promised. How soon will you hear back from Brinole?"

"Tonight at the latest. A rider could be here before sunset."

"Excellent. He may have to ride to Aepoli to learn *everything* I need to know, but any shreds of information he finds along the way will serve me well. And of the ... local matter?"

The innkeeper frowned. "Which one is that?"

"The druid hiding here in Marzelle. Have you learned anything about her yet?"

He shook his head. "Nothing yet. I did put around the description you provided, but no one in Marzelle recognized it."

"Ah," Corin said, disappointed, and the innkeeper hurried to reassure him.

"It should be much easier to investigate now, because of what you've done. I am sure if she's still here, we'll find her for you."

"It warms my heart to hear it. In the meantime, bring me wine and bread and something roasted. And how is Charlie Claire? Any news from your physician?"

"He is here! His wounds are patched, but he needs rest and better board than pirates tend to get."

"Can you attend to that?"

"Already done. He has a room here for as long as he desires, and I will see he's fed as well. In fact, he's lunching even as we speak."

"In his rooms?"

"Indeed."

"Then bring mine there as well. I'll join him."

The innkeeper did not immediately respond, but something in his expression caught Corin's attention. He cocked his head. "Is something wrong?"

"No. But perhaps he will not want an interruption. He has a guest."

"Another sailor?"

"A woman."

"No! Charlie Claire? In Raentz? He knows no women here."

"Perhaps—"

Corin shook his head. "He has no coin to spend. Show me to his rooms."

"I fear—"

"Not as much as I do. There are those in this city who would harm Charlie just because he is my friend. But he's not always quick to sniff out traps like that."

The innkeeper hesitated a moment more, but in the end he bowed his head. "I do not like this indiscretion, but come. This way." He led Corin up a narrow staircase to the room across the hall from one Corin had used the night before. They were modest accommodations, but clean and safe. The innkeeper went to knock on Charlie's door, but Corin caught his wrist, stepped past him, and cracked the door just wide enough to glance inside.

The innkeeper's discretion was unnecessary. Charlie sat at his table, both hands full, devouring a hearty meal. And his guest waited by the dirty window some way off. She was watching him, perplexed. And Corin knew her.

"You may suspend your search," he told the innkeeper. "We have found my druid."

(11)

The innkeeper pushed into place so he could take a peek. He whispered back, "This? This isn't her at all!"

"That is precisely her!"

"But you said she was petite with flashing eyes and a pointed chin. Dark hair, stiff spine, poised and in control—that is the woman you described."

"Yes!" Corin answered, with a gesture toward the room.

The innkeeper shook his head fiercely. "But this woman ... this woman here ... she is none of that."

Corin frowned. "You know her, then?"

"No, but I know my own eyes. This woman ..." He lowered his voice further still. "She is ... sturdy. Strongly built and wilting at the edges. Her hair might have been any color once, but it is golden now and already going gray."

Corin stared agape at the old innkeeper, but the man just waved toward the room. "Am I wrong? Do you see something different? Or was perhaps your memory of her distorted by the wine or rum? I have seen that oft enough—"

"That must be it," Corin said, if only to silence the old man. There was some mystery before him, but it was not one the innkeeper could solve.

There was no truth in the innkeeper's description. Corin rubbed his eyes, but it could hardly make so great a difference. The woman in Charlie's room was undoubtedly the same Aemilia he'd met in Jezeeli in the distant past. And in an alley just last night. She looked not yet thirty, and her hair was dark as night. But she was a druid too, and they knew things concealed from normal men. Perhaps this was some druid sorcery at play.

Corin licked his lips and eased the door closed again. He turned back to the innkeeper. "No matter how she looks, this is my druid. She is a friend, and I cannot believe Charlie would object to an interruption. So if you would be so good, please bring my lunch up to this room. And something for the lady too."

He hesitated. "You are sure? You're sure it's her?"

"I am. And I suspect we'll need some time for catching up. You'll see we're not disturbed?"

"Of course."

"Unless word comes from Brinole. If your man has found me Ethan Blake—"

"Of course, my lord."

"I'm no one's lord," Corin said. "Just call me 'Corin.' But you are an admirable host." The man started to stammer some modest objection, but Corin had no time for pleasantries. His eyes fixed on the door to Charlie's room, and he bounced on his toes. "Thank you. A million times. Now go."

He waited until the innkeeper was gone, then eased the door open again and slipped into the room. He nodded to the sailor. "Good morning, Charlie! I'm glad to see you well." Then to the druid: "And you, Aemilia. I trust you had no trouble finding the tavern?"

She gasped. "But ... how could you? ..."

"Recognize you? I don't know," Corin said, stepping close and offering a bow. "I see you have the locals all confused, and I suspect that's also why you have been stalking me so brazenly. If you are wearing some disguise, I must admit that I can't see it." He showed his most disarming grin. "All I see here is your own true, lovely face."

She touched her cheek, almost disbelieving. "You see—"

"Aemilia. One of King Oberon's most loyal druids, who was once a moneychanger in Jezeeli and yet who somehow doesn't look a day past"—he barely hesitated—"twenty-five."

"Thirty-three," she answered, almost challenging him, and Corin barked a laugh.

"And centuries on top of that. What is your secret, woman?"

"What is yours?"

He spread his hands, the perfect picture of openness. "How much time do you have?"

She considered him in silence for a moment. Then she set her shoulders and met his eyes. "Honestly, I hold nothing higher in priority than discovering your secrets."

"You'll make me blush."

She growled at him. "Do not pretend—"

"I don't," he said, serious at last. "But neither do I give from charity. If you would have my secrets, you must share some part of yours."

She shrugged. "It seems like you already know them all."

"Oh, more than you can guess. But I need details. I need to know the secret workings of your magic, of Oberon's power, to understand what's happening."

She shook her head. "I will tell you what I can, but there are some restrictions."

AARON POGUE

"Hah! Forgive my indiscretion, but we are far beyond the strictures now."

She gaped again. "How can you—" She shook her head, interrupting herself, and cast a pointed look at Charlie Claire.

He hadn't moved since Corin first arrived. Seated at his table, both fists full of sopping bread, he was watching them in fascination. Now he swallowed hard. "What's this, then, Captain?"

Corin frowned. "She is the woman you brought here. I assume she offered you some reason."

"Two pistoles for an hour of my time. She said she had some questions for me."

Corin frowned. "Oh? What did you tell her?"

"Only the simple truth. That we are Ithalian sailors, out of work."

"That's all you said?"

He thought a moment. "I . . . may have said we'd been in Khera, but then it rather seemed that she already knew, so where's the harm?"

Corin sighed. "You saw no harm in answering a stranger's questions?"

"She offered me *two pistoles*, Captain. For that I would have told her my true name."

"Did you?"

Another thoughtful pause. "She never asked. She seemed more interested in you."

"And you told her?"

"Almost nothing. Although, I *think* I mentioned your new magic trick. The traveling. She did seem quite impressed."

Corin restrained himself against an angry outburst. Instead he went closer and lowered his voice. "And what if she had been a justicar? Would you be glad you'd shared so much with her?"

Charlie just looked confused. "But she's a *girl!*"

Corin sighed. "Forget it, then. What else did you say?"

"Nearly nothing. Once my meal arrived, she got pretty quiet."

"In shock, I must assume," Corin said. "Shall we leave you to eat in peace? I suspect I can answer all her questions."

"It sounds that way. But . . . she did promise *me* the coins."

"Of course. They're yours regardless."

"But I would prefer to hear everything you have to say."

"And I would prefer for you to say no more," Corin said. "Gods bless us all, Charlie Claire. You are a good man, but this is *not* where you excel."

The big man gave a heavy sigh. "She's truly trouble, then? I've done something stupid again?"

"Would I let you keep your earnings if you had?" Corin tossed him two pistoles. "No. I had urgent need to speak with her, and you have brought her to me. That's good work, sailor. But now it's time for me to take the helm."

Charlie brightened and took another sloppy bite of bread. "Aye, aye, Captain! You're right as ever."

Corin nodded back, then offered Aemilia his arm. He led her to his own rooms, secured the door, then leaned his back against a wall. He left her time enough to catch her bearings.

She never took her eyes off him. He could almost feel her gaze, measuring every inch of him, weighing, calculating. He left her to the task and made his plans.

He'd met the druids in Jezeeli, but he had learned precious little of them. They were better organized than the Nimble Fingers, better educated than the scholars, better informed than the blasted justicars, and in some ways they were better armed than the gladiators. And yet, despite it all, they were not even a minor power. They skulked around the edges of society. For all their amazing secrets, they had no *impact.*

It was a puzzle, a mystery he would be happy to unravel, but first and foremost, it was an opportunity. Every secret could be made a weapon. If the druids couldn't see the way, Corin would be happy to do it for them. He had to learn the rules behind Oberon's dream magic. He had to learn how she had tracked him clear across the world. With any luck, the same technique could lead him straight to Ethan Blake.

But first, he had to get her on his side. He chose to open with a show of generosity. Reaching beneath his cloak, he produced the stolen dartgun and tossed it to her. "This is yours."

She barely glanced down. "It's spent."

"Aye. It is a useful toy."

"It's not a toy! It is a sacred artifact. If one of these fell into the scholars' hands—"

"I know, I know, the strictures," Corin said. "Now say you're grateful that I chose to give it back."

She glared at him. "It's not enough. Even the dart you fired—"

Corin cut her off again, tossing her the tiny glass and silver cylinder. He'd hoped to get away with that one, for it would have fetched a pretty price at the University, but such thinking was habit more than anything. Gold was not his problem now.

"You have your artifact; your strictures are secure. Now bend them a bit for me, and tell me how you found me."

She scowled. "'Bend them a bit?' It is a strange experience to meet a man who knows the secret words and phrases of my people, but who clearly doesn't grasp the point at all."

Her analysis was perfect, but Corin wouldn't let that stop him. "I know the point," he bluffed. "You live in fear of going back to yesterworld."

She staggered back as though he'd hit her. "How can you know this? Who *are* you?"

Corin took a step toward her and spread his hands. "I am just what Charlie told you, a sailor—"

"Pirate."

"—who went where he never should have gone. I found a scholar's map and notes that spoke of an ancient, secret knowledge buried in the Endless Desert."

Her knees gave out and she sat down hard on the end of Corin's bed.

"I found a buried city," he went on. "Empty except for books."

She nodded in sudden understanding. "That's where Charlie found the tome he meant to sell in Khera. And ... that is where you learned these tricks? From something written in the books?" She sounded doubtful, and Corin had to laugh.

"I never had the chance to read them. I was betrayed by my first mate. He put the city to the torch, burned all but a handful of the books, and left me there to die."

She groaned so sharply that it was almost a wail. "The city burned? You found Gesoelig and you let it burn?"

"I didn't *let it*," Corin snapped. "I was betrayed. They tried to burn me with it. But why do you seem so surprised? You've heard this tale before."

"I—what?"

"I didn't die in the fire. Some magic in the dormant city—in the books themselves—it dragged me back into an ancient memory. It transported me to Jezeeli while Oberon yet reigned, and I arrived outside your door."

"My door?"

"You had a moneychanger's shop by the city's gates."

She placed a hand to her forehead. "I ... I did."

"And Ephitel himself came to see you, to ask of you another Writ of Provender, to buy more black powder from the dwarves."

"You know *everything*!"

Corin threw his hands up. "Of course I do! I was there with you. A thousand years ago, while Ephitel was waiting in your shop, Oberon's power deposited me on the busy street right outside your window. You came to give me aid. You summoned Jeff, who put a boot on my foot. You lectured us about the strictures and then took me to see Delaen."

"Jeff...and Delaen..." She stared at nothing, eyes wide, voice thin and faraway. "You have so many details right—"

"Of course."

But she went right on over him. "And yet you lie. I remember everything about that day and the days that followed. For centuries I have relived the memory of Gesoelig's fall, and no matter what you say, I know for a fact that you were never there."

(12)

Corin barked a laugh. "You can't be serious! I saved you from Ephitel's prison coach."

"No. Jeff and Delaen did, with a little aid from an elf named Avery."

"And Maurelle! I know—I led her there."

Aemilia shook her head. "Your story falls apart. Maurelle came later. At that time, she was still a pawn of Ephitel."

Corin sank down on his heels, completely shaken. "What are you telling me?"

She raised her chin. "I see through your charade as easily as you saw through my disguise. Do not let it hurt your pride. I will admit, I am astonished at how much you have been told."

"I have been told nothing; I lived through all of this. Just days ago. But ..." he trailed off, grasping at a memory. He groaned. "Oberon tried to warn me. It was a dream within a dream. He tried to explain it to me, but I didn't understand."

Aemilia found her feet and withdrew a pace, a newfound worry clouding her expression. "I don't think I understand either. What are you saying?"

"It wasn't real—not *this* real—but it *felt* real. It was another dream, a special dream made just to show me what had happened when Jezeeli fell."

She backed another step away, though there was nowhere to escape. "You grow more worrisome with every word you speak. Do you know that?"

Corin shook his head. "It was always complicated. Summon Delaen. If anyone can understand, it will be her."

"I dearly wish I could, but Delaen died in Ephitel's first strike."

"No. She was in the throne room when the city moved."

The woman snapped, her calm restraint shattered as she stomped her foot. "That isn't real! Stop speaking of your fantasies! This is my life. These are my memories!"

"And they are mine," Corin answered, quietly calm. "They are not the same, but they are just as real for me. I made new friends in Avery and Maurelle. I watched the coward Kellen become a hero. And I remember Delaen advising Oberon upon his throne before he moved the city. My experience may not have changed the world you know, but Oberon invested much...he sacrificed much to share that glimpse with me. If you still serve his goals, you must respect the things I've seen."

"And *you* must understand how this all sounds to me. You suffered an ecstatic dream about a tragic history—and that is *only* if your story's true—and you would have me trust your vision more than my own memory?"

Corin went a step toward her, stretching out his hands. "I would never ask for that. I only ask that you trust *me*."

"A pirate?"

"A fellow servant of King Oberon. An ally in the war on Ephitel. One other person in the world who can remember the city that once was and the wretched things that happened there."

After a moment's hesitation, she dipped her head and came a little closer to him. "You do have a silver tongue."

"Some say gold."

She barked a startled laugh, and Corin went to meet her. He could not doubt that this was the same woman. So serious, so worried, so anxious to do right. He tilted her face up to his and said softly, "I know how difficult this all must be for you. Imagine how it was for me, an unsuspecting Godlander, to be tossed into a fire and emerge in ancient Jezeeli."

"It is a wonder you survived."

"More than you know. I picked a fight with Ephitel."

She gasped. "You didn't!"

"Oh, I did. I think that's what Oberon most wanted from that dream—to find a champion to avenge his death."

Aemilia frowned. "That does not much sound like Oberon."

"Perhaps. But it is what I most remember." He thought about the dwarven pistol tucked safely beneath his cloak and gave a grim smile. "I shot Ephitel. In the dream. I very nearly killed him."

A hungry smile touched her lips, but it quickly faded. "It wasn't real."

"No," he said. "But I wish I'd done it all the same." He thought a moment and gave a little shrug. "I suppose there is some worthwhile advantage there."

"Where?"

"In that it wasn't real. You do not remember me, and that's a shame. I was a dashing hero, and the other you was *most* impressed."

She smirked. "This is an advantage?"

"No. It is the contrast. It is a shame you don't remember me, but quite a comfort to discover Ephitel does not remember either."

"Oh. I suppose that must be true. You said you shot him."

"In the back. On two separate occasions."

She laughed. "You would not have survived one day in Ephitel's Hurope if he remembered that."

"But I do," Corin said. "And that gives me an advantage. I know things he doesn't know."

"And you will use this advantage?"

"Haven't I already said as much? I mean to make him pay for everything he's done—in your memories as well as mine."

She touched her chin, considering. "And just what would he have to fear from some outraged sailor?"

"A pirate captain," Corin corrected. "And a hero of the Nimble Fingers. A well-traveled rogue who's most resourceful."

"Oh, but you are more than that," she said. "What happened to you in the dream? What power did you gain there?"

An instinct for survival barely conquered Corin's vanity, but it made him hesitate before he named the sword on his hip, the dwarven pistol on his belt, or the magic that propelled him over continents with no more than a thought. These were not enough on their own to make him a match for Ephitel, but they gave him a chance. And with the druids' help, with a little careful planning, Corin finally believed he might succeed.

But something stayed his tongue. He frowned, searching for the cause, and found it in the druid's eager gaze. He caught her shoulders gently in his hands and pushed her back to arm's length again.

"If you did not remember me," he asked, "why have you been stalking me?"

She blinked, surprised. "I ... what?"

"You found me two times in as many days in sprawling Khera. And then, months later, you tracked me down across the sea here in Marzelle. Even after I disarmed you, even after I named you to your face, you tried to trail me when I went to face Tommy Day. And then, when I had shaken you, you searched out Charlie Claire where I had hidden him, to pump his dear, soft head for information."

She tried a teasing smile. "You must admit, you are a captivating subject."

She was trying to manipulate him—and not too subtly at that—but it was a pretty smile all the same. Corin tucked the thought away and shook his head. "Has it even been ten minutes since you said discovering my secrets was your top priority? What set you on my trail, Druid? What do you want from me?"

She dropped her smile and ducked out of his grasp. "Charlie told me something of your new abilities. Your . . . travel magic. We did not yet know what it was, but every time you used it, you triggered warnings in our systems."

"Warnings? Of what sort?"

"Technical. It is our job, before anything else, to keep this world intact. To keep the dream—as you have called it— running smoothly. When you twist the dream to propel yourself across the Medgerrad, everything else has to bend and twist to compensate."

Corin nodded, thinking of the months he'd lost when he'd used the magic before. "Time?"

"It can be time. It can be space. It can be histories or random chance or causality itself."

"Can it be controlled?"

"Of course it can. By fairies. Elves. It's how they work, the same way you and I might breathe or keep our hearts beating. They twist reality around them, taste a dozen different samples, and choose the one most closely suited to their needs."

"That!" Corin shouted. "That's what I must learn. Teach me that, and I will be your hero."

"Can I teach you how to breathe? It is not a human thing; it is a fairy thing."

"But *I* can travel through the dream. Just as Charlie told you and as I'm sure you had already guessed."

"It could have been teleportation. We did not know for sure until you skipped across the sea. It could have been great fortune. Or temporal manipulation. Or you might have been some new visitor from Fairy. The only thing the warnings told us was that a new anomaly was here. But ..." She sighed and looked away. "None of the options would have been good news. Any anomaly is a threat to the world we're sworn to protect."

She seemed genuinely distraught, though Corin did not entirely understand why. He offered her a smile. "Ease your heart, because you've found your answer. I am the anomaly. I do have this ability to travel through the dream. And you have nothing to fear, for it was Oberon himself who taught this trick to me. *Gave* it to me, even. If *he* trusted me—"

She shook her head. "He never understood enough of what we do to judge that rightly. There are many things the fairies do, and all of them wreak chaos on causality, but they can all use their sampling to avoid the worst of consequences."

"How does the sampling work?"

She gave him a theatrical shrug. "How could I possibly describe something so far from human experience? It's nothing I have ever known."

"Is it ... could it be like a gray fog hanging over everything? Could it be time playing forward to some point, then skipping back and doing something slightly differently?"

She narrowed her eyes. "It *could* be like that. I've never really heard it put in words."

"But I've experienced that," he said. "When I tried to travel through the dream across the sea. I ran into … well, into you. And into Ephitel himself. And into half a dozen people I don't know, men and elves looming out of nothing to interrupt my path."

"Focus points," she said. "The men would have been druids. When you try to shape the dream, you can come into conflict with others trying to do the same."

"It bounced me back. I nearly died because of it, and Charlie with me."

She weighed this for a moment and shrugged again. "I do not know. I've never known a man who could step through dream before, so perhaps what you describe is just a symptom."

"Ah, but I have also seen it somewhere else! When you shot me with your precious toy."

She gaped a moment, then looked away with a blush on her cheeks. "I never shot you! You took it away."

Corin grinned. "You shot me on four separate occasions. Every time, the world went gray and then started over, until at last I was smart enough to disarm you."

"I wondered how you knew."

"Sampling," he said. "That's what you called it."

She nodded, looking stunned. "That's it. And if you have that ability … I have never heard of any but an elf who could control *that* power. If you have that ability, you may not truly be the danger we thought you were!" She bounced on her toes, relief and excitement in her eyes. "Show me. Show me!"

And she slapped him. Hard.

Her face fell. "I'm not impressed."

"I cannot summon it at will! That's what I'm asking you to teach me. It just happens sometimes."

Her shoulders sagged too. "I'm sorry, Corin. It is not something that can be taught."

"But I already have the ability, clearly. I only need instruction!"

She met his gaze with sympathy in her eyes. "There is nothing in our lore to explain how fairies work. I doubt you'd find it in theirs, either. They just do. Some things can be figured out in time—"

"Like going miles at a step," Corin said. "It works the way a normal dream works."

"Precisely so. Our glamours work the same way."

"Your disguise? The one I saw right through?"

She cocked her head. "Yes. And as it happens, I have never known of anyone but Oberon who could do that."

"Oh?" Corin rubbed his chin. "What does that suggest to you?"

She sighed. "It suggests to me … that perhaps the things you say are true. I cannot imagine how you could have gained these powers *unless* he gave them to you."

"You see? I am a hero. You should welcome me with open arms."

"Unfortunately, no. You are a wild card. Perhaps if you had come to me with Oberon's wisdom in your head or with complete control over the sampling, then I could trust you. But as you are, you represent a severe risk to this reality."

Corin licked his lips. "I don't like where this is going."

She shook her head. "Don't misunderstand me. You have some charm. And I take some heart in hearing that you are opposed to Ephitel. But you seem reckless."

He cocked an eyebrow. "That I am."

"And I find that most alarming. You could destroy the world, Corin. We cannot afford to let you run free."

"I beg your pardon, lady, but I'll be no one's prisoner."

She came closer. "No. Please. I don't mean it like that. But this ... this *gift* you have been given could change the world, for good or ill. I have *seen* the way you gallivant. You're reckless in everything you do, and if you use Oberon's power with so little understanding, you will break the world."

Corin didn't answer right away. She was right, but the truth was even worse than she knew. Oberon had told him once that reality itself—all of Hurope—was no more than a memory of a dream, now trapped in Corin's head. If he died, the world died with him. That seemed a greater risk by far than *using* the gifts that Oberon had given him.

And none of that was information he meant to share with the druids. They'd lock him in a cage and never let him see the light of day. He'd decided long ago that if he couldn't *act* to make this world a better place, then it wasn't worth preserving anyway.

So he met her eyes with perfect confidence and said, "He *chose* me, milady, reckless as I am. Have you considered it might be *because* I'm fool enough to use this power that he gave it to me?"

She bit her lip. "I ... I haven't."

Corin shrugged, as though it were the plain and simple truth. In fact, he knew it wasn't. Oberon had not chosen him at all; any manling who had stumbled on the city's tomb would have served the old king's purpose. But Corin saw no benefit in sharing that with her.

"I have a mission, Aemilia. I have unfinished work to do. Some of it was given to me straight from Oberon's mouth. I will

avenge the death of Oberon and of Jezeeli. I will free the nations
of Hurope from Ephitel and the pretender gods. I will restore the
druids to their full … custodial authority. But I will do none of
this on your leash. Do you understand?"

She touched her chin, thinking hard, but found no answer.

Corin sighed. "I am not negotiating. I tell you as it is.
Remember what you know of me. I can see through your
disguises. I can step across the world with just a thought. If you
try to capture me, to coerce me, to control me … I swear, I have
less regard for the survival of this dream than I have for my own
freedom."

She sighed, frustrated. "I believe you."

"You should. You've said the dreamwalking is dangerous,
and I'll avoid it if I can, but you must remember that you cannot
contain me."

"I wouldn't dream of trying. You've made yourself quite
clear."

"Very well."

She came closer still and raised her hands in pleading. "But
I must beg you: Do nothing rash. You are something precious,
Corin. If you are half the things you claim to be, we *need* you. I
will not try to restrain you, but I would beg you to allow me to
advise you."

Corin considered her a moment, then rolled one shoulder
in a shrug. For all he hated the idea of submitting to the druids,
Aemilia would not be a bad companion. Still, he pretended
reticence. "Perhaps I will allow it. If you can show some service
to me."

"What service?"

"Find me Ethan Blake."

"What?"

He shrugged. "You have shown a knack for finding elusive figures in the crowd. You tracked me across the Medgerrad; now find me the man who once sailed under the name of Ethan Blake."

"I ... we don't really work that way. I found *you* because you kept setting off alarms. Is this Ethan Blake twisting reality everywhere he goes?"

"Umm ... probably not. He is a Vestossi. Does that help?"

She glared at him. "This is the man Charlie told me of. This is the sailor who betrayed you, who took your ship and sank it."

"He is a wicked man, in league with Ephitel—"

"You already named him a Vestossi."

Corin sighed. "And he has done worse than wronged me. He has enslaved an innocent woman who deserves her freedom."

"This is more important than the world?"

Corin nodded. "This is my responsibility. I will serve Oberon. I will slaughter Ephitel. But *first* I must atone for my mistakes. I must find some way to help her."

"This sounds like just the sort of thing I warned against," she started, but Corin cut her off with a raised eyebrow.

"This sounds like you are trying to restrain me. If you want my cooperation, earn it. If you want my full attention, then help me set this other task aside."

She sighed and shrank away. "Very well. If those are your demands, then I will see what I can do."

"You are not the only one I've asked to gather this information. I might have word as soon as sunset from my brothers in the Nimble Fingers. And *they* have no desire to lock me up. So if you wish to impress me with your usefulness ..."

She nodded, impatient. "I understand. I understand."

"Good. Then you are free to go. I'm sure the Council waits with bated breath for your report. You may tell them what a try-ing scoundrel I proved to be. It will hurt my feelings none."

"No, but it could see you dead. There will be those on the Council unwilling to risk an agent—even an agent apparently anointed by Oberon—with such power outside our control."

"Oh. Aye? And you will convince them otherwise?"

She bit her lip, thinking for a moment. "Honestly, I don't yet know if I disagree with them."

"But—"

"You've said your piece. I go to Council. You will … discover our decision. One way or another."

He reached out a hand, anxious to renew the conversation, but she brushed lightly past him and out the door. He watched her go, and even after she was lost to sight, he stood a moment, staring hard at nothing.

Then he smiled. "A fine woman, that." He thought a moment more. "This should be interesting." Then he shook himself and raised his voice. "Charlie! Has my food arrived?"

(13)

Aemilia did not return that afternoon. Nor did Big Jack Brown stop by the tavern. Corin took a stroll late in the afternoon, looking in on some of the more popular pirate haunts, but he found none of his old contacts and learned little new. In all, it was a frustrating afternoon.

A rider did come from Brinole at dinnertime, but only to report that Francois had found none of the information he needed there and that he was riding on toward the Ithalian border. Corin gave the messenger a handsome tip and showed the innkeeper an apathetic shrug, but in his heart he raged.

Tommy's words kept ringing in his head. *"He keeps her clean enough. And not too badly bruised."* Every hour that slipped away left Corin feeling helpless, weak. He paced his room long after he should have gone to bed, still hoping Aemilia would arrive with useful news.

He was not much afraid of her parting threat. It had always been a risk. In fact, the woman he'd met in Jezeeli likely *would* have voted hard against him. He remembered how she'd clung to the strictures like a shipwrecked man might cling to a broken bit of mast to keep himself afloat. She'd been a true believer.

But Corin doubted she still felt the same. After all, she'd seen the limits of the good king's honest plans. There were always wicked men prepared to flout the law for private gain. Even among gods, Ephitel was not the first, and he would not be the last. Aemilia had seen it. She'd lost true friends and watched this precious dream become a nightmare. Surely she'd embrace a chance for revenge.

Surely.

Right?

He twitched aside the curtain to peek out on the empty street. He eased the door to look down the hall. What other magic did the druids have? He should have asked before provoking her. Regardless, he'd only said what had to be said. He *would* prefer an execution to a life in chains. He nodded to himself, repeating the words in his head. *"I will not wear a leash. I am no one's slave."*

And more of Tommy's cruel words answered him. *"How would you treat a girl you owned?"*

He growled and clenched his fists and stomped across the room. Ethan Blake. Where was he now? *Who* was he now? A Vestossi. That was all Corin knew, and it was not much help. The noble house had strongholds all across Hurope, from Rikkeborh to Sesille. From darkest Dehtzlan to the Dividing Line. Their strongest presence was in Ithale—in Aepoli and in Aerome, where Ipolito sat upon the throne—but Blake might just as easily have come from Pri or Lihon or Désanton. Corin could spend a week traveling south to Aepoli only to learn he should have gone north or west or east.

No. Far better to bide his time here. There were other affairs still to settle, other intelligence to gather, and with a little patience, he could better arm himself for whatever battles awaited him at his destination.

He knew these things, but they did not help him sleep.

❦

The morning brought a visit from Big Jack Brown. Corin met him in the common room, and after his initial greeting, Jack said nothing for a long time. Corin tried some pleasantries, but in the end, he let the man have his time.

"I've been thinking," Jack said at last. "I've been thinking awful hard. What are you scheming, Captain?"

"I told you yesterday," Corin said. "No tricks, no complications. I just want to find Ethan Blake and make him dead."

"But there's always a scheme. I know that about you. You're always scheming. What's it this time?"

Corin spread his hands. "You aren't wrong, but right now I don't have enough information to scheme. And I don't have the patience to play things smart. Right now, all I have in mind is some bloodletting."

"I like it," Jack said. "Honest. Proper. And you've learned where the snake is hiding?"

Corin shook his head. "That's the one thing I'm still missing. But I have some lines out in the water."

"Of course you do. I never would have doubted it. Only, I was thinking about yesterday. ..."

"Aye?"

"And you'll recall I offered to point you after Dave Taker."

"Aye."

"Well ... there you have a man who knows Blake's secrets."

Corin didn't answer right away. He considered it a moment, then shook his head. "It's not a *fast* solution. How long would it take to find him in the Wildlands?"

"Four days at sea. Then, at most, two more at the rendezvous. He checks in often, so I'm told."

Corin cocked his head. "What has you so anxious to send me west, Big Jack?"

"You remember yesterday?"

"Aye."

"I did as I promised."

"A proper sailor's burial?"

"Right. Exactly."

"No problems?"

"None that couldn't be overcome."

Corin sat a little straighter at that, but he tried to pretend nonchalance. "Oh? What problems were there?"

Jack shrugged. He kept his eyes fixed on the table. "One of the men got jumpy. Swore he saw Tommy Day was breathing." He avoided Corin's gaze. His voice held steady, but his hands were shaking. "Barely at all. Like an old man on his deathbed. But still…"

Corin swallowed hard. "Aye? What happened then?"

Now Jack met Corin's eyes. "I did as I had promised, Captain. I told him he was seeing things. Corpses can get odd sometimes, you know. I clapped the corpses up in irons and dropped 'em over."

Corin caught a heavy breath. "You're a good man, Jack."

"That I am. That I am. And I've spent the hours since then thinking hard."

"About?"

"Doing justice. Like you said. A good bloodletting."

"Ah."

Big Jack nodded. "Exactly. And whatever grudge you hold against the little tyrant, I promise you, the world needs to see Taker dead more than Ethan Blake."

Corin leaned across the table and held Jack's gaze. "Listen close. I appreciate your reasoning. I really do. But you're forgetting Iryana. Blake has her in his power."

"She's just a desert slave," Jack said.

"She's a living will," Corin said. "She was free. I stole her from her people for a purpose, and because of that, she ended up in Blake's possession. That is wrong, no matter where she had the misfortune to be born."

Big Jack frowned. "Beg pardon for saying, but the slave don't mean a thing to me. You know? She's nothing to me. And Ethan Blake? He was nothing worth speaking of. A lousy captain, but you get those. He saw it soon enough and ran away. I'll credit him for that."

Corin shook his head. "This is about more than pirate honor."

"Maybe for you. I can see that. But Dave Taker—same as Tommy Day—he used me, Captain. He made me his tool to hurt these folks. That blood is on my hands."

"They were orders, Jack."

The big man shook his head. "That lady in the house? I heard her screaming. Heard it all the time, after. You know? And when Pete swore he saw Tommy breathing, I thought... I thought maybe it takes blood to wash the stain of blood. You know? And when I put him in the water, that screaming stopped, Captain."

Corin didn't move. He didn't blink. This was the face of vengeance. It was an echo. Corin wanted to tell Jack to let it go, to walk away. He *was* a good man. There was plenty of work for an honest sailor, if he wanted to go that way.

But Corin couldn't say the words, because he did know. He'd killed his share of evil men. Sometimes that was the only way to stop the screaming.

In the end, he gave a short, sharp nod. "I understand you, Jack."

"Then I'll say it plain. I'm going after Dave Taker. I don't need you coming with me. I'm up to the task."

"I believe you are."

"But I thought there was a chance you had some bloodstains of your own. Thought maybe you had some business with him, too, and I can't pretend my honor outranks yours."

"I don't know," Corin said. "I wouldn't want to see them side-by-side. But are you *sure*—"

"I'm sure. That's not the question."

Corin nodded. "Then you do what you have to do. And I'll sleep easier knowing it's done."

"Glad to be of service, Captain."

Corin shook his head. "I'm no one's captain anymore."

"Not how it works. You know? It's been six years since you left the chariot, but Old Grim ..."

Corin gave him a dry chuckle and nodded along. "Aye. You've got me there. Old Grim will always be my captain."

"And you'll be mine. You were a good one."

"So what's your plan? Need any help with the scheming?"

"Nah. It's a pretty simple one. I know the boys who run Dave Taker's news, supplies, what have you. They'll be stopping through tomorrow night, little smuggler's dock out west of town. I usually have a pint or two with them before they move along. I'll make some excuse to join them."

"It's Tommy Day," Corin said. "That's your angle. You'll have to play it cold, but Tommy's death is big news. Tell them you were there, you saw it all, and you need to carry the report to Taker personally."

"That's good. You're a smart man, Captain."

Corin shrugged. "That's tomorrow night? Four days along the coast, and you said two at the rendezvous."

"That's at most."

"So by this time next week, Dave Taker will be dead."

"That's what I intend."

Corin took a moment to review the plan, searching for some other flaw, but it seemed solid. Simple, like the man had said. Eventually he nodded. "Find me when it's over. Can I beg that favor? Find me when it's over, so I can hear the tale and drink your health."

"Sure thing," Jack said.

He rose to go, but Corin stopped him. "Jack!"

"Captain?"

"You're a good man. I'm proud to know you."

"Clear skies, Captain. I'll see you when it's done."

Corin watched him leave, then he shook his head and muttered, "Clear skies, sailor. But storms are brewing."

(14)

Corin spent the morning making contact with his old acquaintances. It wasn't hard. He picked a dockside tavern, almost at random, took a table in the corner, then sat and waited. Within half an hour, word had spread, and sailors from his past started dropping by. Yesterday's encounter at the *Espinola* was the talk of the town, and it seemed like everyone wanted a chance to shake his hand, thank him for chasing the wretches out of town, and perhaps glean a bit of truth from all the rumors.

Corin let the rumors stand. He held hard to his claim that he'd stopped Tommy's heart with a touch of his hand. A lie like that could sometimes serve a man better than cold steel, so he protected Aemilia's secrets and fabricated some of his own. It was a double victory.

His real intention, though, was to find crews for any of Taker's men still stuck in town. He was surprised to learn how many of them had responded to his threat. More than a hundred men had booked passage yesterday, some at enormous rates once word got around, but there were those who'd been too stupid to skim from the plundered booty, too poor now to pay their way, and by and large those were the same men who'd shown some sense of guilt for their betrayal.

Even lacking that, Corin had no wish to see two men left together from Taker's old crew. He would spread them to the winds. So now he asked around and traded favors, paid for some and bartered for others, and most he managed on nothing more than his swollen reputation. In three and a half hours he found stable work for two score of rotten pirates, and by noon he was already bored again.

Shortly after lunch a new messenger arrived at the Nimble Fingers tavern. This one came from another postal stop along the road to Ithale. Apparently, Francois had ridden hard throughout the night, and he insisted he would do the same again. By the innkeeper's calculations, the man might already be at the border, and by tomorrow they could have word from northwest Ithale. From Nicia by the weekend.

That gave Corin hope, but alas, there was no actual intelligence to report. There would be more once he reached Ithale—the Nimble Fingers there were much better organized—but it chafed at Corin's heart to have to wait.

He spent an hour playing cards with Josef, Charlie, and the innkeeper. Then Charlie Claire excused himself to take a nap, and the other three spent another hour or two talking business. They discussed the Nimble Fingers organization, and Corin made some recommendations that could easily make Marzelle's the finest chapter anywhere in Raentz.

But all the while, Corin's mind was drifting. He felt the hours sloshing past like breakers on the shore, rising up to tower over him, full of promise, then smashing at his feet as so much froth. His fingers itched. He had somewhere to be.

Night brought no news from Francois, and still no visit from the druid. Corin went out for a walk, searching every common room, every busy street corner, for any sign of Aemilia. He went back to the docks and spent two hours buying beer for sailors newly arrived from distant ports. Some of them had heard of Ethan Blake, but none of them could tell Corin his true name or what town he now called home.

Heading back to the shady tavern, Corin cut down through empty alleys every chance he got, just hoping he might crash into Aemilia again. He never did. He spent another sleepless night, then rose at dawn and headed back across the town to see if any new sailors had come in with the tide.

Exhaustion drove him back to the shady tavern early in the afternoon. He announced himself with a knock on the door, nodded absently to Josef as he went past, and then scanned the room for messengers and thousand-year-old ladies. It was depressingly deficient.

"Any news?" he asked the innkeeper.

"Have patience, Captain. It is a long road."

"Longer than you know." Corin sighed. "I'm going to my room. If you hear the sound of things breaking, send up rum."

The man looked a little more alarmed than necessary at Corin's quip, but Corin didn't feel like soothing him. He slunk away, down the hall and up the stairs, and then let himself into the modest room.

Aemilia waited by the window. She didn't turn when Corin entered, so he took his time addressing her. He shed his cloak and unbuckled the sword belt, then collapsed onto his bed and lay there staring at the water-damaged ceiling. For a while, he just breathed.

At last, he pushed up on one elbow and asked, "Well, are you going to join me here or what?"

She rounded on him, unamused. "This is no time for joking, Corin Hugh. Our destiny hangs in the balance—and yours more than most."

Corin quirked an eyebrow. "And? What's the verdict?"

"Six to one against."

"Against what?"

She came a step toward him. Her expression showed no sense of humor. "Preventive homicide."

"Oh. Then I guess I won." He breathed a moment more, then frowned, "Were you the one?"

Just a hint of a smile. "I was not."

"I'm glad to hear it."

"You haven't heard the details yet. You will not like the details."

"I haven't liked much since killing Tommy Day. Tell me anyway."

She came to stand at the foot of his bed, staring down at him. There was pity in her plain brown eyes, but no compromise. "You're going to have to come in. The Council wouldn't budge. You cannot be allowed to run the risk—"

He growled at her like a cornered animal. "I already said—"

"And I repeated everything you said. I argued for you, Corin. What do you think took so long? But this is a chance we'll never have again. This is a final gift from Oberon. This is an opportunity to—"

"No! This is my life," he said, unyielding. She flinched at the severity of his tone, and he regretted that. But he did not relent. "It's not up for discussion."

She sank down on the end of the bed and stared at her hands in her lap. "This is not imprisonment. Far from it."

"But you would bring me in? You would restrict my movements?"

"For your own protection! And it's not *that* bad. There are some special luxuries among the druid circles. It's certainly far more comfortable than ... this."

"I don't ask for comfort. I ask for freedom."

"You will have it. And you'll offer it to millions of other lives. Can you imagine that? If you make good on what you've promised, you will offer a new kind of liberty to all the sons and daughters of the Godlands."

"If I do as I am told? If I bow and scrape before the druid council?"

She closed her eyes. "It's not like that. We're not like that. You claimed you met some of us in the past. You knew about the Council."

"Aye. And I helped Jeff and Delaen save you from Ephitel. Do you know what happened next?"

She shook her head. "No. The timelines were divergent."

"So you said. But I will tell you now. Jeff and Delaen scampered off like rats and left me and the Violets to face Ephitel and a hundred of his men."

"But you've admitted that was not the real—"

"It was real enough to me," Corin said. "And you..." He trailed off, almost smiling in spite of himself. "You are so much like the you I met in Oberon's dream. And honestly, your organization doesn't seem much different either. They'll do what they deem best according to the strictures, and woe befall the manling caught up in the works."

"That isn't fair. We've given our lives to serve the sons and daughters."

"And now you're ready to give mine." Corin shook his head. "I told you my terms. They're not negotiable."

She sighed and met his eyes. "As it happens, I have not come to negotiate. I came to warn you."

Corin blinked. "Warn me?"

"Indeed. The Council voted to detain you. They have extraordinary means."

Corin's lip curled in a snarl. "They're not the only ones."

"Please, Corin. I shouldn't even be here, but I came to ask—"

He cut her off. "Will you help me, Aemilia? Are you truly my friend? Will you help me evade them?"

For a moment she said nothing. Then she gave a tiny shake of her head. "I can't."

He leaned toward her. "I'm not asking for a big betrayal or a life on the run. I'm only asking for a brief diversion and a bit of information."

"Why?"

"I have to get to Ethan Blake. More than one life depends on it."

"Oh." She looked away. "The girl you love?"

Corin shook his head sharply. "I don't love her. I never … why do people keep saying that?"

Aemilia gave him a quiet smile. "It shows when you talk about her."

"I don't love her! I owe a debt, and I take that personally."

She watched him for a moment, saying nothing. Then she shrugged. "Sure. I did tell them about her. Perhaps there's something we can do."

"I can't trust this in someone else's hands. And I owe Ethan Blake more than you'd be willing to give him."

"That's precisely *why* we need to bring you in! Can't you see? You're talking about a war with the Vestossi!"

"Just one."

"There's no such thing as just one Vestossi! And war with the Vestossi is war with Ephitel."

"Isn't that what you want?"

"Yes! On our terms. You said yourself that we have the advantage of surprise. Will you squander that to kill some wretched little man?"

Corin opened his mouth to answer, but he couldn't. Not right away. It only made him angrier. "There's ... no. No, but ... Listen, we will still have the advantage. If I slaughter Ethan Blake, will Ephitel really come after me over one stinking, worthless cousin?"

"His authority is built on the threat of power. He will leap at the opportunity. I'm surprised that you don't know this of him."

Corin hung his head. "I do. Then let us make a trap of it."

"You see? That's a brilliant plan. That's why we should work together. Come back to the circles."

Corin met her eyes. "How long will it take them? How long will they dither? How long will they make me prove myself?"

She licked her lips. "It is not so bad as that."

"How long?"

She didn't answer.

Corin smiled, lips pressed tight. "I appreciate your honesty. That's why I'm asking you this favor."

She wrung her hands, trembling. "I cannot defy the strictures!"

"But you can delay. Surely you can delay. Lose track of me for a moment. That's all it really takes."

"And then what?"

"I'll disappear. They can't blame you for that. I am a sneaky scoundrel. I only really need three days of liberty. Maybe four, depending on where he is. Find the rodent for me and step aside, and I'll deliver myself to your Council when the week is done."

"If you are still alive."

There was a touch of real concern in her voice. Not for the world, not for the druids' plans, but for Corin himself. It stunned him for a moment, and then he snorted dismissively to cover his surprise. "I've tangled with Blake's sort before. Gods' blood, I've tangled with him. He thinks he's lightning with a sword, but I am not looking for a duel. I will settle him and then I'll melt into the shadows. Let them look for me then. Let even Ephitel come after me. He will not find me."

"You're something, Corin Hugh. Such confidence..."

He shook his head. "Experience. I've been doing this since I was still a child. Please, Aemilia. Give me a name. Tell me where he is. Then turn your back for but a moment. That's all I ask of you."

"So you can go do murder."

"For the greater good," he insisted. "And in exchange for this small mercy, I...I will bow to your Council. Think how many millions of lives you could benefit by bending this one small rule."

She shook her head, an admiring smile tugging at the corners of her mouth. "You are a force of nature."

"I am justice dressed in black." Then Corin saw something in her eyes and grinned outright. "Storm's fury, you have his name already, don't you? You tracked him down while you were with the Council. Tell me. Say it's true."

"I...did not come to send you after Blake. But I did bring another offer."

"You think I am so easily distracted?"

She smirked. "Like a ship in a gale."

"Oh! You wound me!" But then he hesitated. He rolled his eyes. "Oh, very well. What's this other offer?"

"I want to try to teach you how to work a glamour."

"This is more dream magic?"

"Yes. It is a power specifically conferred by Oberon, so if he did not share it with you—"

"He gave me dreamwalking and sampling. I can't imagine he restricted that."

"We'll learn in just a moment. And if it works," she heaved a hopeful sigh, "it might just keep you alive a little longer."

"It warms my heart to know you care."

She rolled her eyes at him, but she was smiling. "It isn't hard to do," she said. "If you can, I mean. The dream itself does all the heavy lifting. You just…sort of…ask it to pretend you're someone else."

"Ask?" Corin said. "Pretend? This doesn't sound much like my dreamwalking."

She shook her head. "No, I'm just trying to explain it. It's dream magic, right? Have you ever had a dream featuring someone you knew but…they were also someone else? Like a celebrity? You don't have those. But…well…nobility, I guess? Like it was the girl next door, but it was *also* the royal princess? I don't know exactly how to—"

Corin showed her a smile to shut her up. "I know the feeling, yes."

"Well, that's how the glamour works. You are you—you know you're you—but you ask the dream to make you *also* someone else."

"How?'

She shrugged. "Close your eyes. Think about yourself. Then think about the replacement. And remember that it's all a dream. That helps somehow."

"But what about my clothes? My possessions?" He thought about the Raentzmen in the common room, and his own

THE WRATH OF A SHIPLESS PIRATE

uniquely Ithalian knock on the door. "What about your voice? Your accent? Do you have to study someone before you can become them?"

She shook her head. "No. The dream takes care of that. The people you're interacting with ... they're not seeing your playacting. The dream is *showing them* the person you're trying to be."

"Fascinating."

She nodded. "It's a fascinating world we made. Worth fighting for."

Corin felt the weight she put on those last words, the demand that was almost a plea. He met her eyes. "You have my promise. And now that you've given me another level of protection, you have even less reason to worry. So you can give me Blake's name and tell me where he lives."

She tried to hide her smile. "You are persistent."

"I have been called a 'force of nature.'"

She laughed.

He slipped closer to her. "Please, Aemilia. This is important. What's his name?"

She opened her mouth to answer, then hesitated for one heartbeat too long.

Someone knocked on the door. Corin cursed and flung himself from the bed. He crossed the room in two long bounds and ripped the door open. "Gods' blood, what is it now?"

The innkeeper stood in the hallway, terrified and small before Corin's onslaught. Old Josef and some other wiry Raentzman Corin hadn't seen before stood there as well. All three of them shrank away from Corin's anger, and he felt a pang of guilt.

But all of his attention fixed on the stranger. The man looked worn out, dusty, and exhausted. His eyes were bloodshot, wind-burned from a furious ride perhaps. His boots were scuffed and caked with mud and his clothes all disarrayed. He looked like a man who'd come directly from a long, hard journey. He looked like a messenger.

Corin caught a calming breath, then slipped forward gracefully. He gave a little bow to the newcomer and said, "Good afternoon, my friend. Are you the same Francois I've heard so much about?"

The stranger shook his head, mute.

Corin shrugged. "But you are a messenger? You bring news from him?"

The stranger bowed his head, but he gave a little nod.

"Well? Speak, man! I know you must be weary, but I am more so! Speak, and afterward we both will find some comfort. Speak!"

The stranger sighed. "Francois is dead."

The Nimble Fingers gasped. Aemilia stepped up behind Corin and took his arm, as if to comfort him. But he could not yet understand. He caught the stranger's shoulder and shook the little man more roughly than he had intended. "What do you mean? Francois is dead? He only went for news."

"He was asking the wrong questions. He crossed into Ithale and found an inn. Not a Nimble Fingers inn, but he was so anxious to find news that he asked his questions anyway."

Corin whispered, "Gods preserve."

"No. They didn't. Some of the Vestossis' muscle dragged him in an alley and beat him to death. They hung his body in the streets as a message. He found no answers for you. I am sorry."

Corin shook his head, stunned. "No. He should not have had to give his life. I never would have guessed..."

"For what you did, for all Marzelle, I am sorry that he failed you."

"No," Corin said again. "Don't be absurd. I ... I am sorry he is dead. I never met him."

"He was good and true."

Corin nodded. "Go and have a drink on me. I'm sure there are others here who need to know as well. Thank you. Thank you for bearing this grim news. Now go and grieve."

Corin didn't move, even after they had left. Aemilia stood close beside him, breathing in his shadow. Eventually, she tugged his arm, the barest pressure, but it was enough to turn him. He found her staring up at him, her dark eyes wide and worried. For him.

"What are you thinking, Corin?"

"I think another man is dead because I have not yet found Blake."

She clutched at his shirt. "I think we've just heard why you shouldn't try! A man is dead just for asking questions."

Corin arched an eyebrow. "So he is. But I won't have to ask them, will I? You already know."

She shook her head, frantic. "I will not help you chase after him. You could be hurt!"

"I've made my case," Corin said. "I am a force of nature."

"That was before—"

"Nothing has changed! Your Council has made its demands—"

"This is not about my Council. Don't you see? A man is dead. And ... that could have been you."

He smiled sadly and caught her shoulders in a comforting grip. "Aemilia ... I have always lived a risky life. I am not afraid of dying."

Tears touched her eyes. "I am. For you. I don't want to see you hurt."

He offered her a smile. "I appreciate your sympathy."

But she blinked, and all the sympathy was gone. She was hard again, precise and sure. She released his arm and stepped back a pace. "I won't help you, Corin. I don't want to see you hurt."

"Aemelia—"

She shook her head. "I'm sending for the Council, and I will watch you like a hawk 'til they arrive. You are ... you are too precious, Corin."

For just a moment there, he saw her softer side again. He heard it in her voice. But then she raised her chin and her eyes flashed like chips of obsidian. "Don't move!"

She slipped away and down the hall. He hadn't lied before. He would not make himself a caged animal. Not if it meant letting Blake go free. And he was more than willing to use Oberon's power to evade them if it came to that.

But he could not afford to lose another day in chasing Blake. He could not afford to spend any time negotiating his release or fleeing the Council. He had to move. And he had to move *now*. It would only take Aemilia a moment to find the innkeeper and give him some message. Or perhaps she had some other means, some druid sorcery he'd never seen.

It didn't matter. He didn't need that long. He scooped up his cloak and belt as he went by, and in two quick heartbeats he was out the window, down the wall, and off to find a former friend.

(15)

Corin buckled on his belt while running, slung the cloak around his shoulders, and jerked the cowl up to hide his face as he emerged from the back alley. He heard a cry somewhere behind him, but it came far too late. He was free.

He dashed across the courtyard there and took the first right turn, which sent him north, away from the docks he'd gone so often to frequent. That would buy him time. The druids knew him as a pirate, and if they asked anyone, they'd know the taverns on the pier that had been a second home to him in Marzelle.

He had no intention of going there now. He was heading for a smuggler's dock two miles west of town. If he could meet up with Big Jack Brown before Dave Taker's henchmen sailed, he could tag along. That would serve him well; it took him out of the druids' reach and sent him straight to Ethan Blake's closest confidant. Corin pounded over the cobblestones, fury hammering with his every heartbeat. He'd wring Blake's secrets from Dave Taker, and Big Jack could do the rest.

But just to baffle his pursuers a bit, he held straight a couple blocks before turning to the west. As he went, a rain began to pour—slowly at first, but thick with the promise of a summer storm. He thanked sweet Fortune for that, crossed two more streets, and then stole a saddled horse from a poorly guarded stable. There was no sign of pursuit, and the sleeting rain would make it that much harder, but Corin's true enemy now was time. Big Jack's ship would surely sail with the tide, and Corin had to beat it to the smuggler's dock. He whipped the poor beast to a gallop through the rain and raced toward the setting sun, praying he was not too late.

Corin left the city's edge and started measuring distances. Two miles west of town by his best guess, he found a narrow, muddy footpath through the hills and trees. He splashed down it, heedless of the slapping branches, ducking under low-hanging limbs, until he heard the distant sound of breakers on the rocky shore.

He slowed then, suddenly cautious. If the druids had been waiting for him, they'd have caught him before he left the town. They were not a threat now, but his quarry was. After all, he was rushing to meet a pair of Dave Taker's henchmen. Corin left the horse on the trail and went ahead on foot, stalking now. Beneath the heavy stormclouds, night had already fallen, but Corin saw the flickering of torchlight some way ahead.

He'd seen his share of smuggler's stops. Usually it was some run-down, one-room shanty. Some of them had furnishings, a place to sleep the night. Most of them had fire pits and a neglected store of dry rations. The most popular were working taverns, stocked with beer and wine and rum to help a man forget his troubles. From Big Jack Brown's description, Corin expected this to be one of that sort, especially so close to town, and the nearer he got, the more accurate that seemed.

Two torches burned in sconces by the door, and a pitiful stable leaned against the outer wall. There were no horses in its stalls, but smoke was rising from the tavern's chimney. Corin watched the door a moment, considering, but he did not dare tarry too long.

Another approach occurred to him. He withdrew into the deeper shadows off the beaten path and stood a moment, collecting his thoughts. He closed his eyes and conjured up an image of himself, the cunning pirate captain with the charming grin. He grinned to himself. Then he imagined Charlie Claire, big and brave and dumb, and he laid that image over his own. He held it in his mind a moment, just as Aemilia had told him to do, and he repeated to himself, *All the world's a dream.*

Something seemed to shift. It might have been his imagination, or it might have been reality around him. It hardly mattered when fairy magic was involved. He opened his eyes and looked around.

The world looked hazy gray. It was not the heavy rain, nor even the same thick fog he'd seen at Ahmed's or in the alley when Aemilia had shot him. This was subtler, a blur around the edges of his vision, like a fine mist hanging in the middle distance. Was that the dream itself? Was that the fabric of reality, exposed, distorted by his borrowed power?

Corin tucked the question away for later. Someday he would have the time to think about such things. For now, he had a ship to catch. Ten paces brought him to the tavern's door. He hesitated on the threshold, eased his sword within its scabbard, and then stepped through the door.

The first thing he noticed was the stink of blood. The tiny common room was wrecked, its handful of tables smashed or scattered. A crumpled old man who must have been the proprietor lay in a heap back in one corner. Bruises and blood marked his crown, and Corin held little hope for him.

Big Jack Brown was there as well. He was stretched out on the floor, two paces from the door, one arm extended like he'd tried to crawl away. Blood pooled thick beneath him, all around him, and he was still. Otherwise, the room was empty. Rain and hail alike battered at the roof above, loud and angry.

Corin flew to Jack's side. He fell on his knees and pried Jack's shoulder up. The man's chest was a mess of bleeding wounds, and his face a mask of pain, but there was some life left in him still. He gave a wretched moan that was almost a gargle and convulsed, curling hard around his abdomen. Corin caught his shoulder, shifting him into an easier position, and with his other hand he supported Jack's head, striving to comfort him however he could.

Jack's eyes fluttered open. He stared, unseeing, up at Corin for a moment, then knotted a shaking fist in Corin's shirt and dragged him down close. His voice came out a wet rasp. "Charlie. Charlie Claire. The captain sent you."

Corin shook his head, but he doubted there was time enough to waste on explanations. "What happened, Jack? Who did this?"

"Taker's men. Not the ones I expected."

"And they did this? Just because you spoke with them?"

"I asked to go along. They got suspicious. They know Corin's back, and they are scared."

"And now they're gone?" Corin searched the room again, but there was nowhere to hide. "Which way? Did they go into the city, or are they still heading to meet Taker?"

Jack squeezed his eyes tight against some new wave of pain, but he gave an uneven nod to Corin's question. "Just left. Just now. Go get a good look at them, Charlie, and tell the captain. He'll want to pay them back for me. He understands the blood price."

Corin's stomach knotted hard. He'd set Jack on this path. He'd used the man to do his murder for him, same as Taker. He dipped his forehead now and whispered, "Jack, I'm sorry."

But the man was gone. Between one heartbeat and the next, he'd fallen still. Corin sought a pulse, but there was none. Jack's chest rose no more. His wounds no longer gushed, and his brow was smooth. He was beyond the ghosts of guilt and the hard pain of betrayal.

But his killers were still nearby. Corin growled a quiet oath and drew his sword. He closed his eyes and fought to shake off the glamour. "I can't afford to peer through mists at everything. Gods' blood, I'm me! And this is more than just a dream!"

He opened his eyes and saw the room more clearly. The haze was gone. Grateful to know the way of that, he sprang to his feet and sprinted for the door. The downpour came thick and chilly now, and Corin welcomed it. He dashed through the rain, along another path that led down among the rocks and shadows. The path cut sharply to the right and revealed a little alcove, an inlet hidden from sight out on the sea, protected from the fiercest waves. This was the tiny harbor where the smugglers had stopped.

Their ship was still in port; a low, sleek thing better suited to river travel than the open sea, but it could make the trip as long as it stayed close to shore. Even as Corin peered through the rain, he saw them casting off their lines, securing cargo on the deck. They moved with practiced familiarity, preparing for a trip they'd made a hundred times before and completely unconcerned with the crimson stains beneath their cloaks. They went easily about their business.

A bloodthirsty rage pounded in Corin's chest, a hunger to do justice for poor Jack. In his mind's eye, he was already sprinting down the narrow lane, leaping from the rickety pier to the low-slung deck, and ending both these monsters with two fierce and final thrusts.

And yet he didn't move. He lingered in the shadows, watching, thinking. He couldn't kill these men. Not yet. They were heading to some secret spot along the rough, uncharted coast of Spinola. They were heading to Dave Taker, who'd become Corin's last, best chance at finding Ethan Blake. Blake and Taker bore the ultimate responsibility for Big Jack's death. More than these two hired hands.

Corin clenched his fists until the bones of his hands ached with it, but he didn't move. He held his place, calculating, reasoning, until the last line was cast off. Until the sails went up. Until the ship began to drift along the pier.

He watched until the sailors turned their eyes toward the sea. Then he moved. Sure-footed as a cat and just as quiet, he sprinted down the rain-slick pier. He clasped his cloak around him, flitting like a shadow through the night, and as he ran, he watched the sailors' backs. While he was yet ten paces back, he saw one of them twitch his shoulder, and Corin leaped aside before he could be seen. Down into the water with a splash inaudible beneath the storm. He ignored the biting cold, the boggy filth, and pulled hard against the water. He had to race the wind.

He went ten paces in four hard strokes before he headed up for air, and when he broke the surface he was hard in the ship's wake. He darted forward with a mighty effort and caught the rudder with his right hand. He dragged himself closer, hugging tight against the hull as the ship began to tack toward the sea.

One of the deckhands appeared right above him, leaning out over the rail and staring deep into the night. Corin watched the man scan the length of the pier and even search the water's surface, but he could not have picked out Corin's form in the black shadows beneath the ship. Corin held his breath and gripped the rudder for all he was worth, and a moment later he had his reward.

The man above him turned away and called back to his companion at the fore, "Nothing's there, Ezio! I told you they was dead. I know my way around a dagger."

Ezio called back, "Still your tongue!" and both men fell to bickering. Corin seized the opportunity. He struggled up against the water, caught the railing of the quarterdeck, and heaved himself up out of the bog. He watched the other two a moment, arguing across the tiller twenty paces distant, and when he judged the moment right, he climbed up. Over the rail, onto the deck, and through the open trapdoor to the cargo hold.

The hold was shallow, far too low for Corin to stand up or even crouch. He rolled into the gap beneath the quarterdeck, squeezing out of sight, and lay a moment listening for some alarm, or even footsteps on the planks above. None came. All he heard was the driving rain. A hundred heartbeats later, he at last relaxed. He'd caught his ride. Now all he had to do was wait.

(16)

In his time as a pirate, Corin had seen plenty of opportunities to play the stowaway. It always was a boring task, but it was none too difficult. The biggest challenges were staying unseen and staying hydrated. For any voyage longer than a day or two, securing rations became the most pressing challenge.

Corin's first thought, as he analyzed the little hold, was that rations wouldn't be a problem this trip. For a two-man vessel, the little hold was *packed* with crates of food and barrels full of drinking water. Corin broached the first of each he found and stole a drink and a loaf of bread.

But as he lay there in the claustrophobic darkness, something about the ship began to itch at him. He'd never spent much time on river ships, but still, he had an instinctive feel for the basic architecture of the things, and everything about this ship was wrong. Tired as he was, distracted by the things he'd seen, it took him longer than it should have to figure out the problem, but at last he did.

The hold was far too shallow. The slope of the walls wasn't sharp enough, the bottom not deep enough. As soon as Corin noticed it, he understood. He'd known it for a smuggler's vessel from the first, but he had not considered everything that fact implied.

This was a false hold. This was the one they'd open to taxmen and officials. But there would be another, deeper down, with some form of concealed entry. Pirates rarely wasted effort on such sorts of subterfuge, but the years he'd spent in the close quarters of all sorts of ships gave him a clue. He could tell by feel which walls were true.

But even armed with that knowledge, he spent more than an hour searching to no avail. He began to imagine other designs, other places they might hide the entrance to the false hold, but nothing seemed more likely than some false panel, some artificial crates within this space. So he checked them all, and then he checked them all again. He had the time to spare.

Once, while he was working in the crawlspace of the hold, he had a moment's warning at the clomp of boots above him. He wedged himself into the very farthest corner and went still as midnight when the hold door flew up. If it had been day, the sun might have betrayed him, but not even starlight peeked past the heavy stormclouds, so Corin's dark clothes concealed him in the shadows. He watched from perhaps a pace away as one of the two sailors stooped to draw a mug of drinking water.

Corin didn't breathe until the door fell closed again. Then he waited in his hiding hole another hundred heartbeats, just to be safe. But no one came back for him, and it was boredom as much as anything else that eventually drove him forward again.

A little after midnight, by his best guess, his questing fingers found the latch. It was an uneven plank on the floor. A water barrel sat atop it, and Corin's first attempts to budge the thing drew a heart-stopping groan from the scraping wood. Corin froze in panic, ears straining hard for some sound of alarm, but no one came.

After that he sat and waited for another of the frequent spats between the sailors. When he heard voices rise in anger, he planted his back against the heavy barrel, shoved with his legs, and, inch by inch, he slid the thing aside. That might have taken half an hour, though it felt like days. Still, when that task was done, the rest seemed almost too easy. He crouched above the false panels, trying all the edges with his fingers, until he found the spot to press, the spot to slide, and then the whole thing fell back to show him the true cargo hold.

It was mostly empty now, and that was no surprise. Corin couldn't think of much worth smuggling *to* the Wildlands. They'd simply chosen this ship for its speed and stealth. But he also discovered he was not the first passenger to stow away down here. The lower hold was outfitted with a bunk and a bucket, a tiny table with a stub of candle, and a tinderbox. And there was a spot on the forward wall just high enough that Corin could stand straight.

He marveled at the space, after hours crammed inside the false hold. Then he went back to secure the panel, and in the process he discovered a locking latch. Not a hold for chattel, then, but for paying passengers. He grinned at that and threw the bolt, and then he sank down on the bed.

He'd gone three days now without sleep, and barely any food to eat, and now he found himself with a cabin and a locking door as well as provisions. He had no way to slide the water barrel back, but even if they discovered it, he'd have some warning when they had to break the door. He'd have time to make a plan. At worst—at absolute worst—he could always step through dream.

But in the meantime, he had a place to sleep and time to kill. He stretched out on the bunk and closed his eyes, enjoying the

THE WRATH OF A SHIPLESS PIRATE

old, familiar pitch and roll of a ship at sea. In no time at all, he was fast asleep.

·❦·

He couldn't easily guess how long he slept, but when he woke, it wasn't to the shouts of discovery or a pounding on the door. Everything seemed pretty calm. Corin rose and went back to the forward nook so he could stretch his arms and back, and while he was there, he discovered another perk of the smugglers' hold: It offered excellent acoustics. Standing in just that spot, he could hear the sailors up on the deck as though he were standing right beside them.

The sailors called each other Ezio and Gasparo. Not pirates, then, or they'd have taken pirate names. Instead, they used good Ithalian names, which suggested these were formal attendants of the Vestossis. There seemed no clear distinction between the two in power, but Ezio clearly fancied himself the leader. Gasparo was the brute, uninterested in the little plots and schemes that Ezio got up to, but still he showed no deference. These were Ethan Blake's errand boys, carrying messages to Taker. That was no more than Big Jack had already told him, but Corin felt some measure of comfort to find a point of confirmation.

Alas, for all the clarity with which he could hear them, he could do nothing to steer their conversation. He would have given much to hear some gossip concerning their master, some idle speculation concerning their current task, but all they talked about was wine and women. Corin spent an hour listening, hoping, searching for some clue within their prattle, but he heard nothing useful.

In the end, the only real advantage he could take from eavesdropping came when he abandoned it. He could wait until they were most distracted by their boasts and bickering, then steal into the upper hold to fetch more water or more food.

Ezio asserted his assumed authority in little ways. As the first day waned toward night, Ezio took the first watch, sending Gasparo to get some rest in a pretense of generosity that Corin saw right through. By midnight, Gasparo's turn came up, and Ezio slunk off to snore beneath the stars while Gasparo sailed on alone through the darkest part of night.

That single fact provided a tantalizing opportunity. Corin sat in darkness and considered. He could use the glamour to impersonate one or another of the sailors. Of course, that would require the removal of the man he chose, but Corin had no compunctions against that. The only real challenge was choosing which man to replace.

The quickest answer was Ezio because of the role he played. Corin had no doubts that he could boss around Gasparo just as easily as Ezio did. But Gasparo had bragged that he'd done the stabbing back at the smuggler's tavern. Corin's lips pulled back at the memory. Gasparo needed killing.

The real decision depended entirely on information. More than he wanted either of these men dead, Corin had to find Dave Taker. Until Corin learned the rendezvous location, or at least learned which of these men held the secret, he didn't dare move against either of them.

So he waited. His second day yielded him nothing but frustration, and the third was even worse. Big Jack had said it was a four-day trip, so Corin tried to bide his time, but every hour trapped in that tiny room, listening to the inane yammering of Gasparo and Ezio, drove him closer to madness. He did everything he could to learn their speech patterns, information that would be useful in his masquerade, but even more intently he searched for some subtle clue, some hint of where on Spinola's coast they were heading.

And then, late on the third day, just as Ezio was sending Gasparo off to bed, he dropped a juicy morsel. "Get some rest," he said, his voice ringing in the hidden cabin. "Tomorrow we'll meet Taker."

"You know the place?"

"I'll know it when I see it."

"You ever seen this guy before?"

"Once, I think. At a gala for the princess. He's a dirty pirate, same as all the rest, but he has his uses."

"And what's he gonna want from us?"

"The don said to facilitate him. Whatever way he needs. But he sent you and me, so ..."

"Killing, then."

"Gotta be. A killing or a kidnapping, and who's to kidnap in the Wildlands?"

"You're the smart one, Ezio."

"Don't forget it. Get some sleep. I'll take first watch again."

"Wake me when it's mine." Then Gasparo plopped down in his place on the deck and set to snoring like a man at work.

Corin sank down on his bunk, grinning so hard it almost hurt his cheeks. Ezio knew the rendezvous location. Two hours until the watch changed, and then Gasparo would be up for four. Plenty of time to put his plan in motion. Corin closed his eyes and waited.

An hour into Gasparo's watch, Corin slid aside the panel and crept out of his hidden cabin. He eased himself into the upper hold and lay a moment on his belly, motionless, surveying the open deck.

Ezio was curled under a thin blanket off to starboard, fast asleep. A strong wind blew dragging at the sails and making masts and rigging creak, making waves slap *pap pap* against the hull below. That would be more than enough noise to cover Corin's actions.

Gasparo stood at strict attention in the bow, staring out across the waves, alert for any hidden rocks. Corin slipped out of his hiding place and stole across the deck, silent as a stalking cat. Two paces from his target, Corin grabbed a corner of his cloak and balled it in his left hand while he drew his dagger with the right.

He slipped up behind Gasparo and jammed the makeshift gag over the sailor's mouth, dragging his head backward. "This is for Big Jack Brown," he whispered in Gasparo's ear. "You're not the only one who knows his way around a dagger."

Gasparo struggled, his arms scrabbling frantically, but Corin squeezed tighter with his left arm, then slipped the right past a flailing elbow and, with a short, sharp gesture, inserted his dagger just below the sailor's sternum. One thrust did the job. Gasparo fell limp against him, and Corin eased him to the deck.

He threw a glance back at Ezio, but the self-appointed captain of this little ship was still sound asleep. Corin took a moment to consider the corpse, paying special attention to his face; then he closed his eyes and repeated the same process he had used outside the smuggler's tavern. He borrowed Gasparo's appearance for his own, and when he opened his eyes, he felt the same strange gray mist hanging in his vision once again.

Then he moved fast. He heaved the true Gasparo overboard and scrubbed the tiller and deck for any sign of blood. It was an easy task by starlight, quickly done, and through it all, the other sailor never stirred. The whole ordeal took no more than half an hour, and Corin realized with some surprise that he'd secured himself a sailing job. Two hours still remained of second watch, and Corin fell into his old routines, adjusting trim and tack and watching hard for little signs of danger. The Spinola coast was brutal, but no one on the Medgerrad could navigate it quite like Corin Hugh.

He corrected Gasparo's course to a safer angle from the shore then went below to clean up any signs of his time within the hold. He secured the hidden plank again, shoved the water barrel back in place, and went back to the bow to man the tiller.

It had been a hard three days hiding in the lower hold, and now he stretched his arms and legs and bent his back to honest work. Wind in his hair, salt breeze in his lungs, he rode the waves, alive and free, as the distant sun began to rise.

Then from behind came a sour curse, and Ezio cried out in fury, "You stinking blackguard! What have you done?"

(17)

Corin spun around, panic scraping at the back of his breastbone, but the thin gray haze still hung over his vision. The glamour held. Still, he watched Ezio stalk across the deck toward him with accusation and murder in his eyes. Corin shifted, trying to find the best stance to meet his opponent. Behind his back, Corin gripped the threaded hilt of his dagger and hoped he wouldn't have to use it.

Before he had the chance to decide, the other man burst forward. Ezio didn't strike, though. He shouldered Corin roughly aside and dove upon the tiller.

"You senseless dog. You stupid oaf. I knew you for a fool, but I never thought—" He cut himself off, fighting the sluggish tiller as he tried to force the ship to shallow waters. "Even you ..."

Corin frowned, bouncing on his toes. For all his bluster, the other man seemed genuinely concerned with the situation, and that lit a fire in Corin's belly. He'd seen too much of shipwrecks, the worst of them in these very waters. He pressed forward and asked, "What? What do you need from me?"

"Get overboard and push! That's all I'd trust you with. Or, here, lean hard on this!" He ceded his place at the wheel, and Corin took it, fighting current to drive the ship in closer to the shore.

Corin swallowed hard. "Are you sure? I saw some rocks—"

"Of course there's rocks! That's why we brought the river boat. But you drove us out to sea! This ship ain't meant for that. One good wave could kill us!"

He watched a moment until he was confident that Corin would hold to the new course. Then he sprang away to trim the sails. "I swear to Ephitel," he called back while he worked, "if this stunt gets us killed, I'll curse your mother's house."

Corin nearly missed his chance, but he'd heard enough of their bickering to find the right response. "Hah. You try it. She'd serve you up for stew."

"Still your tongue and steer the ship," Ezio called back. Then from his place in the rigging, "Rocks! Rocks, you fool! Hard a-post!"

Corin saw them, but the ship felt dumb and sluggish compared to the ones he knew. He fought the tiller as hard as he could, but still had to shout, "Brace yourself!" Two heartbeats later, the lower hull ground up against a knot of submerged boulders. A seagoing vessel with a deeper keel might have broken through the formation, but it'd just as likely have smashed to pieces. This one scudded over the top.

It was no easy ride. Timber groaned and screamed, and the whole ship set to bucking like a wounded horse. The whole ship speared upward, driven by the wind and waves, and then dropped away beneath Corin's feet. While he was still falling to meet it, the deck kicked up again and smashed the wind from his lungs. He skidded across the main deck, ricocheted off the railing, and barely caught a grip on a trailing line before he skipped up and over the edge. The line snapped taut above him, stripping flesh from his palm and nearly jerking his arm from its socket, but Corin didn't dare let go.

He smashed hard against the outer hull, and then the ship rocked down again and plunged Corin up to his shoulders in churning seawater. His feet struck stone, and Corin kicked up hard. He heaved against the rope at the same time, and the two moves helped him spring high enough to catch the railing with his free hand. He went up and over onto the deck again, then sat a moment, fighting breathless lungs and a hammering pulse.

Then he heard a cry from the riggings. Corin looked up just in time to see Ezio lose his grip. A wave crushed over the edge, driving hard past Corin, and slammed into Ezio just as he hit the deck. The man went over.

The only man who knew where to find Dave Taker.

"Oh, gods' blood!" Corin shouted. He sprang up and pounded across the deck, drawing his dagger as he went. He skidded up against the port railing, hauled out several loops of rope from the tacking there, and tied the end fast around his dagger's hilt. He spun in place, and heaved with all his might, flinging the rope toward the last spot he'd seen Ezio go under.

The dagger's weight dragged the line out straight. Corin watched for several heartbeats as the line stretched out behind the ship, and then the dagger and the rope's own weight began to drag it downward. Corin cursed again and raised one boot to the railing, ready to dive for the sunken sailor. But then the rope jerked. It twitched once, which might have been anything, but then a weight heaved hard against it.

Corin dropped back to the deck and caught the rope in both his hands. He pulled it in, arm over arm. While he was busy fighting that, the ship finally cleared the beds of rocks. It kicked once more, just as Corin dragged a spluttering Ezio to safety, and then settled back into a low, smooth wallow among the shallow breakers.

Ezio reached up and clasped both hands behind Corin's neck. His arms were shaking. His face was pale, and there was a fever in his eyes. "I never would've guessed it, Gasparo. That was fast thinking. You saved my life. Now get back on the blasted tiller, or you'll have to do it again!"

Corin lowered the other man gently to the deck and then did as directed. It was not so urgent a matter as Ezio had guessed. Corin bent the ship's course back west, still sticking to the shallower waters. He spent a moment watching the rise and fall of distant breakers, then shifted ever so slightly to port. But now that he understood the sailors' plan, he saw its advantages. He'd never have chosen a river ship for the open sea, but the shallow draft allowed it to cruise inside the most dangerous parts of the reef.

"We're through," Corin called back, once he felt confident of their bearing. "Safe enough until you can take the tiller again."

"How badly is she damaged?"

Corin shook his head. "I can only guess. Fortune's grace, I didn't see any flotsam trailing in our wake, but that's no proof."

"Check her out," Ezio said. "Hold. Bilges. Lean over the sides if you have to, but watch your step."

Corin showed him a smile. "Aye, aye."

Ezio narrowed his eyes a moment, and then he hung his head. "Thank you, Gasparo. Gods' favor. I owe you my life."

That earned a more genuine smile, and Corin ducked his head. "Clear skies, Captain. I'll get you a report."

Corin did a visual inspection of the outer hull first. The sides showed no sign of damage, but the worst of the ride had been right along the keel. He leaped up to the quarterdeck and stood a moment watching their wake, but still he saw no signs of flotsam torn from the hull. That was a promising sign.

He threw back the hatch and groaned at the sound of sloshing water, but he quickly discovered the source—not damage to the hull, but broken water barrels. Corin eased himself down into it, then felt blindly through the wreckage across the hold's floor until he found the panel that opened on the secret cabin. When he finally found it, it wouldn't budge. The weight of water above it held the panel fast. Corin tried his dagger against it, stabbing down at the thin wood plank. It threw a violent splash of water and the dagger's point landed with a hollow *thunk*. Nothing else came of it. Corin tried again, and again he got a faceful of bilge water as his only reward. Then, on the third try, he felt the wood splinter beneath the blow.

The water poured through the narrow hole. Corin dragged his dagger back and drove it down again, adding to the flow. That suggested at the least that the lower hold wasn't flooded yet. Corin tried to slide the panel again, but it needed more time. He punched another hole, hoping to drain the water faster, then he went topside for a bucket to do some bailing.

Ezio was on his feet by then, if still a little pale. He was leaning on the tiller now, his eyes fixed hard on the distant shoreline. Watching for the rendezvous spot. Corin prayed Fortune it was close; then he went back below.

It took him half an hour to get through to the secret cabin, and then he saw it by daylight for the first time. It looked even smaller than he'd guessed. The bunk was now soaking in the broth that Corin had emptied through the panel, but the hulls looked secure. Corin knelt there in the upper hold and watched the water level, but it never seemed to rise at all.

He was just about to go and deliver the report when Ezio spoke right by his ear. "Ephitel's name, man, what have you found here?"

Corin looked sidewise at the other man, and then he remembered his disguise. "I can't guess. Some kind of lower hold? Riding over the rocks busted open this trap door."

Ezio nodded in admiration. "Good on you for spotting that. And I'd say you're right. This is a smuggler's ship, ain't it? I suspect that's where they keep the precious cargo. How bad's the leak?"

"Can't see one at all," Corin said. "That's the water from our drinking barrels."

Ezio clapped Corin on the back. "Seems like we survived your miserable piloting, then. Gods favor indeed!"

Corin turned to him. "We're there?"

"Close. I'm starting to recognize the shoreline. Give it another hour. If the ship'll hold together that long, we're safe."

"I'd wager on her," Corin said.

Ezio bent over to peer down into the lower hold. After a moment, he whistled softly. "That's a fancy setup. You sure the water ain't rising?"

Corin checked again, but it was lapping right at the lower edge of the bunk's frame. It hadn't moved a finger's width in the time they'd been talking.

"Positive."

"Good. Then let's get topside and try to bring this thing in to shore."

They chased along the shore for perhaps another half hour, Corin squinting just as hard at the rugged coastline as his companion did, but it was Ezio who spotted the narrow passage between two rocky bluffs that gave access to a sheltered cove. It was no easy task maneuvering the ship through the pass, but once inside they found a deep blue lagoon and a sandy beach hidden from the world.

Another ship already waited in the harbor—this one a single-masted cutter that would have paired well with the mighty *Espinola* that Dave Taker had left docked in Marzelle. Corin nodded toward it. "Is that Taker's?"

Before Ezio could answer, Taker himself appeared on the deck. He considered the newcomers through a battered brass spyglass, watching as they approached. Corin had to fight to suppress a shudder. Even at sixty paces, Corin had no trouble recognizing his old deckhand. Dave Taker had been a brutal infighter and a capable steersman, but the last time Corin had seen the man was when Dave Taker hurled him into the fires of old Jezeeli.

Corin focused hard on the strange gray mist that still hung at the edges of his vision. The illusion should be strong enough to keep him safe, and Corin didn't dare do anything to shatter it. This was what he'd come for, after all. Of course he'd have to face Dave Taker. And if he meant to find Ethan Blake, he'd have to find some cooperation from the scurvy dog. That meant playing his part, for now. So Corin steeled himself and waited.

As soon as the smugglers' ship came within hailing distance, Dave Taker lowered the glass and cupped his hands around his mouth. "Who goes?"

Ezio hollered back. "Friends from Ithale. The don sent us."

"About blasted time! Tell me you brought guns!"

Corin frowned. "Flintlocks?"

"Guns, man!" Dave shouted, furious. "Guns! Cannon! Didn't Blake get my message? If you're not here ahead of an armada, you should've stayed home. Blake's a madman, and we're all gonna die."

(**18**)

Ezio waited, tacking closer, then answered in a more normal voice. "You've been on your own a while. We don't bring any guns, but we are ... specialists. We're here to see you finish what you came for."

Dave Taker frowned. "What became of Greg and Benson?"

"The don had his doubts that they could do the task at hand. He had no such doubts about us."

"I sure as stormwinds do! You don't know what we're up against!"

Closer now, Corin got a good look at Dave Taker, and he began to understand the man's agitation. Taker had always been a brawler, but in the few short months since Corin had seen him last, the big man had gained four new scars—one atop his bald head, one along his jaw, and two crisscrossing his bare chest. His left shoulder showed the ugly puckering of a fairly fresh burn too, and his worn breeches showed the black stain of old blood.

What manner of beast was he hunting here? The Wildlands were rumored to be home to any number of fantastic monsters, but Corin couldn't guess what might have drawn Ethan Blake's attention. Unfortunately, he didn't dare ask the question. After all, it might be information Gasparo should have known.

That severely limited Corin's role in any conversation with both of the other two men. His best move, he realized, might be to find a chance to do away with Ezio in secret and then question Taker directly. Or if it came to it, he could remove Ezio right out in the open. He didn't plan to depend on terribly subtle means to get his information out of Taker.

One thing stayed his hand: He couldn't know for sure that Taker *had* the information he needed. After all, Taker had just referred to Ezio's "don" as "Blake." Perhaps the secrets were still in full effect. Corin silently cursed the famed Vestossi paranoia, and settled for restraint. He would not kill anyone at all. Yet.

Ezio tossed a line across to Taker. As Taker secured the ships and lowered a boarding plank, he grunted back. "Well? What are your instructions, then?"

Ezio crossed to the deck of Taker's larger vessel. He looked around, appraising the situation, then spread his hands. "We're here to assist you in whatever way is necessary. The don was very clear, though: You are to complete the task assigned to you and then return with us."

A spark of curiosity lit in Taker's eyes, and he raised his eyebrows. "Return where?"

Ezio showed his teeth. "You'll have that answer in due time. The don suggested you might ask, and he encouraged us to preserve every discretion until the deed is done."

"He doubts me, does he?"

Corin chuckled. "You sounded pretty unsure yourself."

Taker answered with a snarl. "I've seen storms you can't imagine, friend, and I've learned a thing or two. I know when to fight and when to cut and run."

"But there's so little reward in running," Ezio answered smoothly. "Whereas one last valiant effort now will see you to the satisfaction you've been waiting for. The don has bid us bring you home, where he will grant you a new name and drape you in every luxury—*if* you first accomplish what he's asked."

Taker considered that a moment. "What's changed?"

"Pardon?"

"Don't play dumb with me. Blake's been happy enough to let me rot here in the Wildlands for weeks now. Pay's been worth it, but never any talk of drapes and luxury. Now... now Greg and Benson disappear, and you two blokes show up. Now there's suddenly some rush. Spill, or I'll have you overboard. I ain't afraid to fight two men."

"You won't have to. This, at least, I'm authorized to tell you. In fact, I'm obligated to. The don's official message to you is as follows: Finish what you're about and come home. Do not delay, do not deter, and watch the skies. Corin Hugh is still alive."

Corin had to stifle a grin at the final line. It was rewarding to hear, even secondhand, that Corin's return struck such fear into Ethan Blake's heart.

It didn't do the same for Dave Taker. The big man shrugged and spat. "I've killed him once. I'll do it again."

"You won't," Ezio answered. "At least, not until we've completed our task. It's my sworn duty to see you follow the don's instructions to the letter."

Dave Taker sneered down at him. "You're going to make me?"

"As I said before, we are experts in our field. There is a reason he sent *us* to meet with you."

Taker measured Ezio up and down and then gave Corin a cursory glance as well. After a moment, he shrugged. "Sure. I believe it. But I've already told you, we're going to need more than a couple hired killers to bring this one down."

"We came all this way," Corin said, his patience wearing thin. "Perhaps you can at least tell us what has you so scared."

"The target," Dave Taker spat. "The same bloody farmboy that Blake sent me out here to kill."

"Farmboy?" Corin repeated, trying to mask his surprise.

"I ain't afraid to say it. He's a nameless farmhand just like Blake said. Sounded like an easy job, but the boy's some kind of bloody hero."

"One man? By himself?"

Taker frowned and shook his head. "He'd be bad enough by himself, but he's got a little army!"

Corin bit his lip. An army changed things, but what would a nameless farmboy be doing with an army? What would anyone be doing with an army in the Wildlands?

Ezio seemed to be thinking the same thing, because he cocked his head and asked, "How many?"

"Eh?"

"How many men in this farmboy's army? The don didn't mention them."

"You don't understand. 'Men' isn't the right word for them. They're beasts. They're nightmares."

Corin pressed forward. "How many?"

Taker sighed. "Four. Five with the wizard, but—gods be praised—he left a fortnight gone. Even without him—"

"Four men?" Corin asked. "I can understand you shying away from the task, but this hysteria—"

"Don't you sneer at me, you city rat! I've faced down admirals and kings. I've survived ghosts and the Vestossis' grays. Just last month I buried a justicar beneath the sea. So if you think I'm overreacting—"

Corin put out a soothing hand. "No disrespect intended, then. You've been on your own for weeks. All I meant to say is: You're not alone anymore. We're the best, you understand? We'll do this thing, and then we'll all go back home as heroes."

"Stormwinds take your heroes, pal. I'd rather be alive."

Corin almost cursed. He should have known better than to try that angle with Taker. He'd gotten sloppy, but an answer sprang to mind. "Forget the glory, then. How about revenge?" He gestured at Taker's new scars. "You want to punish the man who did these things to you?"

"Not enough to die trying."

"No one's dying here. That's why Blake sent us, right?"

"You seem like good boys," Taker said. "I'll give you that. Go home. Tell Blake I'm dead. Tell him you couldn't find me. I don't care. He doesn't have enough money to send me into that fire again."

Ezio said softly, "He does."

Taker looked up, surprised.

"He does," Ezio repeated. "And more to the point, I will *not* lie to my master. If you insist, I *will* go home and tell him you are dead. But I will not tell a lie."

Taker backed up half a step and balled his fists. "You think you can bully me—"

Corin stepped between them. "I think we can all get exactly what we want from this. Blake sent us to help you because we are the best in all Ithale at what we do. Like Ezio says, Blake can afford to buy the best. Point us at your problem; we solve it for you. If you get your revenge in the process . . ."

Dave Taker nodded, thoughtful. "I like you better'n him. I like the way you think. With three of us . . . if you're even half as good as you say you are . . ."

"We're better," Corin said.

Taker turned back to Ezio. "But I'm not doing anything until you talk. I'm tired of sailing blind."

"I've already said, the don insisted on the utmost secrecy—"

"I'm not asking for his family name," Taker snapped. "I'm asking for the rest of the story behind this farmboy. Should've asked that from the start. Why in the names of all the gods does Blake want his man dead?"

Ezio pursed his lips. After a long moment, he nodded to himself. "This, perhaps, I can tell you. I do not speak for the don, but only from my own conjecture. I've heard a thing or two at court."

"Spill."

"The princess—Sera Vestossi—rumor claims she has taken a lover. Some nameless farmhand born within a stone's throw of the Dividing Line."

"You think that's him?"

"I think that if it is true, it is a … reckless indiscretion. A Vestossi princess should not be toying with a commoner from Raentz. Or perhaps the don wishes only to inflict distress upon the princess. They have ever been unfriendly."

Taker shook his head. "That's it? Some family politics?"

"The fate of nations is decided on such things."

Taker heaved a weary sigh. "I'll give it a try. For revenge, if nothing else. Once more pays for all." He glanced toward the sky. "Best to wait for nightfall, though. We'll try to kill him while he sleeps."

Corin sucked a sharp breath between his teeth. He had no particular compunctions against killing some Vestossi's peasant paramour, but he had his doubts about Dave Taker. If they killed the man, Taker might still keep his promise and disappear. Corin wasn't sure how things would play out with Ezio if that happened. But if they could satisfy Blake's requirements and keep Taker in their custody, Ezio would take him straight back home to Blake. Corin liked that idea.

And it suggested a new plan too—a way to keep Taker on the line and drive Ezio back to Blake as quickly as possible. So Corin shook his head and put on his most earnest expression. "Fool move. Killing him'd be a waste."

Ezio chimed in, his voice cutting. "Killing him is our assignment, Gasparo. It's time for you to still your tongue."

"Kill or kidnap," Corin corrected. "How much better would it be to take him hostage?"

"I'd rather see him dead," Taker growled.

"I don't doubt you'll have the chance," Corin said. "Have you ever known Blake to release a hostage once he's gotten what he wants? But *first*, he'll be able to wring a ransom out of him."

"What could a farmboy have for ransom?"

"Information. Blackmail. Leverage against the princess. Can you imagine how much fun Blake would have with a prisoner like that?"

Taker nodded, something like hunger in his eyes, and Corin knew that fight was won. Taker had always enjoyed his hostages. But Corin had a new problem. Ezio was watching him with narrowed eyes and pursed lips. When he caught Corin's gaze, Ezio stepped closer and lowered his voice. "I think I've rarely seen you scheme so well, Gasparo."

Corin puffed up. "I came a long way to see this done, same as you, but you're looking ready to let things spoil. Me? I want to see some profit from all this effort."

"Gods favor, man, ease your heart. I meant it for a compliment. Might be the first time I've heard you argue *against* brute force."

Corin threw a shrug. "Maybe I've been paying attention. Maybe I've learned a thing or two."

Ezio grinned ear to ear. "Maybe you have at that."

"And I'm not done," Corin said, raising his voice for Taker too. "I have a plan."

"It had better be a marvel," Taker said.

"Brilliant in its simplicity," Corin said. "You said you've tangled with this man before? And you can lead us to him?"

"By darkness, aye. I wouldn't risk it by day. One of his scouts has an eagle's sight."

"That only serves our ends," Corin said. "My plan is to be caught."

"You're a fool. He may be a humble farmhand, but he goes well armed. And every blade he owns has run with blood."

"Yet you've survived," Corin said. "You've gone against them more than once, and you've survived. They must know you're out here."

Taker nodded.

Corin spread his hands. "Then there's our plan. You point the way. Ezio and I will go in. We'll pretend we're stranded sailors, shipwrecked near here, and we ran afoul of some raving madman."

Ezio quirked a smile at Taker. "I think he means you."

Corin nodded. "We claim that we escaped your camp and beg them to grant us refuge. It might take a day or two, but once we've earned their trust, we'll overpower them as they sleep and drag the farmboy back to you."

"Stormwinds blow, that ain't a lousy plan."

Ezio nodded, too. "You're coming along, Gasparo. There's promise there."

Corin grinned. "Seemed wise to build on the work Taker has already done."

"That's the genius of it," Ezio said. "And that's the part that I'll endorse. But don't allow a small success to carry you away. You may have learned a thing or two from me, but remember who's the master."

Corin frowned. "What?'

"Your plan has great potential, but it is also rash. Allow me to … adapt it to a better end. After all, we would not play dice with the don's commission. He has placed great faith in us."

Corin had to bite back a sarcastic response. "What would you suggest, then?"

"I will wait with Taker. *You* will go into the farmboy's camp and do as you've suggested. But in the meantime, we will lay an ambush of our own. If anything goes wrong, if they suspect you, you need only break away and lead them on a chase back here— right into our ambush."

Corin sighed. "I can see the reason."

Ezio raised a hand. "That's not all! If you intend to study, study closely. For if they buy all your lies, you can lead them, all unsuspecting, straight into our ambush. And even if you fail, even if they slit your throat before you get to say a word, *we* will still have another plan in place to capture them. Just … make sure to point them our direction before you die."

Corin didn't have to fake his look of awe. It was a genuinely cunning plan. It also left Ezio and Dave Taker together outside Corin's influence for hours or days. He did not much like the thought. "I see all your reasons," Corin said, "but couldn't Taker lay an ambush on his own? I'd feel safer with you by my side."

"Of course you would. But no, for two reasons. First, he is a pirate. It's not a career with much subtlety. I would not expect him to have much facility at laying traps on land. And second, I am honor bound to keep an eye on him at all times. I wouldn't trust the blackguard not to run as soon as we were out of sight."

Taker thumped his chest. "I'll black yer eye if you say something of the sort again."

"You will attempt to. But returning to the point, Gasparo...you must go alone. I have every faith in you. After all, you do know your way around a dagger."

"That I do," Corin said, deflating.

"Watch for your chance. Kill the others while they sleep, and drag the farmboy back to us."

"As quickly as I can," Corin said.

Ezio glanced toward the sky. "Within reason, eh? I will need some time to lay a perfect trap. Wait 'til nightfall if you can."

Nightfall gave them half a day to compare notes and make plans without him. Corin wasn't fond of the idea, but he could see no easy way around it.

Ezio clapped him on the shoulder. "Take heart, Gasparo. It is a simple enough task, and I expect you to excel. I'm sure the don will reward you for your part."

Corin closed his eyes and sighed. "I suppose you're right. For that—for the chance to stand before him and claim my right reward—for that I'll go."

"Good!" Ezio clapped his hands together in satisfaction. "Then I will set to work designing a most perfect trap. Mister Taker, if you'd be so kind, please point my companion in the direction of these ruthless killers."

(19)

The Wildlands deserved their name. Civilization had never thrived in the lowlands and river valleys of ancient Spinola, and only the savage tribes of nomads had ever flourished here. Corin had always assumed trade couldn't survive along the treacherous coastlines, but following Dave Taker through the thick undergrowth west of his cove, Corin began to suspect that had just as much to do with the land itself.

Narrow coastal plains gave way to steep, unforgiving mountain ranges that hemmed a vast highland plateau, cutting it off from the world as surely as the Dividing Line along Raentz's border. Corin eyed the high mountains nervously, but Dave Taker turned north, following the coast through dense forest that almost felt like jungle.

In the distance, something screamed.

"Gods' blood," Corin whispered. "What was that?"

Taker shook his head. "Don't know. Don't want to know. There are more monsters in these lands than that blasted Raentzman." He went a few paces in silence before adding, "But none I hate as much."

"Give me a day," Corin said, "and you'll have your revenge."

They went for some time soundlessly through the trackless wilderness. Then Corin asked, "How will I know him?"

"Shut yer yap!" Taker hissed. "They could be anywhere."

Corin lowered his voice, but he persisted. "You said there were four of them, including the farmboy."

"Sometimes five. The wizard comes and goes."

"There might be a *wizard* to contend with?"

Taker shrugged. "He's not the worst of them. The farmboy is the worst. Besides, I haven't seen the wizard in a while."

Corin shook his head. "How will I even know who I'm to bring back? Does he have a name?"

"You'll know him. You'll know him as soon as you see any of them in action. They *worship* him. But look for the golden hair. Now shut yer yap before you get us killed!"

They went more than an hour before Taker finally paused beside a wide, shallow stream. He caught Corin's shoulder and dragged him close, pointing to a small pile of rocks on the opposite shore.

He spoke in a whisper, his breath hot and foul on Corin's face. "That marks the path to their camp."

"You placed it?"

Taker shook his head. "They come here for water. It's a short journey from here. Half a mile?"

Corin rolled his eyes. "Then they might come by here at any moment! Get out of sight. You'll ruin everything if you're spotted."

"Want me to rough you up a bit first? To help sell the illusion?"

Corin shook his head. "I can handle a farmboy and his hunting pack. I'll see you tomorrow."

Taker snorted. "You'll probably be dead in an hour, but your partner seems to have some good ideas. Gods favor, either way."

"Clear skies," Corin answered.

He licked his lips, caught his breath, then slipped away across the gravel creek bed and into the water. It churned and splashed at every step, but Corin did his best to move silently. He wanted to save the theatrics until he knew exactly who was watching.

His only real plan was to find the camp, then dash in shouting, "Help! Save me!" He briefly considered trying it in the Raentzman's native language, but he suspected a man who dallied with the princess of Aerome would have no trouble with honest Ithalian. As Corin left the stream and started down the path toward their camp, he found himself distracted by the question of this man. Was this really Princess Sera's secret lover, some unknown commoner exploring the godless Wildlands?

He barely knew what to make of that. He'd never had much interest in the affairs of court, so the princess was a complete unknown to him. As far as he was concerned, they were all the same Vestossi snakes wearing different titles. But he had to wonder what would tempt Ipolito's own daughter to risk her honor and her father's disfavor on some farmhand from another nation. What sort of man was he that she could not buy ten better off the streets of Aerome with her father's money? The closest thing he had to a clue was a passing comment from Dave Taker. *"They worship him."*

Before he could imagine what that might mean, Corin broke free of the heavy forest. The narrow footpath burst onto a sprawling clearing where green grass grew beneath a brilliant sun. The makings of a mighty bonfire marked the center of the clearing, and half a dozen tents clustered around it. From twenty paces off Corin spotted several figures—this farmboy's army— mostly sprawled at leisure.

There was the wizard Taker had mentioned. He lay stretched out on his back and staring at the sky, hands clasped behind his head. The boy was pale and scrawny, with a melancholy look about his features, but even at this great distance Corin caught a spark of genius in his eye. He should have been no more than an apprentice, for he looked to be perhaps sixteen summers old, but he wore the robes of a journeyman—grass-stained now, but no less opulent.

Near him sat a mountain of a man, a hulking giant who might have dwarfed even Dave Taker, and a look at that one figure alone led Corin to understand Taker's new scars. He hovered near the wizard, a huge two-handed sword strapped to his back, but the man had hands the size of brandy casks. He hardly needed a weapon.

But this giant was not the only warrior in sight. There was another some way off, dressed in the full uniform of a foot soldier from the army of Dehtzlan. He stood outside his tent, one hand on his sword's hilt, his spine straight as a pole. He alone looked sharp, alert, and ready for battle.

Near the fire pit stood three more men deep in conversation. One had his back to Corin, but he had a frame much like the wizard's—small and wiry—though this one dressed in far more ordinary clothes. The second man in the conversation was perhaps the most amazing of the whole troupe. He had the rich red-brown skin of the Wildlander nomads and wore nothing but a raven-feather skirt. He should have been in full bloodrage, warring with the Godlanders who'd dared to visit his ancestral home, but there was no sign of violence here, no struggle. The three spoke at ease like gentlemen.

And the third man in the conversation was tall and broad of shoulder, with thick golden hair and a hard-worn arming sword on his hip. This was the famous farmboy? He was a handsome man, but not extraordinarily so. The giant had him beat for size, the soldier for polish, the wizard for flair, and the Wildlander for ferocity. Of everyone on the field, this farmboy was the only one who looked truly ordinary.

Corin gathered all these details in a glance, and the array of mysteries might have been enough to make him hesitate, to concoct another plan, but he had no chance. The soldier in his uniform spotted Corin as soon as he appeared, and without a moment's hesitation, the young man cried alarum and drew his blade. The others all responded just as quickly, and between one heartbeat and the next, every man was on his feet and searching for the threat. Three sharp swords, two daggers, and a Wildlander bow all appeared as if by magic, and all of them spun toward this new intruder. All at once, Corin understood Dave Taker's fear.

He quelled a curse and sprinted forward, doing his best to pretend he'd been running all along. He cried out, "Help! Save me!" and that, at least, drew some looks of surprise and doubt among the fierce warriors. He went four paces forward at full tilt, and on the fifth he slammed hard into some unseen barrier. Empty air might as well have been forged iron. He smashed hard against empty nothing and then spilled to the earth.

Head spinning from the impact, he still held to his plan. He pushed himself up on hands and knees and groveled in the dirt. "Please! Please help me! I've just ... I've escaped from a madman. He means to kill me. Please, protect me!"

He pressed forward until he found the mystic force he'd crashed against. It was still in place, still unyielding and completely invisible, but he leaned against it, feet scrabbling, in a pitiful show of fear. "Please help me! He's coming!"

And then he saw what Dave Taker had predicted. Five deadly men, all armed to the teeth, turned like curious school-children and looked to the golden-haired farmboy for directions. The farmboy didn't seem notice, nor did he spend any time coming to a decision. His expression softened at Corin's pleas, and the sword went back in its scabbard. Before any of the others could move, the farmboy was sprinting across the field toward Corin.

"Ridgemon!" he cried as he went. "Drop the wards. A'Gileen, get water. Tesyn, come aid me. He might need patching up."

That last name struck a sharp shard of ice into Corin's heart, even before he'd fully placed it. Tesyn? It was too familiar. And then the wiry man who'd been speaking with the farmboy turned, and Corin knew him. Tesyn. He'd learned that name when the young man was his hostage, but he'd never used it much. Corin mostly just called him the Scholar.

This was the same young man who'd made a deal with Charlie Claire, the same who'd recognized Corin in Khera and called the caliph's guards on him. And Corin remembered what he'd said about Jezeeli. *"It's not enough to read the books; you have to risk your neck. You have to go adventuring to find anything worth having."* Now Corin had one paralyzing moment of stark fear as their eyes met across the clearing. ...

But a thin gray mist still hung across his vision. Oberon's magic preserved him. He still wore the illusion of Gasparo, and it served him here. The scholar Tesyn came timidly forward, eyes fixed on Corin, but he showed no real signs of alarm. He sheathed his dagger and knelt to take Corin's pulse.

Before Corin could guess how to react, the scholar withdrew and gave his report. "He's greatly agitated, but I see no signs of serious harm."

The farmboy nodded, real relief in his eyes. Then he sank to his heels before Corin. "You say it was a man that attacked you? Not a vicious beast?'

Corin caught a ragged breath and fought to reassemble his plans. "I ... yes. You ... could almost call him a vicious beast, but it was truly a man. A pirate by the look of him. Tattoos on his arms and face. Hideous scars. And ... what looked like a fresh burn on one shoulder."

The farmboy grinned from ear to ear and spun around to call back toward the wizard. "You hear that, Ridgemon? I told you that one hit him!" He turned back to Corin and clapped a firm grip on his shoulder. "Rest easy, friend. You're safe now. We've met the man you're speaking of, and he's no match for us. He wouldn't dare cross us again."

That comment drew a booming laugh from the giant, who came forward with a dripping waterskin. A'Gileen, he'd been called. And Ridgemon seemed to be the wizard. Corin tried to catch every little detail for use later, but the details bombarded him, every one a fount of puzzling questions. Who were these men, and why were they here? How had the scholar come to join them? Corin reminded himself that it had been *months* since they'd crossed paths in Khera, but still it seemed impossible. And where would this farmboy—even one beloved of the Vestossi princess— have found himself a journeyman wizard? And a friendly savage?

"Hartwin," the farmboy called, "Go and search the woods. Make sure our friend here wasn't followed."

The Dehtzlan soldier snapped a smart salute and followed his orders, but the farmboy wasn't even watching. He was already turning back toward the fire. "Longbow ..." He paused when his gaze fell on the Wildlander, and he barked a startled laugh. "Put away your bow! He is a friend."

The savage never relaxed. He held a massive bow at full draw, a clothyard shaft ready to pin the newcomer to the earth. Corin hardly dared breathe. The Wildlander stared him down. Without ever glancing away, he answered the farmboy. "A friend? How can you be certain?"

The farmboy shook his head. "He is in need of aid, and he has asked it of us. That is all I require."

The Wildlander snorted. "Perhaps you are a fool."

The arrowhead never even trembled. Corin stared at it, transfixed, while he tried desperately to imagine some place he could escape to. If he dared to step through dream—to sacrifice time and opportunity to random chance—where would he go to escape a deadly bolt? And could he go fast enough?

Before Corin found an answer, the farmboy grew frustrated and said, "Longbow! I gave an order. At ease."

The savage arched an eyebrow. "You do not order me, Godlander."

"And you do not threaten those under my protection, or I will take it as a threat to me. Will you break your promise so soon?"

The Wildlander lowered his weapon, but a fury flashed in his eyes. "Do not question my honor, Godlander!"

"And do not threaten my friends," the farmboy answered. He turned back to Corin at last and extended a hand. "Can I call you 'friend'?"

Corin accepted his help up, nodding furiously. "Aye. Indeed. I could use a friend like you."

"I'd say so. How'd you even get here?"

"Shipwreck," Corin said, finally returning to his prepared material. "We were trying to fish the unclaimed waters—"

"We?" the farmboy asked, concerned.

Corin hadn't really considered that aspect of the story, but a two-man ship did make more sense for these waters, so he ran with it. "Aye. Me and a companion. We ran hard against some hidden rocks and our boat broke to pieces underneath us. Had to swim for shore, and when we got there, we found the pirate waiting."

"He's a pirate? You're sure of it?"

Once again, the farmboy's questions caught Corin off guard, but he couldn't see any use in denying it. "Aye. He had the look, anyway."

"And you said he's sticking to the coast. We hadn't expected that. Most folk are smart enough to stay beneath the tree cover."

Corin frowned. "Why's that?"

"Wyverns'll grab you around here, if the sea serpents don't pluck you off the sand. Up on the plains, you'd be more worried about the rocs and manticores. Still, always better to stay under cover."

Corin stared at the farmboy for a moment, then snapped his jaw shut with a *click*. "Manticores? They have manticores?"

"Not *lots*, but … yes. Why do you think we've never colonized the Wildlands?"

"I thought … I thought it had to do with … you know … agriculture and … and trade routes."

The farmboy laughed. "Hah! There's that too. Manticore raids wreak havoc on trade routes."

Corin stepped back and looked around the clearing. The wizard and the giant had settled back into a quiet conversation, but everyone else was gradually drifting toward Corin and the farmboy. Those close enough to have heard his last comment nodded in quiet agreement.

Corin waved his hands at the clearing. "Then what are you doing here? Where's your cover?" He stopped himself, remembering the wall of nothing he'd crashed into before. "Ah. Does your wizard hide you?"

The farmboy grinned. "Nah. We're here to be seen. We're hunting monsters."

Corin shook his head. "Perhaps you're the madmen."

"We're adventurers with nothing to lose and everything to gain! We've been out here months and we've survived. Haven't lost a man yet! In fact,"—he waved toward the Wildlander—"we gained one!"

Corin looked that way, and the savage answered his glance with a friendly nod. It was such an ordinary gesture, such a perfectly civilized act, that it shattered Corin's restraint. His curiosity overcame him, and he said, "I thought your people lived on the high plains."

The Wildlander nodded, silent.

Corin spread his hands. "Well? You're an awful long way from your wigwams."

"And you're an awful long way from your gods. Which of us will suffer most?"

Corin considered it a moment, then shrugged. "Ephitel's never done anything to keep the rain off my head."

Several around the circle roared with laughter at Corin's little sacrilege. The savage only offered a shadow of a smile. It was a pitiful thing, there and gone, but the farmboy clapped Corin on the shoulder as though he'd accomplished some great feat. "I think you're going to be very welcome among our little band," he said. "Now! Enough interruptions! You were telling how you shipwrecked and this . . . pirate captured you and your crewmate."

"Aye, just so," Corin said, playing for sympathy. "I made it out alive. Poor Ezio wasn't so lucky."

Somewhere in those words, every trace of good humor evaporated in the little camp. Corin felt it happen even before he saw the stormclouds in the farmboy's eyes. For an instant he didn't even know what he'd said wrong, but then the farmboy caught Corin's shoulders in his strong hands and pinned him with his gaze. "He killed a man? You're telling me he killed a man?"

Corin licked his lips. "Oh ... aye." He could hardly reverse the claim now, so he just pressed forward. "I told you he was a madman. I thought you'd been fighting with him."

"We thought he was a raider! Out to steal our supplies. We never guessed he was a murderer!"

The Wildlander snorted, but the farmboy didn't seem to notice. His hands were trembling. "We could have stopped him. We never even tried, just scared him off. We could have stopped him, and your friend would still be alive."

Corin stared, baffled. He remembered the fear with which Dave Taker had described his encounters with these men, and now he learned they hadn't even been trying to harm him. It was a terrifying thought.

And on its heels came a terrifying action. The farmboy spun Corin around to face back the way he'd come and propelled him toward the forest path. Corin tried to plant his heels, to resist the motion, but he was helpless as a bit of driftwood on an ocean swell. "Wait!" he cried. "Where are we going?"

"To do justice. Do you think you can find the way?"

"What? No. I ... I'm not prepared to go back there!"

"Longbow! Will you help?"

Instead of answering, the Wildlander dashed on ahead and disappeared into the woods. A native woodsman would have no trouble finding signs of two pirates' tromping passage through the forest. Corin stifled a groan and tried to devise a plan.

Behind them, Ridgemon called, "Auric, wait! I need a moment to prepare."

"Stay here," the farmboy called. "All of you, stay here. This camp is still a beacon for the monsters, after all. I can handle one bloodthirsty pirate."

The scholar asked, "Is that wise?"

"Don't worry, Tesyn. I have Longbow with me. If I see Hartwin, I'll send him back to help protect the camp."

"But ... but ..." Corin sputtered.

"Take a deep breath, friend. I know it's scary when you're not used to adventure, but there's a certain thrill you'll learn to love. Sometimes the best choice is just to rush right in and set things right. You'll feel better when it's done."

For the first time in his life, Corin couldn't agree with the sentiment. Right now he wanted nothing more in the world than to slow down and think things through.

The farmboy never gave him a chance.

(20)

Corin needed time. He had an opportunity here to lead the farmboy, Auric, back to Ezio's trap, without having to kill anyone in their sleep, but if he arrived too soon, the trap would not be ready. He had his doubts this Auric could be anywhere near as fearsome as Taker painted him, but he was not prepared to run the risk of losing his chance at Blake. That meant Ezio had to survive and be willing still to lead Corin back to Blake.

So Corin had to find ways to delay. Ezio had asked him to wait until nightfall. It had been an hour's journey to the camp, and it would be at least another hour back, but still Corin needed to delay the farmboy hero for the better part of the day. But he needed to do that without giving Auric any chance to return to his camp and bring more men along.

It was a delicate task, and one Corin was still pondering as Auric steered him back down the path toward the stream. The farmboy pointed ahead. "You came from this direction. I assume you saw our waypoints."

"Waypoints?"

"Piles of stone, always with one bit of quartz to mark the way back to camp."

Corin shook his head. "I only saw the one. Down by the water."

"Oh! Right. The rest are to the west, and you said you came from the coast."

"Aye." Corin spotted the wide, meandering creek ahead, and it gave him a plan. He nodded more earnestly. "Yes! Downstream from here. I told you the pirate was a fearsome man, and I had no wish for him to track me, so I waded in the riverbed. I hoped the rocky shore would hide any signs of my passage."

"Oh." Auric's eyebrows drooped and his shoulders sagged. "That was awful clever of you, but we won't be able to follow your trail back to him. I don't suppose you remember any details? Could you point us to his camp?"

Corin almost grinned. "I can. But I must warn you, I took a twisting path."

Auric gave a laugh. "There are no other paths in these woods. That's why they're called the Wildlands. Lead on! Lead on!"

Corin started east along the stream's path and toward the distant shore, but also away from the cove down south. He felt a flash of hope, but three heartbeats later it dashed against the return of the Wildlander.

Longbow emerged from the undergrowth opposite the stream with barely a rustle. He held a scrap of torn fabric in one hand and a broken twig in another. He called across to Auric. "I have found the path, and it offers many mysteries."

Auric stepped up behind Corin and clapped him on the shoulder. "No need! Our new friend remembers the way."

The Wildlander narrowed his eyes. "Which way is that?"

"Back east, along the riverbed."

The savage shook his head. "My trail points south through jungle."

"Ah!" Corin said. "That must be the pirate's doing. You said he'd visited your camp before."

Auric nodded. "More than once."

But Longbow wasn't satisfied. "This trail was not made by one man, but two."

Corin licked his lips. "Did you think he was alone? Could any Godlander survive in this place on his own? He had another man with him at his camp."

"You have many answers," Longbow said, his voice heavy with accusation.

"That's exactly why we need him," Auric answered. "We've only ever seen this man when he came to raid our camp, but this one has seen *his* base."

"Even so," Corin said, "I couldn't hope to navigate these woods the way you do. I certainly would not have spotted the pirate's tracks. Perhaps if you scout back that way and we return the way I came, we'll meet up at the end."

"And even if we don't," Auric added, "You're sure to find something useful on the trail. It will be good to know more about his movements. You could even lay a snare or two, just to be safe."

The Wildlander opened his mouth to argue more, but Auric's attention was already focused east again, toward the distant shore. The man was easily distracted and itching for adventure. Corin caught his arm. "I overheard him saying something to his mate about the Carnival in Nicia. Perhaps he tires of this place. If he's returning to the Godlands, we can trust him to their authorities. Let's just go back to camp."

Auric snorted his contempt. "The authorities in Ithale are barely better than he is. No. If this man has done murder right beneath my nose, then I will show him justice. Longbow! Follow that trail and discover all its secrets. I'll see you at the other end!"

Longbow cried, "But wait!" But he did so in vain. Auric was already dashing off along the stream's path, anxious to join the fray. Corin dipped his head toward the noble savage, then darted to catch up with the farmboy.

When Corin caught up with Auric, the farmboy asked, "Is Carnival far off? Do you think he's sailing soon?"

Corin glanced sideways and risked a bigger lie. "I've lost track of time, but I believe it is. Perhaps a week or two."

Six months might have been closer, but the Raentzman didn't catch the lie. He groaned. "It would take that long to sail from here! He might be leaving even now."

"I suspect he'll wait at least a day trying to find me. Or hoping I come back to his camp out of desperation. He seemed most anxious that I not escape."

"No doubt because you were a witness to his crime."

"Ah. That must be it."

"Yet we should hurry all the same. I'd hate to have him slip through my fingers."

Corin pressed forward and pretended to pick a path from memory. He led the farmboy for a while before his curiosity pressed him to speak. "How do you know Longbow?"

"You remember the manticores I mentioned?"

"How could I forget?"

"We were hunting on the high plains and found one attacking a Wildlander village. I drove it off. The People of the Crow were quite grateful."

Corin remembered the raven-feather skirt. "Longbow's one of them?"

"He's their Judgment. Something like a Justicar, but worse. There's a tribal magic to it that I don't understand, but his honor is tied to protecting his people from danger."

"And now he serves you out of gratitude?"

Auric barked a laugh. "Every piece of that is wrong. No. He was furious that I stole his honor. It should have been his to kill the manticore."

"Oh."

"So he challenged me to battle."

"You won."

"I did."

"And now he owes his life to you?"

"You have heard too many wild stories. No. Now he watches me. He claims he's never met a Godlander with the wits to survive two days in these lands, let alone a whole pack of them. So he's observing us. For the good of his tribe."

The farmboy spoke as though it were the simple truth—he must have believed it was—but Corin spotted several flaws in that explanation, wild stories or not. He went in silence for a moment, considering, then asked offhand, "So he's not one of your men?"

"I don't have any men. I'm just a freelance looking for a name."

Corin frowned. "There were five men in your camp ready to kill me if you'd said the word. And when you decided I was a friend, they answered your orders. Those are your men."

Auric shrugged. "I don't know. This venture was my plan, so they let me take the lead. That's all."

Corin didn't believe that for a moment, even if the farmboy did. He had a charisma Corin had seen before, a talent for leadership, and he used it without even trying. Perhaps that was how the Vestossi princess meant to use him. Or perhaps she'd been caught up in his charm as well.

Corin shook his head. "Where in all Hurope did you get yourself a wizard?"

"Ridgemon? He's my brother. He met Tesyn while he was at the university, and A'Gileen was our neighbor back in Raentz."

"And the Dehtzlan foot soldier?"

Auric frowned. "I ... don't remember where we picked up Hartwin. Some campaign while I was still with the regiments, I suspect."

"And now you're here, a hundred leagues from civilization. Why?"

"I told you. We're adventurers."

"Is there good money in it?"

Auric didn't answer right away. He thought about it, and finally he shook his head. "Renown. That's the word. Everything we do is for renown. We were nothing in the Godlands—well, except for Ridgemon, and he could only ever afford his training because of the freelance work I'd done."

"A noble sacrifice."

He shook his head. "No. That's just it. It's a common sacrifice. If I ever mean to change the world ... If I ever mean to do anything that matters ... I need a name. Can you understand that? I need a name that's recognized through all Hurope."

Or only in the court at Aerome, Corin thought. A hero might be worthy of a princess's hand, no matter where he'd been born. It was a romantic plan. There was a certain beauty to it, and for a moment Corin wrestled a pang of doubt, of guilt, at what he meant to do. This young man was not what he'd expected—not a posturing hero or a dumb Vestossi brute. He seemed brave and true, and before he'd seen his twenty summers, he already led a band of men so dedicated they would risk their lives to follow him.

He had potential. Corin cherished that. But could Corin give up his own revenge to let the farmboy go? It seemed the honorable choice, but where was honor in a pirate's life? Corin had a quest of his own, given him by the very maker of Hurope. He meant to cast down Ephitel, and before he could do that, he needed to answer for Ethan Blake. For his own peace of mind. If he had to sacrifice this farmboy along the way...

He thought of Big Jack Brown, dying in the smuggler's tavern, and he shook his head. There'd been the Nimble Fingers messenger in from Marzelle too. Francois? Aye. This wouldn't be the first good man who'd died for Corin's quest.

And there was no good reason Auric had to die. After all, Corin had already convinced the other two to take him as a hostage. Once they returned to civilization, once Ezio revealed Ethan Blake's true identity, it couldn't be too hard a thing to help the adventurer escape. He'd proven quite resourceful on his own, and with Corin's help it should prove a simple thing.

That seemed a happy end to all of it, but still Corin's stomach churned. Guilt and doubt growled inside his chest like a raging storm, and he couldn't bring himself to banter with the other man. He went on ahead, burning daylight as he led the farmboy on a convoluted path that never quite reached the rocky shore. And then, just as the sun was setting, Corin passed beneath the shadow of a huge leaning boulder that looked a bit familiar, and there ahead was the entrance to Dave Taker's cove. He'd arrived at last, and just in time.

The two ships still sat moored out in the bay, and two rowboats stood beached on the sand, but no sign of Taker or Ezio. One pace closer showed him the dark form on the path. The salt sea air didn't quite mask the sharp scent of fresh-spilled blood. Corin froze, eyes fixed on the Wildlander savage. He lay sprawled in the sand beneath the leaning stones, unmoving while his lifeblood pooled around him. His mighty bow lay broken some way off, his arrows scattered and stomped to tinder.

He'd found them. He'd found Ezio's ambush, and this is what Ethan Blake's prize henchman had done. Corin shook his head. He turned away and stopped Auric with a hand on his chest.

"Auric, wait," he said. "There's something I must tell you."

The farmboy frowned, confused, and then his gaze drifted past Corin and touched on the fallen savage. His face screwed up in pain and anger, and he roared his fury at the killers on the beach.

Corin tried to restrain him. "Auric, wait! They're expecting you!"

But the farmboy didn't listen. He spun past Corin and charged ahead, sword flying into his hand as he rushed toward the fallen Longbow. Corin chased after him, searching left and right for some sign of the trap that must be waiting, but he saw nothing.

Instead, he heard an odd, familiar sound. It was a tiny pop, a little whistle, and then a little glass-and-silver dart buried itself in the farmboy's neck. Auric gave a gentle grunt, staggered one more pace forward, and then the druids' poison took its toll.

He fell.

(21)

Corin dashed forward, searching the cove's beaches for some sign of the attacker. He prayed Fortune he'd find Aemilia, or some other druids here to intervene, to capture him. Instead he saw Dave Taker spring from behind a boulder, a cutlass in each hand, and charge toward the fallen farmboy. Ezio rose behind him, and in his hand he held one of the miniature guns the druids used.

Of course. He worked for the Vestossis.

Dave Taker wasn't slowing, and Corin saw almost too late what the man intended. Corin sprinted forward, ducked his head, and met the pirate's charge with a shoulder to his ribs. They both went sprawling in the sand, and it was all Corin could do to avoid the tumbling blades.

He wasn't quick enough to dodge the thrashing fists. Dave Taker clubbed him once on the back of the neck and then hit him with a hook beneath his ear that knocked him away. "What's in your bloody head?" he shouted. "That's a killer! That's a monster on the sand."

"That's a valuable hostage," Ezio answered, his voice that same eerie calm. "We've all worked hard to capture him alive. You might count yourself lucky that my companion only hit you with his shoulder. I've rarely seen him exercise such cool restraint."

Dave Taker climbed to his feet, grumbling all the while, but he made no further move toward the fallen farmboy. Ezio nodded. "Good! Now go and fetch whatever things you need from the other ship. As soon as we have the prisoner aboard, we should leave this place behind."

The prisoner. Corin stared at Auric, fallen half a pace from the bleeding Wildlander. The farmboy was still breathing. They both were. That was some small mercy.

Corin hadn't heard the man approaching, but Ezio clapped him lightly on the shoulder. "That was a clever move, sending the ranger to us first. He'd have put an arrow straight through Taker's heart, but he was not expecting a second man."

Corin winced at that. He could have expected it. If he'd believed Corin's story, he'd have expected Taker to have a companion. But the Wildlander—the Judgment, Auric had called him—had seen through Corin's lies. He just hadn't seen quite far enough.

"He made good bait," Ezio said. "But what were you attempting at the end? It almost seemed you were trying to warn our target."

Corin shrugged, still feeling numb. "Had to sell the lie. Didn't want him suspicious."

Ezio narrowed his eyes. "Risky, but it worked. You and I will have to talk during the voyage home. It will make a pleasant change of pace to have a truly competent assistant."

"Partner," Corin said, just to keep up the part. "I'm nobody's assistant."

"Fair enough. Fair enough. Now, come, let's stow him in the compartment you discovered."

Corin stooped and heaved the unconscious adventurer up onto his shoulders. It was no easy task, but Corin bore the burden. He plodded down the beach, grateful for the potency of the druids' sleeping potion. He would not have wanted Auric to know the part he'd played in this. With any luck, when Corin came to rescue the farmboy from Ethan Blake, he might even come off as a hero.

"I must admit," Ezio said as they climbed into one of the bigger ship's rowboats, "I had my doubts that you'd succeed, and I certainly did not expect it to be so soon."

"You said nightfall," Corin answered. "I came at nightfall."

"That you did, and thanks to Ephitel, we were ready for you. In fact, we have everything worked out. We'll trap the adventurer in the lower hold, keep him sedated with the don's new toy, and sail straight home from here. I suspect we have rations enough for all three of us already."

"On the river boat?" Corin asked, surprised. "We're not taking his cutter?"

Ezio shook his head. "Same reason we brought the river boat here. Without an expert navigator, we're safer on the coastline with a shallow draft than in a deep-keeled ship out on the open sea."

"But the cutter would be faster. We could sail straight—"

He had to cut himself short, because he still didn't know just where they were headed.

Ezio didn't seem to notice. He was already shaking his head. "Too dangerous. Too dangerous by far. Better safe than dead men, especially now that our task is nearly done."

Corin looked across the waves to the other little boat some way ahead of them. Dave Taker was making for the anchored cutter. Ezio had instructed him to fetch his things, hadn't he? Corin frowned. "And Taker agreed to this? I'm surprised he didn't insist he was sufficient to the task."

Ezio shook his head. "On the contrary. He insisted we take the safer ship."

Corin stared after Taker, thinking hard. It seemed most out of place for Taker to agree. He'd never been a man short on bravado, and he'd often claimed himself a master of Spinola's treacherous waters. He'd clearly brought the cutter through them safely, after all. Why agree to take the slower boat, the unfamiliar one, even if Ezio insisted?

Corin could see no clear reason, and it ate at him. *He* would have been so much more comfortable aboard the cutter. He had no doubt that Taker felt the same, but for whatever reason, he was willing to join Corin and Ezio on the low, clumsy river boat. It made no sense.

He puzzled at it while he hoisted Auric's limp form up into the smuggler's boat and then maneuvered him down into the lower hold. He stretched the farmboy out on the bed as comfortably as he could manage, but as he turned to leave, he found Ezio waiting. Watching.

"What's gotten into you?" Ezio asked, calm as the eye of a hurricane.

"He's valuable goods, just like you said," Corin answered.

"He's not our *guest*, Gasparo. He's a prisoner. Chain him up." He tossed a heavy set of iron manacles down to Corin, then disappeared a moment and came back with a huge iron ball. The ball crashed down with such a force that it dented the hardwood planking of the floor. Corin stared at it.

"You really think that's necessary?"

"Mister Taker insisted on it. You saw how he responded to the man. It does seem a reasonable precaution."

Corin sighed. "I'll see to it."

"No mistakes. You can be certain Mister Taker will double-check the locks before he lets us seal the hold. He is *most* concerned."

Corin bit back his curse. He merely nodded, then bent to the task. He clamped the cuffs on Auric's wrists and ankles, and attached the heavy ball. It could hardly slow him any more than the druids' poison, after all, and Corin would have no trouble picking the manacle locks once the time came for rescue.

But even as he thought of the druids' poison, he saw Auric's fingers twitch. That should not have happened. Corin raised his eyes to the farmboy's face. Nothing happened for a moment, and then one eyelid twitched.

How? Corin had no time to consider it. He heard Dave Taker's heavy tread on the upper deck, his booming voice berating Ezio, and Corin knew his time was short. He leaned down close to Auric's ear and whispered, "I am your friend, and your only friend in this place. You must listen to me. Do not move. If they see you are awake, they'll likely kill you. Bide until you hear from me again. I swear I'll get you out of this."

He saw no reaction from the farmboy, no way to know if his message had been heard or if the little twitches had been nothing at all. It didn't matter anyway. He had no time to act further. Dave Taker crouched outside the hold, one big hand on either side of the hatch, and glared down at Corin.

"Have you chained 'im up?"

"Aye. He's secure."

"I'll see about that. You come fetch this chest. Ezio says you're the strong one."

Corin threw one last glance at Auric, then headed for the hatch. He paused partway through it, blocking Taker's way, and met the big man's eyes. "Leave the knife behind."

Taker curled his lip. "What's your meaning?"

"There's a knife on your belt. Leave it here. And don't you touch him, understand? He's worth a lot more to us alive than dead, and I'll have your guts if you cost us that reward."

Taker sucked in a big breath to shout Corin down—his swollen pride would have demanded it—but somehow he restrained himself. He deflated, spread his hands in a conciliatory gesture, and then, with great show, he drew the knife out of its sheath, held it a moment for Corin to see, and tossed it casually aside.

"I've seen the error of my ways," Dave Taker said. "And I need your companion's assistance if I'm going to see any reward for all my pains. I might hate the dog, but my love for silver overwhelms it. I'm not going to touch his sorry hide." He pointed to the knife on the floor. "Satisfied?"

Corin stared into his eyes a moment more, but he saw no deception there. Reluctantly, he climbed aside and let Taker make his own inspection. He checked every link and lock at least two times, but he found nothing to complain of. At last he turned back toward the hatch and seemed surprised to find Corin still watching him.

"I thought I told you to fetch the chest."

"Aye, and you thought I answered to your orders. You were clearly wrong on at least one count."

"Gasparo!" Ezio called from his place near the port bow. "Stop bickering and lend a hand. I'll feel safer once we're clear of this place altogether. I don't much like the sounds I'm hearing from the forest."

"Adventurers?" Taker asked, a touch of panic in his voice.

"No. Creatures. But those are not the cries of the kind of creatures allowed to roam the Godlands."

"Monsters," Taker snarled. "Almost as bad as the adventurers! Grab the chest."

Corin was just as anxious as the rest to get under way, so he relented. He found the rowboat tied alongside the ship, wallowing low in the bay's waters from the great weight of the iron chest it carried. It was a lockbox, wide and deep and secured with three massive, elaborate locks. Corin couldn't see the need; he doubted even he could have picked one of these locks, so three seemed such a waste.

"What's in the chest?" he asked Taker.

"None of your concern."

"It's a fancy piece of craftsmanship, and not a cheap one. Enough to make a man wonder."

"I thought your captain there told you to stop bickering."

"He's not my captain. We're partners. And if you want me to bring this chest aboard for you—"

A scream from the forest cut him short. All three men spun to stare in that direction, eyes wide. It was not a human scream. And it was not far off.

"Storming seas!" Taker growled. "It's Blake's bankroll. Understand? He sent me enough coin to do the job, and your don won't be very happy if I come back without the leftovers."

"Get it," Ezio said. "And let's weigh anchor."

"Not yet," Dave Taker said. "One more thing."

"No," Ezio said. "I do not want to see what made that noise."

"Neither do I," Dave Taker said, "but there are letters from your don aboard my ship. Confidential correspondence, if you catch my meaning. Should we really leave such things for anyone to find? The farmboy's companions, perhaps?"

Ezio compressed his lips to a thin line, and his eyes flashed. "Why didn't you bring these letters before?"

"Forgot. You can stand there and chastise me, or you can go and fetch them while we arrange this chest."

"You get them. Gasparo and I will handle the chest."

"I doubt you're up to the task. It's a very heavy chest."

Corin frowned at him. "But … you managed to load it on your own."

"Dropping's always a lot easier than lifting. Besides, it was empty when I put it in the boat. I loaded it after."

Ezio sighed. "I will be pleased to be done with you. Very well. Where are these letters?"

"In an oiled leather bag inside the cabin. You can't miss them."

"Gasparo, get this sorted out. Mister Taker, please be ready to set sail as soon as I return."

"Happy to," Dave Taker said. He watched while Ezio climbed into one of the two boats and pushed off toward the cutter. Then he turned back to Gasparo. "Well? Put your back into it!"

It was indeed a heavy burden. It was all Corin could do to lift just his half of it, and the short lug from the railing to the hatch was like a torture. He had to summon every ounce of strength, and he fought desperately to conceal his struggle. Gasparo, after all, should have been sufficient to the task.

When they reached the hold, Corin dropped his end just inside the hatch, but Dave Taker cuffed him on the ear. "Not there! It goes above the brig's trapdoor."

"What?" Corin asked, panting despite himself. "Why?"

"Ain't you heard me? Your hostage is some kind of hero. I'm not convinced those chains will slow him down, but I'd like to see him bust through this! Eh?"

Corin groaned inwardly, but for Taker's sake he bent his knees and heaved the chest back up again, just to slide it two paces over. It fell across the sliding panel like the lid of a sarcophagus, and Corin knew it wouldn't budge until Dave Taker was ready to help move it.

Dave Taker seemed pretty satisfied of the fact too. He nodded to himself a moment, then stretched his back and craned his neck to look toward the cutter. "I think that has us set. Can you see your partner? Is he coming back yet?"

Corin had to climb back out of the hold to get a good look, and even then he wasn't sure. The moonlight played in broken slivers on the cove's black waters, and the cutter itself threw a huge shadow. Corin went to the railing, raised a hand to his eyes, and stared a moment, but he saw no sign of the rowboat.

"Nothing yet," he called over his shoulder. "I suspect he couldn't find the letters under your directions."

Dave Taker answered with some noise, barely a grunt, but it was enough to catch Corin's attention. The man had never left the cramped hold. Instead he knelt above the lockbox, open now, and as Corin turned that way he heard a metallic *snap* and a rasp, and saw a flash of light. Like flint and tinder. Once, twice, and then a third time brought a sudden flare that was quickly concealed as Taker slammed shut the lockbox's lid. All three exquisite locks snapped shut at once.

Then Taker turned and found Corin watching him. "What was that?" Corin asked.

"Revenge," Taker answered. Then he sprinted to the port bow and leaped the low railing. He landed in the rowboat, cast off the line, and kicked away hard from the low-riding river boat. "Better jump!" he called to Corin. "Better jump real soon. If you swim fast enough, maybe you can join us in the cutter."

Then he pulled hard on the oars and shot away toward the bigger ship.

Paralyzed, Corin watched him go. In the hold behind him, Corin heard the angry, popping hiss of a powder fuse burning toward its charge.

(**22**)

Revenge, he'd said. That was just what Corin had used to entice him, and now he paid the price. Corin remembered all too clearly a story Charlie Claire had shared. A justicar had found his crew while they were under Ethan Blake. They'd trapped him in the *Diavahl*'s hold and blown a hole through the bottom of it with a lockbox full of dwarven powder. Even here, when Corin and Ezio first met him, Dave Taker had bragged about burying a justicar beneath the sea.

Now he meant to do the same thing to the farmboy. And unless he moved fast, to Corin with him. But despite his sudden understanding, despite the threatening hiss of burning cord behind him, Corin couldn't move. He couldn't throw himself overboard. He *hated* dwarven powder and he *wanted* to run, but he couldn't.

He couldn't just leave Auric to die. It astonished him. Despite his every instinct, he rushed *toward* the explosive chest. He dove into the upper hold and wasted half a breath searching the lockbox for some weak point he might exploit. There was none. It was a work of extraordinary quality, and in a moment it would be so much kindling bobbing on the quiet waters of the cove.

Corin abandoned that hope and fell to his knees, pounding frantically against the planks. "Auric! Auric, can you hear me! Wake up! For the love of everything, wake up!"

For a dreadful moment, Corin heard nothing but the burning of the fuse. Then a feeble voice rose in answer. "Who goes?"

"Corin. Corin Hugh. I'm the friend you met in the forest. I led you to the pirate camp."

"They got me, Corin. Must have been some magic. They got me."

"I know. And things are bad. Things are really bad. You have to break out of there."

A moment passed, a distant rattling, and then Auric cried, "No good. The magic hasn't passed yet. I can barely lift my head, and someone's chained my arms and legs."

Corin dropped his head against the planks. He'd done that. He'd attached the chains, and even if the chest's explosion didn't kill the farmboy, that huge iron ball would drag him to the bottom of the cove.

"Listen," Corin shouted, and then he found he had nothing to say. He floundered for a moment. "Auric … I'm sorry."

"Chin up, friend."

Corin shook his head. "You don't understand. They've rigged the ship with cannon powder. In a moment, this ship is going down."

"Ah. Well. That's a challenge."

Corin's shoulders slumped. "I have a plan. It might not work."

"Forget it," Auric called. "Are you chained up too?"

"No. No, they … didn't catch me. I just slipped aboard."

"Then slip *off*," Auric said. "If you can get away, get away. Leave the danger to us adventurers."

"I can't," Corin said. "I can't just leave you."

"It's an order, friend. Don't fret too much over me. I've been in worse places than this."

Corin wasn't listening. Frantic now, he closed his eyes and focused hard. He tried to imagine the cramped little hold where he had spent three days, but in his memory it was nothing but darkness and hard boundaries. Still, he fixed the *shape* of it in his mind and wished desperately to be there. Just as he'd done half a dozen times before. He stepped through dream, then opened his eyes to see the lockbox still before him. He hadn't moved.

"Auric!" he shouted.

"Just go."

"Auric, you don't understand. This was no accident. Someone sent the pirate to kill you. He's a Vestossi, same as Sera, and he wants you dead to hurt her."

"Sera? You ... you know about Sera?"

"Listen to me, Auric! We cannot let them win. We have to find some way."

"No. Forget me. Go to her. Find Sera in Aerome and warn her. If she has enemies among her family, she has to know."

"I can't just leave you here. Auric! Auric?"

But the man answered no more. Corin tried again to step through dream, and again it was to no avail. He braced himself against the wall and propped his feet against the hissing lockbox and tried with all his might to heave it aside, but it wouldn't even budge. His strength was spent.

He pounded on the planks. He cried to Auric, but the man gave no answer. Perhaps the druids' poison had won out again, or perhaps it was from stubbornness that he refused to speak, but he would give no answer, and Corin could find no way into the inner hold.

And still, all the while, the fuse burned angrily away. At last, Corin could contain his fear no more. With a cry of anguish, he tore himself away, sprang up out of the hold and dashed across the quarterdeck. He flung himself across the railing and splashed into the cold, dark waters of the bay one heartbeat before powder caught.

A flash of fire lit the night like noontime, and the concussion touched him even through the water. Corin stroked away, pulling hard against the current and refusing to look back. Behind him, the smuggler's ship splashed and screamed and groaned like some dying thing, before at last it sank beneath the waters and went down.

Corin fixed his eyes on a shadow at the surface, and now he swam even harder. That was Taker's boat. He hadn't reached the cutter yet. Corin was too long underwater now. His lungs were burning coals, his arms a cutting agony from too much heavy labor. But he pushed the pain aside and struggled harder. He pulled and pulled and pulled. Perhaps some vengeful spirit lent Corin inhuman strength, or perhaps Dave Taker paused to marvel at his handiwork, but somehow Corin caught the little boat.

He sprang up alongside it, shooting from the water like a porpoise at play. He hung suspended for a moment, sucking in a great breath of air, then he grabbed the rowboat's transom in both hands, pointed his toes toward the bottom of the cove, and stabbed downward hard enough to flip the little boat.

He flailed before him until one hand collided with Dave Taker's torso. Then he closed his left hand in a death grip on Taker's shoulder and grabbed his dagger with his right hand. He plunged it in. Again and again and again until Corin's lungs threatened once more to burst. Then he released the bloody corpse and struggled upward. He heaved himself onto the capsized rowboat, sprawled across it, and lay a moment, gasping for air. It was all he could do.

You killed a good man, Corin thought, and he wasn't sure whether he meant the accusation for Dave Taker or for himself. The words just kept repeating in his head. *You killed a good man for the sake of a bad one. You're the monster. You're the monster.*

It seemed an age he lay there in the darkness, full of hate and rage and desperate for air. But eventually the world returned around him. He heard a voice crying out high above him. "Hallo? Hallo there, Gasparo? Mister Taker? Anyone at all?"

Ezio. He yet lived. And now Corin understood Dave Taker's plan. He'd never meant to sail the river boat across the open sea. He'd always intended to sink it and Auric with it. That was why he'd sent Ezio back for the letters. He'd planned to join him just like this, rowing away from the wreckage of the smuggler's ship. He'd probably had some lie prepared about an accident. Perhaps he'd hoped to blame Gasparo for it all.

Corin licked his lips, considering. He could be Gasparo. Or he could be Dave Taker. Which form would best convince Ezio to take him back to Ethan Blake? That was the only question that still mattered. In all the world, it was his only hope for satisfaction. Dave Taker was dead in the waters below, but he'd suffered less than he deserved. Ethan Blake would pay the price for all of this.

"Mister Taker?" Ezio cried. "What's happened? Gods favor, is anyone alive?"

Corin closed his eyes, and summoned up an image of himself. Then he drew the ugly face of the wicked man he'd just destroyed. He made himself into Dave Taker, and it was not as difficult a thing as it should have been. When he opened his eyes and saw the thin gray mist still hanging there, he shuddered at the thought of what he had become.

Then he cupped his hands around his mouth and called up to Ezio, "Hallo! I've lived, but your bloody partner sank the bloody ship! Now how will we get home?"

Ezio's sigh carried all the way down to the water. "You did claim you could sail this thing through the shoals."

"Nothing easier. Toss me down a line?"

"Aye, aye. It's coming. Watch your head."

Corin scrambled up the rope. He stood a moment face-to-face with Ezio, and Ezio stared deep into his eyes. There was no doubt he'd seen through Corin's lie—Dave Taker's lie—he merely had to choose whether to address it or let it go. Corin wasn't entirely sure what to expect of either choice, but he closed one hand around the hilt of his dagger behind his back. Just in case.

At last Ezio ducked his head. "It is a tragedy. Gasparo will be missed. Perhaps. And the farmboy ... might have been a useful hostage. But as things stand, I believe every measure of the don's demands have been met."

"Then you will take me to him?"

"Those are my final orders."

"Just tell me where and I will plot the course."

"East. Across the Medgerrad. That's all you need to know for now."

"But—"

"Mister Taker, I do not trust you. I have my orders, and I will follow them to the letter. Take us east, and I will tell you more as it becomes necessary. Do you understand?"

Corin nodded once. "Aye. As long as you get us there."

"And I would ask the same of you."

Corin knew two days into the voyage—and two full days before Ezio revealed it—where they must be heading. It was Aerome, Ithale's capital. That served him well, and Ezio proved an able steersman, so Corin maintained the ruse right to the last.

In all, they spent six days on the open sea. Corin docked the sleek cutter among the fishing boats and merchant vessels at the port town of Ostartia, and while he was still tying up, Ezio leaped down and gave some message to the runners on the wharf.

Corin made some show of bundling up Taker's possessions, but mostly he only cared about the things he carried on his own person. He checked that they were all secure, then made his own way down the gangplank and met Ezio outside the harbormaster's wall.

A moment later, a carriage arrived for them. It was a gaudy thing, oversized and paneled in some dark, expensive wood. It bore no noble's seal; its attendants, no livery colors; but it had all the ostentation of a noble house. And there was none in all Ithale so ostentatious as the Vestossis. Who would doubt this was their carriage?

A doorman hopped down to open a door for them, and Corin followed Ezio inside. The driver cracked his whip and they were off, charging up the hill toward the mighty city. Nor did they slow when they reached its busy streets. The driver only cracked his whip the louder, likely at the common folk that clogged his way as much as at the belabored horses. Corin held his place and bit his tongue. Ezio seemed quite accustomed to such rides. He said no word for the entire trip.

Their destination proved to be some deep, dark alley, tucked between a row of modest homes and a public bathhouse, long abandoned by the look of it. The doorman handed them down, then bowed, ushering them toward a rotting wooden door that gave entry to the bathhouse. Corin looked to Ezio for some explanation, but now he seemed just as confused.

He shrugged to Corin and said quietly, "The don sometimes keeps mysterious habits. He does adore his privacy."

Corin growled a curse against the man, but he went along. This was exactly what he'd come for, after all. He and Ezio stepped into a vast, dark room, the quiet ripples of still water and the stink of mildew their only company.

Ten minutes they waited there. After twenty, a door opened at the far side of the room, spreading a wide, thin streak of torchlight across the stale pool. Corin went forward two steps before he recognized the frame and bearing of the new arrivals. They were only hired guards. He watched the door for someone else, but no one came. Four guards for two men.

It was twenty paces across the pool, and no way around it. Any attempt to reach the other side would require a sprint through waist-high water. No chance for a surprise, then. It was a good location for a meet. Corin felt a touch of grudging admiration. Here on their home turf, the Vestossis certainly knew how to run a show.

But still there was no sign of Blake. In his boredom, Corin took careful stock of all four guards. They were broad of shoulder, straight of spine, with the look of former soldiers about them. They wore daggers on their belts and knives in their boots, and every man among them carried a loaded crossbow. That could certainly do some damage from across the pool. He licked his lips and leaned his head toward Ezio.

"How much do you trust your don?"

"He is an honorable man. Hold your tongue."

"How long do you intend to wait here for him?"

"I would not like my chances of leaving here before he grants permission. He is not a much forgiving man."

"That he's not," Corin said. He sighed and rolled his shoulders. "Fine. I just hate the waiting most."

"You spent three months in the Wildlands alone to earn this meeting. You can wait ten minutes more."

Ten minutes proved too generous an underestimation. At half an hour, the far door cracked again, and the shadow of the man who stepped in front of the distant torchlight did not have the bearing of a soldier. For one dreadful moment, Corin feared it was some retainer, some other hired hand like Ezio instead of Ethan Blake himself. But then the distant shadow spoke, and the voice was all too familiar.

"Master Ezio, what has become of your companion?"

"Regretfully, he did not survive the voyage."

"Ah." There came a whispered conference from the other end of the room, and then the speaker in the doorway raised his voice again. "Shall we wait for his return?"

"Regretfully, he did not survive at all."

"Then he is dead? You're certain of it?"

Ezio looked to Corin. Corin nodded once. Ezio called back, "He is dead."

"And you, Taker? You had a mission to fulfill."

"It is done," Corin answered.

"And I attest to it," Ezio said. "He has done all you asked of him, Don Giuliano."

Corin leaned toward Ezio again. "Giuliano?" he whispered. "That's Blake's true name?"

"Blake was his name for a time," Ezio returned under his breath.

Across the wide pool, Blake was still speaking. "I thank you, gentlemen. You've served me well, and you will be remembered."

Corin felt a deep suspicion as to what was coming next. Everything about the meeting suggested Blake was tying up loose ends, but Corin would not have expected such treatment for Dave Taker. He darted forward, still in his disguise, and called across the pool. "Is that it, Blake? 'Remembered?' You promised me more!"

Blake almost didn't answer. Corin saw him hesitate, one hand on the door, but pride dragged him back into the room. He stood, still just a distant silhouette, and called back in an even voice. "The situation changed. You should understand that. Corin Hugh's back from the dead. You've served me well. Now go with grace."

Corin cried out, "But—"

But Blake spoke over him, even as he turned his back. "Guards, you have your orders."

Corin cursed. He drew his dagger and hurled it in desperation, but through the glamour's veil, through the stifling darkness, and over such a distance, he never had a chance. It was a marvel the blade came as close to Blake as it did. It sank into the doorframe just as Blake passed through. Then the door fell shut, and all four guards raised their crossbows in unison.

For all his claims of trust in his employer, Ezio reacted nearly as fast as Corin had. He sprang aside, reaching underneath his coat and drawing out the druids' dartgun. Still, he had no chance to fire it—to even aim—before two heavy bolts ripped through his torso, and he collapsed.

Corin spun his heavy cloak around him and dropped the glamour. All dressed in black, he disappeared among the shadows, but nevertheless he didn't tarry. He dashed to Ezio's corpse, snatched up the dartgun, and dove toward the outer door a moment before a crossbow bolt ricocheted where he'd been. For all his stealth, his boots rang loud on the marble floor, and this end of the room gave little space to maneuver.

He didn't try. He sprinted straight for the door onto the alley and slammed into it hard.

It didn't budge.

He drove a mighty kick against it, right beside the latch, but it made no difference. The door was barricaded from outside. Some instinct made him dodge aside one heartbeat before another crossbow bolt buried itself to the fletchings in the rotted door. He cried out anyway, as though he had been hit, then drifted farther left, as softly as he could.

The pool. It made too dangerous an approach. He cursed Ethan Blake's black cunning. He'd had the man in his grasp—scant paces away—and now Blake was slipping away. The thought of it burned like coals in Corin's belly. For all his caution, all his fear of losing time, he closed his eyes and called on Oberon's power. There was no quick escape from this place, and nothing in the world could have stopped him chasing after Blake. He drew the sword *Godslayer*, with righteous murder in his heart, and flung himself through dream across the wide, dark room.

Before he opened his eyes, he tasted ash on the air. He looked and saw only burned-out ruins where the bathhouse had been.

Corin cursed. The day was gone, and Blake with it. Night lay thick and cold over the city, and the whole lot was empty now. There was no sign left of the meeting, of the guards, or of Ezio's corpse. Of course. It had always been Blake's plans to tie up his loose ends here. Corin wondered if he'd let the guards escape before he set the fire. It didn't matter. Blake was gone. In a bid to end things here, Corin had lost his chance and lost more time on top of that. He cursed and cursed again.

And then he stopped. And then he smiled. Don Giuliano. Aerome. He was not glad to have given Blake a single extra minute, but that was a problem he could overcome. He had everything he needed now. He traded the glamour of Dave Taker for another face, old Josef from far-off Marzelle, and pressed out through the ruins toward the distant bustle of the city streets.

Aerome. It was not quite home, but it was a city he knew well. And now he had a target here. Somewhere in this town was Ethan Blake—Giuliano Vestossi—and he might well believe his hired henchmen were all dead. He would be satisfied. He would be comfortable at last. After all, his loose ends were tied up. He'd never see the stormclouds brewing.

Corin grinned despite the anger burning in his belly. Ethan Blake was going to suffer for his sins.

(23)

For some time he drifted aimlessly along the busy streets. He needed time to catch his bearings, some familiar landmark to point his way, but he needed time to think, at least as much. After weeks of grueling searching, he'd learned everything he wanted in two words from Ezio.

They were two important words. *Don Giuliano.* And there was more, though it had gone unsaid. *Vestossi. Don Giuliano Vestossi.* The family name showed in everything Corin had seen since his arrival at Aerome. It was the ostentatious carriage, the show of force in a surreptitious meeting, the contemptuous betrayal, and the gall to burn down a sprawling public building just to conceal another villainy. Corin felt a gnawing irritation at that. He wanted Blake to pay for the act of mutiny. He wanted to make him suffer for any and every pain he'd done to Iryana. But now... Blake had become so much more. Now he was a Vestossi—not just in name, but in deed. From half a world away, he'd sent the orders that left a righteous man dead beneath the sea, for no other reason than family politics.

Corin seethed at that. Blake had killed Ezio as well, and given orders to kill Taker, even *after* learning the man had faithfully fulfilled his duties. This was the kind of monster Ethan

Blake could be. He was a wretched dog, but here in the heart of the Godlands, he was called Don Giuliano. He was respected, a noble representative of Ithale's first family.

It was not enough to kill him. Not by half. Corin's first thought outside the bathhouse had been to find Giuliano's estate, to get a good look at all the grounds, and then to come back when Blake was home. Step through the dream and kill him in his sleep. It would be easy with Oberon's power at his command. But Corin had already slaughtered Dave Taker. Dead men slept in easy peace, and Corin wanted no peace at all for Ethan Blake.

But how to make him suffer? Blake loved his power. He loved his luxury. But most of all, he loved the respect of his peers. Corin knew that well. It was pride and vain ambition that had always driven Ethan Blake, and it was there that Corin could hurt him most.

He'd have to cost the man his rank. He'd have to strip him of his standing. He'd have to cast him down to nothing—less than nothing—and somehow bind him there for the rest of his days. Corin went a block or two mulling that, and it felt right. It would be no easy task, but it was a righteous one.

Corin's wandering footsteps carried him to a broad piazza in a modest part of town. He found himself standing in the shadow of some long-forgotten patron, but something in the statue's timeworn face sparked a memory for Corin. It felt familiar somehow. For one strange moment he thought it might be a memory of Jezeeli—perhaps this was a shadow to some elfin legend—but then he glanced aside and recognized the street. He realized where his idle path had brought him.

On the north side of the piazza stood an ancient chapter house. It might once have belonged to carpenters or masons, but its walls were cracked with age and its windows boarded up. The

huge polished wood doors that filled the arching entryway were
sealed, and scrawled signs plastered on the doors declared this
place private property. Closed. Keep out. By the look of them,
those doors hadn't opened in ages.

But Corin knew the other way around. He'd been here
before. He slipped down the alley to the left and found a much
newer door—this one entirely unmarked—set in a bit of darkest
shadow. He glanced back up the alley both directions, assured
himself no one was watching, and then dropped his glamour
altogether. If there was anywhere in the world Corin Hugh might
find true welcome, it was beyond this door.

He announced himself with a patterned knock, just as
he'd done once before in Marzelle. The door opened and Corin
went in.

And this ... *this* was a Nimble Fingers. Marzelle's smoky
cellar had been a breath of fresh air after so long away from
civilization, but it had been a poor excuse for a Nimble Fingers
compared to the organization in Ithale. Back home in Aepoli
they did things right, but even there they didn't have anything
like this.

Behind the modest façade lay a sprawling parlor. From
the entryway, Corin couldn't see the back of the room. Tables
spotted the floor and closed booths lined the walls, but none of
them were too close together, none too large to allow a whispered
conversation. The lights were few enough, the shadows thick; it
would have been easy for a man to visit here unrecognized and
carry on his private business. The waiters wore tiny silver bells
on their wrists and ankles, just loud enough to announce their
presence.

The arrangements were a marvel, but a Nimble Fingers tavern
was only worth as much as the quality of its patrons. There too

Aerome seemed ready to impress. The sprawling common room was packed, bustling with quiet activity, and even as he lingered in the doorway, Corin watched more than a dozen men arrive and melt into the crowd.

It was everything a Nimble Fingers ought to be. Corin breathed a deep, contented sigh and waded down into the throng. He'd barely gone ten paces before a man in black stepped up to walk beside him. This one wore no silver bells, but on his left hand he bore the ring of a Nimble Fingers tavern keeper. He walked tall, eyes always moving as he tracked the movements of his patrons. They never quite touched on Corin, even as the tavern keeper addressed him.

"You're new to Aerome, but not here for the first time."

"I've been before, in my younger days."

"Oh, so careful. You can speak more plainly than that. I remember Corin Hugh, even before he was a pirate."

Corin glanced aside, but he couldn't place the other man's face. He shrugged. "Beg pardon, but you have my advantage."

"Oh, no pardon necessary. There are so many tavern keepers in the world, and none of them as famous as Corin Hugh."

Corin chuckled. "I'm hardly famous."

"You're getting there. Especially among the Nimble Fingers. We heard what happened in Marzelle."

"Already?"

"Already? Hah! It has been days."

Corin slammed a fist against his hip. *Days?*

But the tavern keeper pressed right on. "But you should know that's not all we've heard. We know you asked a Raentzman brother to bring you some information, and one of our noble countrymen ... interfered with his task."

The messenger Francois. Corin growled. "Aye. I know it well."

"Then you'll be glad to know the countrymen responsible have paid a dear price for their actions."

"The ones responsible? Or just the ones who swung their clubs."

The tavern keeper ducked his head in a bow. "You have me there. We are not so powerful as to punish those with names, but we can keep our own streets clean."

"We must do more than that."

The tavern keeper spread his hands. "We've heard rumors of this too. You are no longer satisfied with the Nimble Fingers' mission. You think we should be warriors? An army?"

"I think we should aim so high, if not precisely in that direction. We are a brotherhood—"

"Dedicated entirely to private gain." The tavern keeper forced a chuckle. "We cannot all be heroes, Corin Hugh."

"Then what purpose do you serve at all?"

"We are a home. We are a refuge in the storm. That is a service I take great pride in providing. If some among us strive for greater things, they can do so in the knowledge that there's always someplace safe to run."

"Oh, very well. I suppose that's noble in its way. Do you think I ask too much?"

"If you didn't, if that weren't in your nature, then I suspect I wouldn't know your name."

Corin smirked. "You have me there. Then I will only ask for refuge here. I have some grim business in Aerome, and I fear I'll find enemies on her streets."

"I fear you are correct. I understand the city watch have your description memorized, and they're perhaps the nicest of the men looking for you."

"I appreciate the warning. Can I count on a room as well?"

"Of course. No favors asked. I have a cousin in Marzelle."

Corin smiled. "You're a good man, and I'm deeply grateful. I apologize if I didn't seem that way before."

"From what I hear, you've seen hard times."

"And harder times ahead. It's a pirate's life."

"Well, trust your brothers in the Nimble Fingers. Even pirates need a soft bed and a warm meal from time to time."

"You're a godsend, tavern keeper."

"And about the other matter?"

Corin frowned, trying to recall. "Which matter is that?"

"The messenger from Marzelle. You sent him for information. It's my understanding that information was never gathered."

Corin spread his hands. "I have found some part of it on my own, but you're correct. I could use some fresh intelligence."

"Then ask. I'd like to see that old debt paid."

"That debt was signed in blood, and it will be repaid before I'm done in Aerome. But here are the things I need to know. Where is Ben Strunk?"

"The crazy dwarf?"

Corin grinned. "Good man! In Marzelle, they didn't know his name."

"Gods favor 'em."

"Hah! Yes. I owe him a minor debt, and I would like to get it paid before I die."

"He's here in town."

"Truth? Thank Fortune for that."

"Thank the Vestossis! They're paying him handsomely to mint their coins."

"And he does it?"

"Something has to pay for all his gambling debts."

"Fair enough. Then I'll forgive him that. Can you get him word that I'd like to meet him here? Quietly, I mean."

"I can, but it might not reach him before he comes here on his own accord. Check back tonight. He likes our common room."

Corin nodded. "He loves to lose to thieves. He says that saves him time. Otherwise he loses half his pot to honest men, then ends up paying the rest to thieves on his way home."

The tavern keeper laughed at that, though it couldn't be the first time he'd heard it. Corin let his smile linger for a moment and then turned back to business. "After Ben, I need current information on a man. A powerful man from a powerful family in this town."

"The way I hear it, they're a powerful family across Hurope."

"Then you already know?'

"I know you bear some grudge against the Vestossis."

"Every one of them. But especially against one who used to sail under the name of Ethan Blake."

"Many nobles' sons take to the seas at a certain age. It's no easy task to unveil some particular fellow's pirate name—"

"Giuliano," Corin said. "I've done that work myself and paid a handsome price for the information. Giuliano Vestossi was the pirate known as Ethan Blake. He mutinied and stole my crew and sank my ship with a justicar in it."

"Gods on high!" The tavern keeper reeled. "That ... that was you? That was Blake? That was Giuliano?"

"You've heard rumors."

"I've heard a lot of rumors. I never believed they all were attached to one man. The justicar? It's true?"

Corin nodded. "Buried beneath the sea, and Blake sent my ship down with him."

"Dreadful waste of perfectly good timber."

Corin chuckled. "Giuliano. He's the one I'm after. What can you tell me about him?"

"He's relatively new to the city. Trying his hand at court intrigue, but he's fumbling. He's made more enemies than friends so far, and some of them have names. Vague as it is, that's as much as I can tell you now. Give me an hour—"

"Take a day. I'm sore in need of rest."

"Give me a day, then, and I can tell you everything you want to know."

"Make sure no one dies this time."

"We are not Raentzmen, Corin Hugh. You should know better. We are the true Nimble Fingers."

"Hah. You speak true. Good. I look forward to that report."

"And that is all?"

"Aye. That's all. Now show me to a bed and send me something stewed."

He made it halfway up the stairs before one other request occurred to him. He sprinted back down, scanning the busy common room in vain, but half a heartbeat later the tavern keeper appeared at his elbow once again.

"Can I help you further?"

"Aye," Corin said. "I need another Vestossi."

"Oh, this town is rotten with them. It shouldn't be hard."

Corin showed his teeth. "This one might prove a challenge."

"I am prepared to impress you, sir."

"I look forward to it. But I need more than information. I need a meeting."

"Even that should be within our reach. What is his name?"

"Her," Corin said. "I need to meet with Princess Sera."

(24)

It took less than an afternoon. Corin barely had time for lunch and a quick nap before the tavern keeper knocked on his door. As soon as Corin slid the bolt, the tavern keeper darted into the room and closed the door behind him.

"Who are you, really? You must bear the favor of some powerful gods."

Corin spread his hands. "A dead one, actually." He waved away the confusion in the tavern keeper's eyes. "I am just the man you think I am."

"And yet you change the world wherever you go. You saved Marzelle from a tyranny, and now a humble thief can somehow demand an audience with Sera Vestossi."

Corin cocked his head. "You've done it then?"

"Indeed. You have a meeting with the princess, but you must hurry. She expects you in an hour."

"That's fast indeed!"

"She grew anxious when she heard the name you gave me. Who is Auric?"

"That is not my secret to share. Not yet. We'll see how this rendezvous proceeds."

"Very well. Then you take this." He produced a delicate handkerchief embroidered with a curling S in gold, of a fabric so fine it felt like water between his fingers.

Corin stared at it a moment. "What's this?"

"It is at once your map and your passport to see the princess."

"Do elaborate."

"Of course. You see ... I have a cousin who works at the palace."

"You have a lot of cousins."

"Cousins are a valuable resource to a tavern keeper."

"I believe you. Go on."

"This cousin has a daughter who works directly for the princess. She's a linen maid."

"And a trusted confidante?"

"Just so. So when you asked to meet the princess, I went to speak with my cousin, and he with his daughter, and his daughter with Princess Sera. When she heard I bore a message from this Auric, she sent back the handkerchief."

"And how am I to use it?"

"Make your way to the palace. There is a servants' gate off Prince's Way. Tell the attendant there you mean to speak with Signor della Porta."

"Signor della Porta. Your cousin?"

"Just so. When he arrives, speak no word to him, but deliver him this handkerchief, and he will escort you to your meeting with the princess."

"Such measures! Is this truly necessary?"

"The Vestossi princess does not lightly meet with some vagabond off the street. She has more than a lady's honor to concern herself with."

"Aye. I know it well." Corin played the delicate cloth between his fingers, thinking. Then he nodded. "I understand. I'm ready. And have you gathered any news concerning this Giuliano?"

"I have done naught but run from here to the palace and back. You did give me until tomorrow."

"That I did. Take no offense. I'm most impressed by what you have accomplished."

"I'd gladly take a secret as reward."

Corin waved an admonishing finger. "Not yet, I said. Let me meet with this Vestossi girl and see what she can do for me. When I am through with her, I'll share her indiscretion."

The tavern keeper turned to go, but Corin caught his arm. "One thing more. Can I count this room secure?"

"If there is any honor in the Nimble Fingers, you may trust this room. I will swear on behalf of this ancient chapter house."

"Then I will trust you," Corin said. "See that no one enters this room unless I accompany them personally, no matter what they tell you. See that no one brings anything in or takes anything out unless I am here to supervise."

"You are a careful man."

"I am stalking lords. If I were not careful, I would not still be alive."

"I will do everything you've asked."

Corin dipped his head. "You set my heart at ease. Many thanks."

"You will tell me how your rendezvous unfolds?"

"I will tell you all I can. It seems only fair."

"Then I will leave you to it. The palace is some ways from here. You should set out soon."

"I will. Do not fear on that count. I couldn't bear to tarry."

The tavern keeper lingered a moment more, but seeing Corin meant to share no more, he ducked his head and went on his way. Corin waited until the door was closed behind him, secure, and then he went to the tall armoire against the outer wall. He prodded at the inside bottom panel until he found the spot that yielded, then searched with his fingers to find the hidden edge.

Every room in every Nimble Fingers tavern had its secret hiding spot. They didn't start out that way, but when a tavern's only patrons are practicing thieves, they tend to follow certain patterns. Someone long before him had picked the armoire as the perfect hiding spot and carved a false bottom into it.

Corin lifted the panel aside and dropped his purse into the cavity. It held perhaps a hundred livres in Ithalian silver. Not a fortune, but enough to catch attention. Enough to satisfy an idle pickpocket.

Then he went to the bed and peeled up its mattress. It lay on a wooden frame—nothing more than a shallow box—and that served Corin's purpose well. He fished inside his robe and drew out three precious artifacts. The druids' dartgun went in first, and then the dwarven pistol. Finally, he drew forth the book— the cracked leather tome that the elf Maurelle had spent her final years filling with the memories of a dying god.

It told of Oberon's demise, and Jezeeli's with him. It told of Ephitel's betrayal in plain words. It was the long-forgotten history of Hurope's men and gods. It was a precious thing, beyond any price, but it was more than that. It was a weapon.

Corin stared at it for some time, unmoving, before he shook himself and tore his gaze away. With great regret he unbuckled his glorious sword, *Godslayer*, and placed it in the bed frame too. Then he dropped the mattress back over it all and surveyed his handiwork.

It wasn't bad. It wasn't bad at all. He doubted he needed take any such precautions at all. There were few places safer in the Godlands than a Nimble Fingers tavern. But these goods demanded special care. He went back to the wardrobe and cracked the door just enough to catch the eye. If anyone clever enough get past the tavern keeper *did* come in to search the place, they'd surely be clever enough to find the purse. With any luck, they'd overlook the bed.

He took a deep breath and realized his nerves were running high. Too much at stake. He didn't dare take these treasures to a meeting with a Vestossi—a meeting in their very palace—but he hated leaving them. He paced the room three times, fighting with himself, and at the last he had to tear himself away. He ripped the door open and dashed through it, slamming it shut behind him, and all the way down the stairs he fought an urge to go back and grab the sword. Or just the book.

He didn't yield. He crossed the busy common room and left by the alley door. The evening met him, sharp and cool, and fresh air cleared his head somewhat. A brisk pace cleared it more. When he'd gone a mile, he no longer felt the urge to rush back to his room. When he'd gone two, he forgot the treasures altogether. His attention turned completely to the task at hand.

The princess. She was the key to his revenge. For she could do what Corin couldn't hope to: She could cast down a Vestossi lord and keep him down. After all, she was Ipolito's daughter and third in line to Ithale's throne. And Ethan Blake—no, *Giuliano*— had made himself her enemy. It was a situation ripe for Corin's purposes.

She certainly had her own reasons to go after Giuliano. The man had killed her lover. Or … tried to. That's the story he intended to tell. As soon as he caught sight of the palace, he found a quiet side street and slipped into its shadows. Aemilia hadn't given him much hint how it would seem to people watching while he wove the glamour, but it seemed safest to keep the thing a secret. He made sure no one was looking, then closed his eyes and focused on a memory of the farmboy.

He'd made Corin one request before he died. Warn Sera. That much, at least, he could do. Corin clenched his fists and focused on the face in his imagination. He held it a moment and murmured to himself, "The world's a dream. It's all a dream." Then he blinked, and he was a gold-haired farmboy. He strolled back out onto the broad King's Way and proceeded to his meeting.

It wasn't hard to find the servants' gate, and the name "della Porta" drew a prompt obedience. Someone ran to fetch him, and a white-haired gentleman with a kindly face came in answer to the call. Corin stuck to his instructions. Without a word spoken, he presented the embroidered handkerchief.

The old man looked Corin up and down. Then he beckoned and turned away. Corin followed him through the outer gates and into the palace courtyard, but they did not go far. Ten paces from the gate, a carriage waited. Big and black, without a crest or seal. Corin shook his head.

"This again?"

"Beg pardon?" the old man asked.

"We're not meeting in the palace?"

Signor della Porta spoke volumes with a turned-down mouth. "You know better. You should not have come at all."

"I bear important tidings."

"I'm sure you do." The old man shook his head, then waved impatiently toward the carriage. "Go. She's waiting, and if it's noticed she is missing, we will all regret this visit dearly. Do you understand?"

"Of course," Corin lied. He went ahead, up into the coach, and della Porta himself climbed up to the driver's perch. He leaned back and slammed the door shut, blocking Corin's view, then cracked his whip and rumbled off. He crossed the courtyard and exited through the main gate, then went down twisting city streets unfamiliar to Corin.

Ten minutes he drove, long enough that Corin began to worry he was riding to some other careful ambush. But why show such disapproval if this was a trap? Why threaten him in such a way? They'd *all* regret it if Sera were discovered? Was her position not enough to protect her, at least?

There were questions here. And he had barely scratched the surface when the carriage settled to a stop, and the door swung open. Signor della Porta raised a finger to his lips, requesting silence still, then gestured farther down the narrow lane. It was a quiet part of town, where the lords and ladies kept their homes far from the noisy bustle of the markets. Tall trees spread their branches above the road, making a lovely colonnade, and walls lined either side of it, carved stone that pleased the eye and also offered privacy to the privileged homes.

And there, where the old retainer had indicated, Corin saw a swooping archway through the wall, an entrance to some private garden. As he approached, he found an iron gate, its lock open. It struck him, then. She was waiting for him there. The royal princess was waiting for her secret lover in this secluded, lovely garden.

He almost hesitated. But, after all, there was work to do. If some sacrifices were required ... well, he'd do what he had to do to destroy Ethan Blake. He ran a hand through his hair, and perhaps he stood a little taller—though with the glamour it would make no difference. Then he strode ahead and through the gate, with all the swagger of a returning hero.

But then he saw her, and she stopped him in his tracks. She was nothing like the woman he'd expected. At a glance, she looked young and soft and sweet. Seventeen at most, but there was a quiet sadness in her clear blue eyes that spoke of wisdom. Her dress was white and of a simple, modest cut, and the only jewelry she wore was a thin gold chain around her neck and a narrow silver ring on her right hand. Her brown hair hung loose, and two tendrils curled around her soft face, brushing at her slender neck. He'd expected sharp lines and hard edges. He'd expected a viper's grace, a vixen's cunning. He had not expected softness, but in the moonlight she looked gentle as a lamb.

And then she noticed he was there. Her eyes grew wide and the most precious smile lit her face. She dashed toward him, arms outstretched, but two paces off she caught herself. Pain tugged at the corners of her eyes, but she forced her arms down to her side and gulped a heavy breath that did nothing for her modesty. She licked her lips and almost met his eyes.

"Good knight, what brings you to Aerome?"

Corin shook his head. "Grim news. Grim news indeed."

"Oh?" Surprise flashed to disappointment, and she took a step away. "Tell me, then."

"You have an enemy at court."

She hung her head. "I have a thousand of them. What's one more?"

"This one is a cousin," Corin said. "Giuliano. And he is acting against you even now."

"How? Giuliano? I barely know the name. What could he do to me?"

"He tried to kill me, Sera. He sent three agents to dispatch me while I was in the Wildlands."

"But you've survived." She flashed a little smile. "You always do survive."

He shook his head. "Can you believe he'll stop with one attempt? Would anyone in your family stop now?"

She heaved a sigh. "Of course not. Are you afraid? Do you really think he can hurt you?"

"I am more afraid he will hurt you. If he changes his designs—"

"Why? Why would he come after me? What could anyone gain by hurting me?"

Corin tried to hide his frown. It was a senseless question. She was in line to Ipolito's throne. She should have been a major power in the city. Everyone but the king himself had motive to manipulate her or remove her from contention.

But she seemed earnest. She took half a step toward him, and he felt an urge to wrap his arms around her and comfort her. It was what she wanted from him—from the man she thought he was—and something deep in Corin's heart wanted to comfort her, to wipe that pain from her expression.

But he was not her lover. He had to think the words, to remind himself. She was a Vestossi snake, however soft her skin, and he meant to use her as a tool against her cousin. Comforting her would not aid him there. He needed her to feel this anguish, this dread, so he could direct it. He turned his face away and forced some steel into his voice.

"You cannot wait to find the answers to those questions," he said. "Do you understand? If you wait until Giuliano reveals his true intentions, it will be too late for you."

"But what of *our* plans?"

He shook his head. "Everything has changed. He came after me, Sera. Do you understand that? He came after me to get at you, and when he learns his agents failed, it will be too late."

"Then we will run," she said. She came forward another step, close enough that he could smell the perfume in her hair, and she caught his hand in both of hers. "We'll run away somewhere where we can't be found. Take me to the Spinola, if that's the only place that's safe. I trust in you."

Corin started. "You would leave Ithale? You'd lose everything. There's nothing in the Wildlands—"

"There's you. That's all I need."

Who was this woman? Leave the lap of luxury? Leave her power? Leave her name? This was no Vestossi! But the woman here before him was a perfect match for the noble hero he had met in the Wildlands. Bright-eyed and innocent, courageous and naïve.

She was not the cold steel blade he'd hoped to use against Ethan Blake, but she was the only weapon that he had. He dropped her hands and caught her shoulders. Grim and midnight, he held her eyes for a moment and said, "Sera ... if you want to live ... if you want me to live, we have to deal with this threat."

"Not if we run. Not if we hide. I trust in you. No one will ever find us."

"He tried to kill me, Sera."

"But he failed."

"He tried to kill me, and he will do the same to you. We'll run. We'll live the life you're dreaming of. But first, we must eliminate the threat."

"What do you mean?"

"We must crush Giuliano. We must strip him of his power. I can find a way, if you will help."

"Auric—"

"You've said you trust in me."

"I do."

"Then help me in this. Give me a day or two. Give me time to make a plan, and then do only what I ask of you."

"To what end, Auric?"

"To Giuliano's end. We can destroy him. I'm sure of it. And once he's crushed, we can live, happy ever after."

She withdrew a pace, her gentle gaze still fixed on Corin's face. She stood there for a moment, lovely in the moonlight, and then she cocked her head to the side and whispered softly, "Who are you? Why are you here? And what's become of the true Auric?"

(25)

"Sera, I—"

She raised her eyebrows, glaring, and for the first time since he'd seen her, she looked like a Vestossi. "No more lies, stranger. I must admit, you do look just like him. You sound like him. You ..." A little shiver shook her. "You smell like him. But you are not the man you claim to be."

His mind raced. "Much has changed. I've seen the darker side of man—"

She cut him off with a burst of laughter. "No. You fail again. But it is a compelling disguise. Are you a wizard?"

A wizard! Of course. Corin hung his head and closed his eyes. "Not I," he said. "But Ridgemon is."

"Auric's brother?"

Corin nodded. He let the glamour melt away, then raised his gaze back to the princess. "Forgive me this deception, Princess Sera. Forgive Auric too. He feared that you would not trust the message of some stranger, so he asked Ridgemon to send me in this guise."

She shook her head. "That is not my Auric either. Tell me the whole truth, or I will end this interview immediately."

End the interview. That was her gravest threat, when she had murderers and justicars at her beck and call? Corin couldn't fathom the woman standing here before him. He couldn't find an angle, an edge to pull on. The Nimble Fingers had a rule: "You cannot cheat an honest man." He'd always taken it to mean there were no honest men, for he'd never yet found an opportunity he couldn't twist to his advantage.

But this princess...He'd mistaken kind and honest for naïve and innocent, but she was no fool. She seemed to see right through his lies, and no matter how he'd tried, she showed no interest in revenge or even justice. But then, he'd concealed the worst of it from her. If anything would compel her, it was the truth. And if that didn't work, at least he'd know he'd honored a good man's last request.

So he cleared his throat and stared at his own feet. "Forgive me, Princess Sera. I am a vagabond and a rogue. The truth does not come easily to me, and I do not often treat with nobility."

"At last I hear a genuine voice from you."

"But not a happy one. The message that I brought to you was true, even if my form was not. You do have an enemy in your cousin Giuliano. He did conspire against your lover, Auric."

"How did he know? We've kept a careful secret."

Corin shook his head. "There are no secrets in Ithale. Not from the Vestossis. You should know this as well as anyone."

She sighed but gave no other answer.

Corin pressed on. "I chanced to meet with Auric just before the killers found him. We spoke but—"

"How?" she interrupted.

"How?"

"How did you chance to meet him? He is hunting in the Wildlands, or was the last I heard."

"Aye," Corin said. "It was there. I shipwrecked off the coast and ran afoul of the same men who'd been sent against Auric. I escaped their clutches, dashed into the woods, and found Auric's hunting party gathered around a fire. They took me in."

"That sounds like him."

"And when I told them that there was a murderer on the shore, Auric insisted on delivering him justice."

A sad smile touched her lips. "That sounds like him as well."

Corin shook his head. "But they had placed a careful trap for him. They ambushed him on the beach and killed him. I'm sorry, Princess."

For a long while she said nothing. She didn't move. She barely breathed. And then she touched her cheek with a delicate hand, turned away a moment, and asked him softly, "How?"

"The details aren't pleasant."

"I don't care. Tell me how."

"They trapped him in the lower hold of a pirate ship and exploded a charge of dwarven powder just outside. They sank the ship to the seabed with him still trapped inside. Even if the blast was not enough to kill him—"

"You didn't see it, then?"

He stared a moment. "Aye. I saw the blast. It lit up the night like noon."

She shook her head. "No. I mean you didn't seem him dead."

"Oh, Princess. Don't hold out hope for him. No man could have survived that."

She raised her chin. "My Auric is no ordinary man."

"Princess, I was there at the last. I tried in vain to rescue him, and all he said, all he asked of me was that I get away—that I find some way to reach you in Aerome and warn you of the danger against you."

She smiled, though tears still touched her eyes. "That does sound so much like him."

"I wanted so much to save him. You must believe me."

She came forward and laid a gentle hand on his shoulder. She caught his gaze and held it for a moment, every inch the noble princess. "I do. How could you not? Anyone who spent an hour with Auric would have thrown his life away to save him."

Corin winced as though she'd stricken him, but she squeezed harder at his shoulder. She raised a finger to his chin and lifted his face to meet her gaze again. "I absolve you of whatever guilt you carry here—"

"That's not within your reach," he said.

"Vagabond, do not argue with your princess."

He offered her a conciliatory smile but argued anyway. "You are not my princess."

"Your Aepoli accent and the laws of Ithale would say otherwise. And as I *am* your princess, I will absolve you of this guilt because I know that Auric would if he were here. I know it as I know my own true heart, and if you knew him at all, you'd know it too."

"Oh, gods' blood, he likely would."

"He would. And I assure you, no matter what you've seen, that he's alive. He has survived far worse things than this trap that you've described."

"Princess—"

"Please. Call me Sera, if he sent you to speak with me. If he trusted you that much, then I do too."

"Then you must trust his message as well. Giuliano is a grave threat."

"He is not the first. Auric and I had our plans."

"But Auric's gone. Or ... even if he did survive, he isn't here to protect you."

"And you're prepared to take his place?"

"Against Giuliano, aye. If you will help me, I can crush him."

She shook her head, a sadness in her eyes. "You cannot crush them all, vagabond. They *are* Ithale."

"But if I can crush just this one."

She smiled, sad. "I used to think the way you do. I used to try to find some way through the twisting maze of my family's politics. I never wished to be like them, but I always assumed I had to use my family's power to survive it."

"Now's the time."

"No. That's what Auric showed me. Evil can't be fought with evil, and filth cannot be cleaned with filth. He convinced me to pursue a better life and went himself to do the same, thinking that between us, we could change the world."

"And now the filth has taken him from you," Corin said, as gently as he could. "Princess, it was a precious thought, but good men do not thrive in this Hurope."

"Then I will run away. That was our plan. We would do everything we could to change the world through hope and noble deeds, but we always knew it might not work. And if worse came to worst, we would run away. We would leave the vipers to their nests and find some quiet place of our own."

"But ... you can't go on your own. I've told you, he's—"

"He'll find me. I have faith in him. He'll find me, and we'll be happy again."

"That's no kind of plan. Don't you understand what this man has done to you? To Auric? You're about to throw away a life of luxury because some wretched snake—some stinking dog—believed that he could treat human beings like chattel. I won't accept it, Princess. He needs to pay."

She considered him a moment. "Run away."

"That is no answer!"

"It is the only answer. I can see it in your eyes. You hate this society at least as much as I. But I can tell you from long experience, it will not change. You can spend your life hating them, fighting them, but you cannot defeat them. There is a wide world outside the Godlands. Go explore it. Find some hidden corner all your own, and make it what you want it to be."

Corin's hands clenched into fists. A rage burned behind his breastbone—not at the princess, but at the things she spoke of. His voice rose louder than he meant it to. "That is no answer."

"I'd hoped for another. I thought perhaps I'd found the one man in this world so charmed that he could change things, but you tell me I was wrong. If Auric couldn't do it, no one can. The only hope is running."

"No. Here it is *I* who speak from long experience, and I can tell you this plan is just as broken as the other. I've tried it, Princess. I've run."

"Perhaps not far enough?"

"There's nowhere farther than I've been. All my life I ran away, and still they found me. Everywhere I've gone, in space and time, they've found me. There is no escape from tyrants. They must be challenged, and they must be cast down."

She shrank away from his intensity. Her lip trembled, and once again she looked but a girl. Alone. "I ... I don't know how. I can't. I made a promise."

"And a noble one, but we must face the truth."

She shook her head. "I can't. I can't betray that promise. Even if he's dead. No, especially if he's dead. I can't."

Corin considered her a moment, then dropped his gaze. "I understand. It was unfair to ask of you. Everything I've done has been unfair to you. I should have honored Auric's wishes and nothing more."

"You had a good intention."

"But I hurt you with it. Princess, beware your cousin Giuliano. He means you harm. Watch out for every sign of danger."

"I always do."

"Good. That's all you need for now."

"But what do you intend?"

"I will do what you cannot. I still believe there must be some way to break his power. I will find it. I will cast him down."

"And ... what do you ask of me."

He met her eyes and offered her a smile. "I ask only that you keep your promise. Fight for nobility, because someone has to."

She stood a moment, weighing Corin with her eyes; then she shook her head and moved toward the gateway. As she approached, the windowless, unmarked black carriage rattled up and stood waiting for her. She stopped beneath the arch, though, and turned back to Corin.

"What *will* you do?"

Corin spread his hands. "I will take your cousin's evil to his own door. I'll hang him by the knot of his misdeeds."

"Gods favor," she breathed, horrified.

"No gods at all. Just me."

She shuddered, head to toe, then turned and climbed quickly up into the carriage. The driver cracked his whip the moment she was closed inside, and the carriage thundered off at a terrible speed. Corin started after it, surprised, and he'd gone perhaps ten paces down the lane before he found an answer lying in the gutter.

Signor della Porta lay there, a vicious bruise swelling on his forehead. Corin rushed to his side and stirred him with a gentle shake.

As soon as the old man's eyes focused on Corin, he spat and rained feeble blows on the pirate's chest. "Scoundrel! Knave! What have you done with her?"

Corin sighed, miserable. "Unless I'm gravely mistaken, I led her right into a trap of Giuliano's."

(26)

The tavern keeper met them on the floor again, and his eyes went wide at the sight of Signor della Porta in such condition. "Cousin! I do bid you welcome to my fine establishment, but is this wise? And tell me what's become of you!"

Corin spared no time for niceties. He caught the tavern keeper by the shoulder. "Have you set someone to searching for my information yet?"

"Not yet. You did say tomorrow—"

"I need them now. I need them right now, but the target has changed."

"What do you mean?"

"Princess Sera has been kidnapped. About an hour ago, she was stolen right off the street and carried away in a big black carriage."

"And ... how does this relate to your search for Don Giuliano?"

"I can only guess. But I suspect it was my action that led to her capture, and I will do what I must to rescue her. Has anyone been to my room?"

The tavern keeper blinked at the sudden change of topic. "No, my lord. I gave my word—"

"Good. I'll grab some things while you catch up with della Porta. Find out where we should start searching. Put all your men on finding the princess."

"And you?"

"I have work of my own to do. I can find the things I need to know. Put all your men on finding the princess. Can you do that?"

"I will do whatever you ask."

"Then help your cousin. I don't want her fate weighing on my conscience."

"Yes, my lord. I understand."

He turned to Signor della Porta for clearer answers, and Corin left them to their conversation. He had to find Blake. His every instinct screamed that Blake had captured Sera, and that gave Corin one more sin to hold against the man. One more potential victim Corin needed to rescue, if there were any time left at all. He darted up the stairs toward his rooms. He burst through the door—

—and found Aemilia sitting on his bed. She held the book of memories in one hand and the dartgun in the other. To Corin's horror, she was reading from the book. For a moment she didn't move, didn't react at all to his arrival. She turned a page, finished a paragraph, and then raised her eyes to Corin with an infuriating calm.

Corin shut the door. He stared at her a moment. How had she found him here? How had she gotten past a Nimble Fingers tavern keeper unnoticed? She was remarkable in her own way. And now she simply sat there, waiting. She didn't point the dartgun, didn't make a threat or plea. She waited for him with a pretty little smile. Most remarkable.

And at the same time, most inconvenient. He couldn't run this time. He'd escaped her in Marzelle, but only by skipping town. He could not leave Aerome. He had to win her over or at least buy time to settle Ethan Blake.

So he smoothed his brow and dipped his head to her in greeting. "You do keep springing up in unexpected places."

Her smile broadened. "And you keep running away. A girl could get her feelings hurt."

"How did you find me here?"

She laid the book aside and climbed to her feet. "The Council caught you traveling again. They know you're in Aerome, but they do not know where."

Corin licked his lips. "You're on the Council. You know where I am."

"On this one point ... the Council and I are at odds."

"Oh?"

"I didn't need to hear you had been traveling, Corin; I've been waiting for you here since you left Marzelle."

"You knew I'd come to Aerome?" he asked, but then he nodded. "Ah. Yes. You'd already tracked down Ethan Blake."

"And I never doubted you would find him too."

"I've found him, all right. But not soon enough. He's committed more atrocities, and I believe he's just abducted the princess."

"We do not meddle in the politics of nations," she said.

"And I don't stand idly by while tyrants ply their trade!"

She widened her eyes, apparently impressed at his sincerity, then came across the floor toward him. "You are something special."

He cocked his head. "Are you warming up to me?"

"Corin ... why didn't you tell me about the book?"

He looked away and shrugged. "I told you there were books."

"But you didn't mention that you'd saved one. You didn't mention that it spoke of you and of Oberon's last design."

"Honestly? I didn't think you'd want to share."

She cleared her throat. "You can hardly claim that this is *yours*. It belongs to the world—"

"You see?" Corin said. "That's just the sort of thing I thought you'd say."

She sighed and shook her head. "I don't wish to fight with you, Corin. I want to be your friend."

It sounded genuine—desperate even—but Corin couldn't bring himself to trust easily. He fixed her with a challenging glare. "That's a cruel lie, Aemilia, especially when you've already said the truth more plainly. You want to use me."

She crumpled, sitting there on his bed. In a tiny voice, she answered him. "The Council wants to use you. I won't deny that. But they haven't met you yet. They cannot comprehend everything you are until they know you."

Corin wanted to go to her, to comfort her, but some old, stubborn pride kept him where he was. He raised his chin. "I'd prefer to keep them guessing."

"I understand," she said, meeting his eyes again. "I truly do. That's why I didn't tell them where to look. That's why I came alone to speak with you again."

He blinked. "You . . . you won't convince me."

"I have to try. Not for their sake, but for yours."

Corin stretched out his hand. "Very well. But first, return the book."

To his surprise, she did. She didn't even argue. She pressed it into his hands and backed away. "It's yours," she said. "For now, at least. I hope someday you'll choose to share it with me."

"You've made a good first move. Now wow me. What's your offer?"

"Me."

He blinked. "I don't know what to say. Maybe... spin around? Show me your teeth?"

She blushed bright red, but she did not back down. "I want to bring you in, Corin. To keep you safe. I want you to stay with the Council."

"I've already said—"

"You won't be a prisoner," she said. "You'll be a guest. I am prepared to guarantee it."

"Do you have so much authority? Can you stop them from throwing me in a pit somewhere? Hiding me from the world? Interrogating me for every last scrap of information? Stealing my *life*?"

She sat a little straighter. "No. But that's my offer. Wherever the Council sends you, whatever they elect to do with you... I'll be right there with you. I will not leave your side. I will not abandon you to them. If they steal your life, they'll be stealing mine too. I am prepared to tie my fate to yours."

"You'd do all that just to get me to submit to them?"

"All that and more. I do not want to see you harmed."

He chuckled. "I must have won you over with my charm."

She surprised him with another blush. And she did not deny his claim. "I understand you are afraid. You do not need to be. You'll have a friend and a determined advocate in me."

He went a step toward her. "Aemilia... are you concerned for me?" He could not quite hide his grin.

"We've been gathering intelligence, you know. We've been piecing together your history. And then... I read the book. I wish … I wish I could have seen you face down Ephitel. I wish I could remember that day the way you do."

"It is no happier for me."

"Perhaps. But it would have been good to find a hero on our side." She cleared her throat and looked away. "It would be good to find one now. Please be on our side."

"Aemilia." He took her hand, and that drew her gaze back to his. "I could use a steadfast friend. I've learned that on this journey. I would love to have you for a companion."

"But?"

"But nothing. There is work in Aerome that I must do, but you already know that. I ask the same thing that I asked of you back in Marzelle, and for a moment you were prepared to grant it. I'm closer now, and since he's captured the princess, the stakes are higher now."

"You still want me to let you start a war with Ethan Blake."

"No war. I mean I mean to vanquish him. Let me finish this one task, and then I'll run away with you."

She rolled her eyes at that, but she could not quite hide the blush that bloomed again on her cheeks.

"You have my word. I won't betray you to them. But tell me what you have in mind."

Corin had no answer for her. He pointed past the bed. "Hand me my sword."

"Tell me first."

He shrugged. "I'd hoped to use the princess. Giuliano has positioned himself against her. He killed a man she loves, and I hoped when I revealed that to her, she'd use her family connections to destroy him."

Aemilia frowned. "Our intel suggests that Sera's out of favor with the family."

"She is, and she's a kind person as well. She was useless to me even before he carted her off."

"So, what will you do?"

Corin shrugged. "I will use more common means." He went to the armoire and fetched his purse. "I'll investigate this, Giuliano. I will spend tonight on questions, trying to find some indiscreet retainer or old associate who might point me to a weakness. If I can find where he is vulnerable, I can exploit it."

"And if he isn't at all?"

"Everyone is vulnerable somewhere," Corin said. "The bigger question is time."

She sighed, exasperated. "I'll keep your secret, Corin. You asked a day, but if it takes a week, a month, I won't betray you."

He showed her a smile. "I know. It's not for you."

"Then who?"

"The women in his power. If he has kidnapped Princess Sera, he must plan something truly terrible for her. He cannot allow her to escape and testify against him."

"Why is she your responsibility? Surely she has her own supporters in the family!"

"As far as I can tell, she has only one old retainer. But more than that, she's my responsibility because she was captured when I lured her from the palace by pretending to be the paramour that I allowed Dave Taker to murder."

Aemilia gasped. "I ... I see."

"Aye. I created this mess, and it falls to me to clean it up."

"Then the second woman would be Iryana? You have said you feel much the same when it comes to her."

"All his victims," Corin said. "I seek justice for the ones he has already hurt, and rescue for the ones he'll hurt if I delay."

"You bear too much upon your shoulders."

"Someone must. I spoke with the creator. I spoke with the man who made this world and I faced down the man who broke it. I can no longer accept that this is just the way things are; I know that wicked men have made it thus. And I can stop them."

"I should come with you."

"I'd beg you not to."

She tilted her head, smiling up at him. "Because it is too dangerous? I know some tricks of my own."

He shook his head. "That's not it at all. My methods ... aren't always pretty. I'll have to go to some dark places to find the things I need. I won't try to hide the truth from you, but I'd much prefer you never see it firsthand."

She paled at his words, and after a moment she nodded. Without another word, she passed him his sword.

"And the dwarven pistol."

"It isn't loaded."

"Praise Fortune. Still, it has served me as a prop."

She gave him the gun as well. He tucked it in his belt, and then he almost kissed her. Instead, he held her gaze and told her earnestly, "I will come back."

"Bloodstained?"

"One can only hope."

She sighed. "Be safe, Corin. I mean it. I don't want to see you hurt."

"I'll do my best."

She opened her mouth as though to argue more, to press the point, but then she let her shoulders drop and looked away. "Will you at least leave me something to read while I wait up for you?"

He only weighed the question for a moment. He did trust her. He bowed his head and handed her the book of memories. "Keep it safe."

"Safer than you. I'll swear it."

He barked a laugh. "I have to give you that one. Good evening to you, lady."

"Clear skies," she said. "And happy hunting."

Corin's hunt took him no further than the common room.
As he stepped onto the floor, the tavern keeper appeared,
bubbling with news. But Corin silenced him with a gesture. He
cocked his head, listening to the noise of the busy tavern.

"Something amiss?" the tavern keeper asked.

"Aye," Corin said, as he caught the sound again. A booming
laugh, and a familiar one. Corin grinned. "And it's something
good for a change." He turned to the tavern keeper. "Send some
dinner to my room, and a good bottle of wine. There is a lady
there, and she deserves a decent meal."

The tavern keeper shook his head. "I can assure you no one
has gone up—"

Corin laid a reassuring hand on the other man's shoulder. "I
keep strange company. Don't let it trouble you, good man. See to
that, and then you can bring me whatever news you have of the
princess."

"You're not going out?"

"Not yet," Corin said. "First, I think I'll win a hand of
cards."

Corin slipped into the crowd and picked a path toward the
distant sound of laughter. He didn't need to listen hard to find

his way. The man he went to meet would be in the center of the room. He always was.

Ben Strunk, the city dwarf. Corin watched him from a distance for a moment. Strunk sat at a table with half a dozen local thieves, trading barbs and sipping spirits and throwing hand after hand after hand into the pot. Corin grinned.

He moved forward then, slipping stealthily behind the laughing dwarf, and when he was just a pace away, Corin drew the dwarven pistol from beneath his cloak. He pressed the barrel's tip against the back of Ben Strunk's neck and cocked the hammer. The click was loud enough to silence all the laughter at the table.

Ben dropped his cards and spread his hands wide, but otherwise he didn't move. He took a slow breath, then spoke distinctly. "I'm sorry, mister. I swear, she said she wasn't married."

Corin had to laugh at that. He eased the hammer and dropped the pistol on the table right in front of Ben. "Still the same Ben Strunk! I bring a gift from out of time."

"Corin Hugh!" Ben shouted, springing to his feet. He clasped Corin's arm in welcome, then waved toward the table. "I'd heard rumors you were in Aerome. Take a seat! Take a seat. I'm sure someone in this rabble will yield you his place. They've gotta be tired of winning my money by now."

"They can go for hours yet," Corin said, waving for the others to keep their places. "It's all part of the Nimble Fingers training. And I have business elsewhere."

"Aye? What business is that? Anything to do with a desert mutiny?"

"You heard about that?"

"I heard a First Mate got sick of sucking sand and left his captain buried in a mountain. Heard the same fellow ended up sinking that captain's ship off Jebbra Point."

"The scalawag!"

"You make light," Ben said, "but there's a specialness to crafted things. To *owned* things. And there are few relationships more dear than that between a captain and his ship. I know this."

"As it happens," Corin said, more bitter than he meant to be, "that was not the only relationship Ethan Blake stole in Jepta. I owe him for a great many things."

"How did that bring you to Aerome? I don't much consider this a pirate port."

"You were doing so well! Have you heard no rumors about a spoiled little lord playing pirate?"

"Happens all the time."

"And do they often come back home when they fail as captains? When their ships sink off Jebbra Point?"

"Oho! Your Ethan Blake was just pretending."

"Pretending not to be a Vestossi," Corin said. He looked around the table, conscious of all the unfamiliar faces, but in the end he did not much care. If he failed in his quest, he might at least spread a little slander on the villain's name. "Pretending not to be Giuliano, in fact. I've chased his trail halfway across the world and found him here."

Ben Strunk sucked in a deep breath. He dropped the playful tone and lowered his voice. "You might be careful using names like that, Corin."

"I used up all my caution days ago. It's past time I answered Blake for his misdeeds."

"Aye, I'll give you that, but going up against a Vestossi in Aerome? It's a risky business. Particularly Giuliano. Particularly now."

"Oh? You know him?"

"Who doesn't? You always did hang out with riffraff. You should spend some time among courtiers—their gossip and their booze are both much better."

"So? What can you tell me of Giuliano?"

"He's the talk of the town, my boy. He's been at every dinner, every ball since summer started. And he has this exotic little trinket on his arm."

Iryana. Corin's eyes must have flashed, because Ben Strunk shrank away and stammered. "Oh. Yes. You did mention other relationships."

Corin growled a warning. "What can you tell me about him?"

"I never thought to look too deep. He seems like your average little lord, if an up-and-comer. He's certainly done something to make a name, though. I've heard King Ipolito means to honor him tonight."

"What? Why?"

Ben Strunk shrugged. "No one knows. Some family politics."

Auric. It had to be. Blake had removed a potential embarrassment from the family name, and now he'd be rewarded. That explained the bathhouse, tying up all his loose ends.

Corin slammed a fist down on the table. "Honor him? Tonight, you said? Where?"

"A gala at his father's house."

"Where is this house?"

"I'd planned to go. Shall I just take you there?"

"Aye! But tell me now. Where is he?"

"King's Way," Ben said. "West of the palace. Half a mile from the playhouse. You shouldn't have any trouble spotting it; they have half the city out for decorations."

"When? When does the gala start?"

Ben leaned back in his chair, thinking. "Oh ... in perhaps an hour. But I hadn't planned to show before midnight. You know, for the sake of fashion."

"That will do for me," Corin said, clapping Ben on the shoulder. He bounced on his toes, anxious to be off. "Bring a blade or two. Things could get nasty."

"Oh, silly pirate. I don't think you understand how galas work."

Corin shook his head. He broke away, heading for the door. "I've waited long enough," he shouted back. "It's time he's answered for."

Ben Strunk jumped to his feet and shouted after Corin. "Wait! What's this toy you bring me?"

"Your legacy! Gift from your father in another version of the dream. It's dwarven mastercraft, commissioned by a god."

Ben's eyes grew wide at that. He nodded a true artist's appreciation for such a priceless work of art.

Corin couldn't linger any longer. He broke for the alley door, but he heard Ben behind him. "You hear that, boys? Dwarven mastercraft. A perfect treasure. I'll wager that and sixty livres blind on my next hand."

King's Way ran along the crest of the city's highest hill, and it featured the stylish mansions of the highest families. The Vestossis owned more than a block of it, not even counting the royal family, but Corin didn't have to ask to know which one belonged to Giuliano's father. Ben had been right; it was obvious.

Torches flared all across the steep, sloping yard as workers rushed to finish decorating. Silken streamers sought to soften the appearance of the spike-topped gates. A band was setting up out on the porch, and from the screech and whine of strings, Corin guessed another was already tuning up somewhere inside. The whole scene was chaos.

And chaos was his friend. Corin picked out the darkest spot along the wide front gate, then camped within its shadows, waiting for some disturbance from the house—or, more likely, some passing beauty on the street—to distract the guards on the front gate. Then it would be an easy enough matter to scale the fence, climb the hill, and find his way into the house.

In the end, it was a disturbance from the house—a shouting altercation between some serving maid and a noble lady. Corin grabbed two handfuls of silk streamer, heaved himself up to the top of the gate, and caught one clear look across the lawn to the front porch.

And spotted Iryana.

She was not in chains. She wasn't bruised or beaten. She wore a sleek black dress and gold enough to buy a ship and crew. Corin gasped aloud. He wasn't close enough to have been heard, but he was in obvious sight, hanging from the gate like that. A servant spotted him and pointed. Iryana and the serving maid both turned his way. The guards on the gate shouted, "Halt! Who goes?"

And Corin ran. He went two blocks, then slipped into the shadows and waited for the chasing guards to lumber past, heads whipping left and right as they searched for him. He waited until they'd gone another block; then he eased back out onto the lane and crept toward the house again.

Iryana was still there. She lingered halfway down the drive, wringing her hands and staring out into the dark night. She'd seen him. She must have seen him. And she'd always been a clever girl. He could count on it. She'd find some chance to slip away—

While he watched, she turned and shouted something back into the house. Then she stomped down the hill to the front gates and waited by the street, tapping one heel. Corin watched her, hoping she'd come farther, desperate to catch any signal she might give him.

He was so intent on her, he was nearly trampled by the little trap carriage that came dashing up the street behind him. It settled to a halt just by the gate, and Iryana climbed up inside. Corin couldn't hear her instructions, but the tone was sharp enough to draw blood. The driver cracked his whip, and they were gone.

For a half a heartbeat Corin didn't move, torn between his errand here and his concern for Iryana. She had not seemed broken. She'd barely seemed restrained. But—no matter what he'd told the druid—this girl was at least half the reason he had come for Blake.

So in the end he chased her. He couldn't guess where she might go, so he abandoned subtlety and set off at a full sprint. The gate attendant cried out when he saw Corin in pursuit. He leaned out in the street and shouted after the missing guards, but Corin was already past and gone. Corin reached the apex of the hill just in time to see the carriage down below turn left onto a crossing lane. He didn't slow.

Lungs and legs both burning, he pounded down the hill and made the turn just in time to see the trap force through a crowd of late-night revelers. The driver never eased up. Perhaps Iryana hadn't seen him. Perhaps she'd planned her own escape, and he'd arrived just in time to see her slip away. He made the block, then leaped onto the platform of a priceless statue to search left and right for some sign of the carriage.

He found it parked beside a tailor's shop half a mile off. He frowned, then cast another glance around, but this was the only carriage of its sort in sight. And even as he watched, Iryana came stomping from the shop and flung herself into the cab again. Corin sprang down to the street and ran that way, but she was already giving her directions. He'd never catch her now.

The trap stopped at a jeweler's two blocks down. This time she did not even go in. She spoke some word to the driver and then sat waiting in the carriage while he went and rapped on the door. The shop was closed, but when he returned to report this, she sent him back to rap all the harder. He raised a racket that might have woken half the street, and in time the jeweler came to open the door for him.

Corin watched this all play out as he crept slowly closer. Once the driver was inside, Corin had his chance to approach unseen. But something stopped him. He moved close enough to give chase again, and that was all. He hid within the shadows of a closed-up bakery and watched the girl he'd come to rescue.

She tapped her fingers on the carriage door. She fiddled with the bangles on her arms. She huffed in irritation and rolled her eyes toward the storefront. She was the very picture of an agitated lady.

Corin stared at her, perplexed. Where was the beaten slave he'd come to rescue? Where was the helpless damsel in distress? But she had never been helpless, had she? That was half of what he'd loved about her. She was fierce and proud and more than able in any circumstances....

And here and now, by all appearances, she was a proud Vestossi lady.

(**28**)

Corin shuddered at the thought of it. She couldn't be. She was an untamed spirit, a wild wind, a mystery. She was no Vestossi trinket.

But *something* strange was going on. He puzzled at it until his head began to ache, but he could find no explanation. He'd almost made up his mind to just go forward, to confront her and discover the whole truth, but the driver beat him to it. The young man emerged from the shop, bearing a small black box. He handed it up to Iryana, and she accepted it with little grace. She said some word, and the driver climbed into his seat and cracked his whip.

For a moment, Corin worried that the errands were all done, that the carriage was returning to the mansion and he'd missed his chance to unravel these new mysteries. But the carriage bore her half a block before it stopped outside a quiet little wine shop. She climbed down from the cab and paid the driver some small coins. He rolled away, back toward the house, and she went alone into the shop.

Two burly guards stood watch over the street. They nodded a familiar greeting to the desert girl. Corin took small hope in that. Perhaps these were Vestossi guards, and this a Vestossi shop.

Perhaps she wasn't really free at all, but always under supervision. Every living body in this part of town could be bought and owned with Vestossi silver. It might be a wide prison, a pretty prison, but it could still be a prison all the same.

He told himself that must be true and went to rescue her. He found a side door on a narrow alley and slipped in behind the kitchens. He went ten paces down a narrow corridor and emerged into the patrons' lounge. He almost laughed in his surprise.

The wine shop fit the neighborhood perfectly. Its storefront was immaculate and understated, but this was not enough to hide its opulence. Inside, it was dark as sin, full of whispered secrets. Corin watched, unseen, while a hostess in black livery led the dusky woman to a corner booth. He waited while she settled herself. Then he slipped across the room, searching every corner as he went. He saw no other skulkers, no other watching eyes. It was a place that prized discretion above all. He strode right to her table and took a seat across from her.

She gasped and pressed a hand to her mouth. Gold bangles glittered on her wrist, and gemstones sparkled on her fingers. They could scarcely compete with her natural beauty, though. Corin smiled for her. "Why am I always saving you from such dark places?"

She leaned across the table, voice pitched low. "You must get out of here!"

"You're not surprised that I'm alive?"

She scoffed. "Surprised? No. I have watched Blake tremble over it for weeks."

Corin grinned. "You always knew how to make me smile."

"I have no wish to make you smile! I want you to leave this city and never look back!"

"I will, and you'll come with me, but first I need to have a word with Ethan Blake."

"You'll have a dagger in your gut and a kicking from the city guard! Ethan Blake is a Vestossi!"

"Aye, I know it well. But I have found a patron of my own."

"Unless it's someone strong enough to challenge Ephitel outright, your patron will not serve you."

"Ephitel's a dog. I serve King Oberon."

Her eyes went wide at that—pools of light within the shop's deep gloom. She breathed the words, "Did you say ... Oberon?"

"I survived Jezeeli, Iryana. I learned its secrets. And now I've come to rescue you and settle with Blake."

"You survived Jezeeli?"

"Aye."

"And you learned something there?"

"Secrets out of time and long forgotten."

She tugged at her ear. "My people have some ancient legends. ..."

"If they tell of an ancient kingdom where men and elves lived side by side, of great prosperity brought low by betrayal, treason—"

"All of that and more."

"Then, aye. I've lived the legends, Iryana, and I can attest that Ithale's patron god was that same traitor."

"Why do you think my people chose to survive the wretched sands? They thought it better to face the tyranny of the Endless Desert than bend knee to your false gods."

Corin showed his teeth again. "I could not agree more, but I have found a better answer."

"And what is that?"

"Revenge. Justice. I mean to make things right, for all the world."

She stared a moment, fascinated. And then she laughed. "You cannot mean it."

"I do. And I am not alone."

She sighed in cruel sympathy. "You are a fool and always have been. If you know any of Jezeeli's secrets, you know what comes of good men who face Ephitel."

Corin grinned. "That's just the trick: I am no good man."

She reached across the table, took his hands in hers, and held his gaze as warmly. "You are not good enough to be a god, and you are not bad enough to best one. Take your secrets somewhere far away, somewhere Ephitel and Ethan Blake alike will never find you."

"It's not in my nature to hide from tyrants."

She laughed. "No? Then what sent you to the sea for seven years?"

He licked his lips. "Well ... I mean ... anymore. It's not in my nature anymore."

"You are a good man, Corin. You're the only one who will not see that. But I know that you are good at heart. You do not deserve what lies on the path you've chosen."

"I have chosen nothing, Iryana. I only do what must be done."

She snorted. "No one makes a slave of Corin Hugh. I know it well. I've tried, and I have tricks even the Vestossis would admire."

He frowned, uncomprehending. When had she done anything of the sort? But he had no time to pursue that now. He shook his head. "There's more to this matter than you could begin to guess. But this is not the place or time to speak of such things."

"It's not," she said, serious. "I am expected at the house."

"Forget the house. Forget the Vestossis altogether. I can take you away from here."

"You don't always have to be the hero, Corin. You were a pirate. Sometimes pirates get to play the selfish villain. Forget me. Save yourself."

Corin faltered. His mouth felt suddenly dry, his lungs too empty. "Iryana—"

"I have made my peace, Corin. I'm happy here."

He forced a doubtful smile. "With Blake? You can't be."

"He has his qualities."

Corin leaned toward her. "I don't know what he's done or said. I don't know what threats he's made, but you don't have to fear him anymore. I've gained a share of Oberon's power, Iryana. I can take you away from here in the blink of an eye."

She breathed a heavy sigh. "You aren't listening."

He was trying so hard not to. He caught her hand. "You will be safe and free. I'll see it's done. Then I will come back for him."

She shook her head, a glistening in her eyes. "I am not yours to save, Corin Hugh. I do not want saving. Go away."

Corin sank back, stunned. "You're no one's." His voice sounded distant, pale. "You are a desert wind. An untamed spirit."

"That is no easy life. For all their sins, these Godlanders can offer comforts liberty cannot."

"You're not Ethan Blake's."

"I am," she said.

"Perhaps . . . perhaps he has convinced you. After all this time—"

"I was always his. I'm sorry, Corin, but it's true. An hour after you . . . recruited me to your mad quest, he took me aside and made me a far better offer. To deceive you. To undermine you. To deprive you of my people's magic."

"No."

She shrugged. "In the end, you didn't need me anyway. But I still earned my reward."

"Money? It was all about money?"

"Oh, Giuliano is far more than money. He is security and power and prestige. These are the things a woman craves." There was a sadness in her eyes as she said this, but not a shade of doubt.

"I liked you better when you were poor."

She gave him a little smile. "Of course you did. You thought you could have me then."

Corin never flinched, but the words were like a gut wound. How often had he claimed he didn't love her? Had he always known it was a lie?

The pain of her betrayal rolled around inside his belly, fighting to get out. He sucked a shallow breath and fought to keep his voice level, to pretend indifference. "I have fought with gods and monsters to get back here. For you. To set you free."

She shook her head. "I am more than free. I am engaged."

Corin held her gaze. "I owe Blake a reckoning. You must understand I will not spare him for your sake."

"Corin, do not be a fool. I allied myself with him because he is the sort of man who will prevail. Not on noble character, not on courage or wits, but on resources. You cannot fight a Vestossi lord."

"I will," Corin said. "And I'll destroy him. Do you have any backup plans?"

She sighed and regarded him with pity in her eyes. "Oh, Corin. Forget this madness. Go find yourself another ship and sail the seas while the world forgets your name. It's the only thing that's ever made you happy."

"It won't. Not anymore. I've developed a certain taste for justice."

"That's a shame. It comes at such a dear price, and there's never enough to satisfy."

Corin showed her his teeth. "I'll manage. I always do."

She leaned forward, elbows on the table, and fixed him with a serious glare. "Abandon your bravado for a moment. I like you, Corin. I always did. It made my task much harder, but now it helps. Because now I can give you true and good advice that serves my own interests as well."

He shook his head. "This is bigger than you and me, Iryana."

"You're right. This is exactly as big as Giuliano, and he can crush you without even trying. He stole your boat. He tried to kill you. You were a pirate, Corin. It's all part of the game."

"Those are not the worst of his sins. By far."

She scoffed. "What, me? I never was yours. You can't blame him for that."

"No," Corin admitted. "No, I'll credit him back for you. It does ease my heart a bit to know you've not been much mistreated."

"On the contrary—"

"I don't want to know. But I've seen good men die by Giuliano's hand. Men who had nothing to do with his intrigues. Better men than me."

"What, some pirates? Some hired help?"

"No. An honest hero who did nothing worse than love a woman who loved him in return."

She stared a moment. "You don't mean the farmboy?"

"You know of him?"

She laughed. "Giuliano's talked of little else. He was not a hero, Corin. He was a national disgrace in the making."

Corin's lip curled. "You've learned their language well."

"I've had some time to practice."

"Stop trying to convince me, and listen for a moment. I hope you've made higher friends than Giuliano. Because he won't be around for long."

She touched a finger to her chin, considering. "Such confidence. You always were a brash one, but this...this speaks of something deeper."

It was nothing but his anger, pain, betrayal, but if she would see it for some hidden card, he'd play the bluff. "I've come to bring him justice. I won't fail."

She blinked. "You said you had a higher patron. I...I took that to mean this mad memory of Oberon."

That was all he'd meant, but Iryana seemed to suspect he meant someone else. He put on his cleverest expression and gave her a theatric shrug. "I have lots of friends."

To his surprise, she answered with a look of perfect pity. "It is the princess, isn't it? You've staked your hopes on the princess."

Corin couldn't guess where she was going, but he played it out. "Sera and I have spoken."

Iryana shook her head. "Oh, you poor thing. You must have thought you held some precious opportunity when you met with her, but I've gauged Sera myself. She doesn't have the spine to play the family game."

"She has found a new mentor," Corin said.

Iryana shook her head. "It doesn't matter. She's finished. She's no longer in the picture."

"A minor setback—"

Iryana leaned forward again, frustration hissing in her voice. "Stop playing games and listen to me! You have nothing! The princess will be dead by dawn."

A fist of ice closed hard around Corin's spine. He shuddered and shook his head in mute denial. "He...he wouldn't dare. Even Blake wouldn't dare."

"I never thought you were naïve, Corin."

Corin shook his head. "I don't mistake him for a decent man, but he's not stupid. He's ambitious. He can't hope to get away with something like that—"

"He has a letter Sera wrote to the wretched farmboy. In her hand and with her seal. She promised she would run away with him, and the family would never know where she had gone."

"Gods' blood," Corin breathed. "That's why he killed Auric. That's why he abducted her."

Iryana nodded. "He plans to share the letter with the king tonight, and the princess will be dead by dawn. Everyone will think she ran away to live with her Raentzman commoner."

"And no one will much bother looking for her."

Iryana nodded, grinning. "And Ethan Blake will have earned the favor of the king."

Corin leaned back in his chair, considering the desert woman for a while. She had a cruel spirit in her, a violence barely restrained. He'd found it alluring once, but now it just seemed wild. Unpredictable. As frightening as dwarven powder.

"Why would you tell me all this? If you have cast your lot with Blake, why would you tell me of his secret plans?"

She smirked. "It will do you little good to know he has a letter. There are many pieces to his plan, and I have revealed only enough to show you that you can't defeat him. Your princess is a shadow, and your patron god is long forgotten. You cannot face the Vestossi."

"So you taunt me?"

"No!" she snapped, exasperated. "From the moment you've arrived, my only desire has been to convince you that you *must leave town.* You are a proud man, Corin Hugh, but I have some hope that you'll see reason."

"Your concern does warm my heart," he said, his tone as cold as ice.

"But you will go?"

"I'll make sure you learn what I decide."

He rose and swept his cloak around his shoulders, but before he could stomp off, she stopped him with a gentle touch on his elbow. "Corin?"

"Aye?"

"You are too clever a man to die in some Vestossi trap. The ones that you lament were weak or dumb. Do not follow in their footsteps."

He offered her a smile. "That I won't, Iryana. That I won't."

He left by the back hallway, out the side door, and down the narrow alley. He'd found out what he needed. He had Blake's plan. But he'd paid a dear price to get it. Now the princess's fate hung in the balance, and if she fell, it would be on Corin's head. He went two blocks as stealthy as a shadow and then, confident no one was watching, he broke into a run back to the Nimble Fingers tavern.

(29)

His heart was pounding hard, his hands clenched into fists. He barely slowed when he reached the tavern's door. He bulled his way across the common room's floor, shouting, "Tavern keeper! Tavern keeper!" as he went.

His path brought him to Ben Strunk's table, where the dwarf was still engaged at cards. Corin jerked his head toward the door. "Settle up, Ben. We're leaving."

"What? I can't leave. I haven't quite lost all my money yet!"

Corin turned to the other men at the table. "My apologies, gentlemen, and your next round's on me. But I require this good dwarf's assistance."

"Oh, very well," Ben grumbled. "Can anyone make change for uncut diamonds?"

Corin turned away as the tavern keeper arrived. "My lord?"

Corin stepped close to him and lowered his voice. "You *must* find the princess. Her life is in danger. Send word to Signor della Porta. I'll do what I can to ... resolve the issue. But if she has any friends at all within the city, it is time to rouse them."

"My cousin is out with a dozen brilliant Nimble Fingers. They have a lead and, last I heard, they were making plans to rescue her."

Corin clapped the tavern keeper on the shoulder. "Good man! You didn't let me down." He started toward his room, then turned back. "One more thing! Can you summon me a carriage."

"A carriage? At this hour?"

"Aye! Think you could get me Princess Sera's?"

The tavern keeper barked a laugh, but when Corin didn't even smile, he considered it a moment and gave a nod. "Not her proper cab, but I can supply one a Vestossi might use in a pinch."

"That'll do," Corin said. "Make it happen."

He snapped his fingers at Ben Strunk and dashed away toward the stairs. He slammed into his room, and Aemilia screamed in shock. She sprang up from the bed and dove across the room, both dartguns trained on Corin's chest.

Corin almost grinned. "And you thought I would be worried about you."

She knelt there panting, flushed, and he saw her hands were shaking. "I'm not ..." she said. "I'm not ... a hero. I'm just ..."

"You are a druid of the Council of King Oberon," he said. "You remember things this world has never known. For a thousand years you've fought a shadow battle against tyrant gods."

Still she panted, but a smile touched her face. "When you put it like that ..."

"You almost seem like one."

"I ... I almost do."

"Good," he said. "Because tonight you go to war."

"I ... what?" she said. "I cannot go to war! What would I wear?"

"A fancy dress and a careful glamour."

"Corin ... what do you intend?"

Before he answered, a knock came at the door, followed shortly by Ben Strunk. He poked his head into the room and looked around. "Are we decent?"

"Come in," Corin said. "You need to hear this."

"Who's the lady?"

"Tonight, she will be a highborn lady of no particular name or nation."

The dwarf looked Aemilia up and down and nodded thoughtfully. "Fancy trick, that."

"Trust me," Corin said. "We're going to Giuliano's gala."

"You found the house, then?" Ben asked.

"Aye. And I found Iryana there."

Aemilia said nothing, but something in her expression caught Corin's attention. She seemed terribly alert. And none too happy.

Corin cleared his throat. "I found Iryana," he repeated. "And I learned that she is Giuliano's woman."

"I could have told you that," Ben said.

Aemilia didn't meet his eyes, but she spoke up. "Not his slave?"

"Not as such," Corin said.

"Isn't ... isn't that good news?"

"It is. For that part."

"Then there's no need for heroes here. We can leave them—"

"No!" Corin snapped. "I've said before, and it has always been as true: This is more than Iryana. This is justice. Ethan Blake must be put down."

Aemilia touched his arm, and it was like the shock of frigid water.

He blinked down at her and shivered. "Aemilia ..."

"You cannot fix Hurope by killing Blake. And we will *drown* before you spill the blood of all the wicked lords and ladies."

"I cannot fix Hurope," Corin said. "But I can fix the things that I have wrought."

"You? What have you done?"

"I gave him a command. I gave him his first taste of ambition. And in the Wildlands, I helped him catch and kill a noble man."

"That was not your doing!"

"But I played my part. And now I've given him Princess Sera. I tried to use her for my own ends, and now he has her in his power. He means to kill her, Aemilia."

Ben Strunk grunted. "Honor from the king or not, he's just a middling lord. I doubt he'd have the nerve to kill a princess."

"He has letters from her to a secret lover. A lowborn Raentzman. She was conspiring to sneak away. He means to make it look like she succeeded."

"Ah." Ben Strunk bobbed his head. "I suspect that might just do the job."

"But what can we do?" Aemilia asked.

"That letter is the anchor to his plan. If I can find it, if I can take it from him, he won't dare to kill her. Then we can rescue Princess Sera and chase him out of town."

"Will it work?"

Corin licked his lips. "It's all I've got. But if we don't act tonight, it will be too late. I'll have her death as well as Auric's on my conscience. I don't think I could bear that."

Aemilia looked down at the dartguns in her hands. She thought a moment. Then she met his eyes. "Can I bring these?"

"You should," he said. "You really, really should." He turned to Ben. "I've heard you're a retainer for King Ipolito."

"Aye, well, a man has to earn a living—"

Corin waved away the explanation. "Could that justify your attending tonight's gala?"

"I'd already planned to go."

"With an exotic foreign lady on your arm?"

"I ... am the Captain of the Mint."

"I'll take that as a yes. Aemilia, can you work the glamour?"

"I should be able to, though I've never tried to play royalty before."

"Not royalty. Just someone interesting and lovely. You're qualified for that, I'll swear."

She blushed and looked away. Ben Strunk laughed.

Aemilia asked, "Are we ... are we really going to do this?"

Corin nodded. "We must."

"But ... now?"

"Right now. Come!"

The carriage waited for them in the piazza. Corin helped them both inside; then he closed the door and took his place on the footman's stair. Aemilia twitched the curtain aside and leaned down to him as the horses clopped across the cobblestones.

"What are we doing? What's the plan?"

"When we arrive, you and Ben make a grand entrance. Circulate among the guests, and see what you can learn about Blake's plans for the evening."

"What are we looking for?"

"I know that he intends to share this letter with the king. It won't be a public thing—that makes no sense—but if you can discover when he plans to meet the king, or where, that might point me in the right direction."

"And you? What will you do?"

"I'll take advantage of the distraction you provide. I'll slip inside the house unseen, and try to find this letter."

She shook her head. "One piece of paper? In a mansion? How?"

Corin smiled. "People are predictable in ways. Once you've seen the structure of a house, you can often make a reasoned guess where they might try to secure a precious object of a known size and nature."

"I can almost believe that."

Corin chuckled. "I spent most of a decade studying the nuance of it. What do you think the Nimble Fingers really is?"

"I…"

"And that's just guessing from architecture. It's even easier if you know something of the nature of the person living there. I know Blake's ambitions and his fears. I'm pretty confident that I can find his secrets."

"But if you can't?"

"We'll manufacture something. If you can't find any news, you and Ben can at least distract him and buy me time."

"And if that doesn't work?"

Corin held her gaze a moment before he answered. "If gray skies turn to storms, we'll get clear of there. I won't risk you or Ben on this adventure. But if we don't succeed tonight, the princess dies."

She rode in silence for a moment, gripping the wooden windowsill and staring out into the night. Then she pressed her face close to his again and whispered, "This is how you live?"

He grinned. "It's exciting, isn't it?"

"It's terrifying. I can hardly breathe."

He glanced ahead and spotted the bonfire glow of all the torches atop the hill, approaching quickly now. He kissed the druid's cheek and spoke over her gasp.

"Don't slow down. Don't hesitate. If you just keep going fast enough, sometimes you can outrun the fear."

He dropped from his perch, rolled twice across the cobblestones, then bounded up and disappeared among the shadows.

.⚜.

Blake's father's house bespoke the Vestossi reputation—twisting, cold, and sinister even with a party going on out front. Hired guards still kept to their patrols down dark corridors, and every room seemed to have open doors in all directions. Downstairs, anyway, there was no privacy. Every corner could be easily observed.

It mattered little. Nothing of any genuine worth would be trusted to such rooms. There were ancient suits of armor, priceless paintings, even a bronze-work bust that had to be Ben Strunk's own handiwork. But there were no precious treasures here. Still, it took him twenty minutes to confirm that, and then ten more to discover that there were no hidden closets, no stairs down to a cellar. Everything was up.

He hated going up.

The second floor was given over to the servants' quarters. Corin didn't even glance that way. It would never cross a Vestossi's mind to hide anything of worth among the help. That forced him up to the third floor, far from any easy exits and where it would be much harder to justify his presence. He told himself he'd seen worse spots, and he pressed on.

There were guards here too, of course—two men in rotation, their lanterns bobbing down the darkened corridor like will-o'-the-wisps. Corin watched them from the shadows of the stairwell, mesmerized, until one passed close enough for Corin to catch the stench of him. He exhaled through his nose, then glided like a whisper forward to fall in step behind the man, two paces back. He followed the guard right down the corridor, observing each of the rooms by the guard's lantern light as he went by.

There was a library, its shelves packed with a thousand books no one would ever read. There was a sitting room. The master's bedroom. The linen closet, locked. Another room, and he guessed this one to be Blake's. A sitting room. An office.

He'd nearly passed the office by when he saw the battered cutlass in its sheath, mounted above the fireplace. It was no antique relic, no bejeweled trinket, just a hard-worn weapon recently retired. Its edge might still be stained with some of Corin's blood.

Only Blake would consider such a thing a trophy. It was a memory of an adventure. Corin licked his lips as the guard advanced to the end of the hall, timed his steps so they would not be heard, and slipped into the spacious office.

Coals glowed in the fireplace, but there was no other light within the room. Corin knew how to search a room in darkness, but it could well take hours, and he'd hoped to do it more quickly. The guards would notice if he lit a candle or a lamp, but he soon saw a risk worth taking. He stole across to the outer wall and drew aside a curtain on the window there.

The window ledge was wide and empty, no glass separating the room from the three-story drop outside. But there was light enough, by moon and stars, to aid Corin in his quest. He saw papers, loose on the writing desk, a leather envelope, a locking drawer. But then he spotted the battered footlocker tucked into a corner, and he dismissed the rest.

It was all of iron, and Corin felt a sudden grim recognition. Three exquisite locks stood side by side in its top. It was the same model Dave Taker had used to firebomb the smuggler's ship with Auric trapped below.

Corin cursed. He couldn't break those locks. Not in any useful time. Not with Blake downstairs and guards out in the hall. But in his heart he knew—he *knew*—this would be the chest that Blake trusted to preserve Sera's letter. Corin knelt over it, running his fingers over the locks, but it was no use. He'd tried when it was Auric's life in the balance, and nothing he had learned since then would aid him here.

While he was kneeling there, a new light, warm and golden, washed across the surface of the chest. Too late he spun around, raised a hand to shade his eyes, and stared past a glowing candle at Aemilia. Corin heaved a grateful sigh. "Praise Fortune," he whispered, "it's only you."

She came forward, lowering the candle and shaking her head. "It's so unsettling the way you do that."

"Do what?"

"See through my glamours. My heart stops every time."

"You near enough stopped mine. What are you doing here?"

"Ben sent me. He charmed a serving girl into sharing her secrets. Somehow. I didn't ask."

"Smart of you."

She gaped. "Truly? We've only been here half an hour."

"He *is* an artist."

She puffed out a breath and shook her head. "She told him Blake keeps a study up here."

"And you thought it would be wise to just come traipsing up? How'd you avoid the guards?"

"I didn't." She did a little twirl. "I traded my glamour for the serving girl's. She does the grates."

"The grates?" Corin said, his gaze flashing to the smoldering coals in the fireplace. A grin tugged at his lips. "I will call you my muse, Aemelia."

"You're the artist now?"

"I dare to say it. Aye. But I'm afraid I'll need a little help."

"With what?"

He nodded to the iron lockbox. This one stuffed with letters was not as heavy as the one Dave Taker had loaded up with dwarven powder, but still it took them both to lift it. They lumbered four hard paces, then set it down among the burning coals. Corin flapped his cloak above them to stir a little life, and all the while he grinned.

Only then did Aemilia ask questions. Breathing hard, she nodded to the chest. "Does that contain—"

"The letter," Corin said. "I'd bet my life on it."

"Then we are done here! We can go."

Corin shook his head. "I'd bet my life, perhaps, but not Sera's. We've gotten lucky so far. There's time enough for me to look around a little more." He frowned. "But you and Ben have done all I asked of you. Go find him. Wait for me at the shady tavern."

She licked her lips and stood her ground. "I won't leave you here."

He sighed. "These are dangerous waters. It's no place for inexperienced hands. Trust me."

"I do," she said. "But I also made a promise. My fate is tied to yours."

"We don't have *time* for this!" he snapped. "Just go."

"And you'll ... you'll be safe?"

Corin nodded. "I always do pull through somehow. Find Ben for me, and get him out of here."

She squeezed his hand, then turned and started for the door. She'd made it halfway there when another inspiration struck Corin. He leaped forward and caught her elbow. "Better yet! Be the princess now. Change your glamour, *then* go downstairs. Let the guards see you sneaking around up here. That will put the fear in him. But do *not* let them detain you."

"Will they?"

"They shouldn't. They should go report what they've seen to Blake. But if they try . . . you have the dartguns?"

She nodded. "Aye."

He grinned at her. "Use them well."

She closed her eyes. He watched her. Her forehead crinkled as she concentrated. Her lips moved soundlessly. Then her eyes opened, and she looked down at her ordinary clothes. "Such a lovely dress," she whispered.

"We'll make Sera buy you one of your own, once this is done. You've earned it." He caught her hand and squeezed it, reassuring, then escorted her to the door. "Remember. Make a show. Be seen, but once they spot you, get away. I'll handle all the rest."

She hesitated at the doorway, still gripping Corin's hand. She bit her bottom lip, a touch of mischief in her eyes. "Have we really done it? Have we really brought down a Vestossi lord."

"I think we have," Corin answered, full of optimism. And then his gaze slipped past the druid to the distant lantern bobbing down the hall. The silhouette behind the flare of light was not a hired guard. It was much too familiar.

"Gods' blood, I spoke too soon. He's here. He's right behind you."

(**30**)

Aemilia spun around, drawing the guns as she went. "Should I shoot him?"

Corin clapped one hand over her mouth and the other around her waist and dragged her back into the room. "No!" he hissed in her ear as he released her. "He hasn't seen us yet. And I have a plan."

"You have a plan? For this? Already?"

"I'm ... making one. Just trust me."

"What do I do?"

"Get out the window."

"What? It's a thirty-foot fall!'

"Well, don't fall. You don't have to hold yourself. Just get behind the curtain. Get invisible." He darted back, but he didn't have to glance down the corridor to see how close the light had come. "Just go! And make no sound!"

She'd already climbed onto the window ledge, and Corin felt a flash of fear when he saw her there. It was a narrow ledge and such a long fall. He stepped close to her and tipped his forehead against hers. "It's almost over. I swear it."

"I trust you."

He breathed out heavily. Then he stepped back and let the curtain fall to hide her.

He caught his breath.

When he turned, Ethan Blake was standing in the doorway. He had the lantern in one hand and a bare rapier in the other.

"I thought you preferred a cutlass," Corin said.

"Oh, the times have changed. Haven't you heard? I am a gentleman now."

"Someone said as much, and I called him a liar."

"Funny," Blake said, coming into the room. "Someone told me you were come back from the dead, and I was smart enough to believe him."

"Not smart enough to act on it, though. You should have run away."

"Run away? From a pirate without a ship? Without a crew? What's there to fear?"

"I have a princess."

Blake chuckled. "That's an empty threat. I have a—" His eyes cut to the corner where the lockbox had been, and his throat closed up. His face went pale.

Corin gestured to the fireplace. "You have char paper and tinder, if you're lucky."

Blake dashed toward the fire, but before he'd made it halfway Corin had his sword in his hand. He lashed it out, within an inch of Blake's face, before the other man pulled up.

"Be careful of your choices, Corin Hugh. We're not pirates on the lawless seas anymore. You know that, right? I am a Vestossi lord."

"You're bilgewater."

"It doesn't matter what you think of me. It's who I am. Do you think a man can just cut down a Vestossi and walk away?

Any man? You'd have a nation hunting you. Ephitel himself might come for you."

"Not over you. They wouldn't waste the effort."

Blake flashed a smile, but the rage behind his eyes was barely contained. "You don't understand. It's a matter of precedent. No one wants the common folk to think there's *any* sufficient reason to spill Vestossi blood. It's a matter of principle."

"I'm not concerned with their opinions," Corin said. "I've come to make you pay for all your crimes."

"That's a righteous sentiment coming from a thieving pirate."

"There are rules, Blake. There are limits, and you have crossed them all."

"And what is it I've done to so offend you? Mutiny? But what's a man without ambition? You'd have done the same."

"You left me to die."

"But look at you! Storming seas, you look better than ever."

"You burned Jezeeli. Do you have any idea what was written in those books?"

"I had no choice. It was the only way to—"

"That's not the worst you've done. By far. You killed a good man, Blake."

He frowned, thinking. "I'll need more than that. I kill a lot of good men. Did you hear about the justicar?"

Corin showed his teeth. "I mean Auric."

"What, the farmboy? Of all the claims you have against me, you would bring up some nameless Raentzman?"

"You might at least show some remorse."

"I wouldn't even know how to fake it, I'm afraid. One of the great joys of coming home is I don't have to try. It's good to be Vestossi."

Corin turned his sword so that the firelight danced along its edge. "You don't seem to recognize the intention I have for this sharp blade."

Blake shook his head. "I'm not afraid. I know you, Corin Hugh. It's not ambition that drives you, though all the gods know you have ambition. No, it's freedom. You long to have the freedom to do anything your heart desires."

"Right now, my heart only desires one thing, Blake."

"That doesn't worry me. Desires change just like the tide. Just like the summer winds. One moment you're rushing up the shore, straining hard against your boundaries, and then things change. That's the key. When things change, perhaps you'll be prepared to run the other way."

"Nothing changes. You know what I've come for."

"I do. You've come for satisfaction. You resent some of the things I've done, and you suspect a little bloodletting will make things right. It won't. It never really does. But I believe I can appease you through other means. You see ... I've recently lost my first lieutenant."

"Dave Taker? Aye. He's dead."

Blake frowned. "Not quite. Not yet. But when my men track him down—"

"Unless they're looking in the bottom of the sea, they're not going to find him. That wasn't Taker in the bathhouse."

Blake showed a more genuine grin this time. "You see? You prove my very point. You are resourceful, and I am in need of a man of resources."

"I'm not interested in working for you."

"Not for me. For all Ithale! The fleet needs a new admiral. That's more than freedom—that's command!"

"I've had command."

"Of a petty pirate ship. I'm offering you an armada."

Corin snarled. "I don't want it, Blake."

"You may not like the alternative."

"I know *you* won't."

Blake barked a bitter laugh and shook his head. "You don't get to kill me, Corin. That's the part you're missing. What you came here for ... that's not an option. I have already explained. I'm not some mutinous scalawag now; I am a Vestossi lord. I have but to raise my voice and two dozen of my guards will fall upon you."

"And yet you ramble on."

"Because I don't want you dead. I've already tried that route, and it proved unprofitable. You have potential."

"Auric had potential."

"The farmboy again? Storming seas, why are you so obsessed with him?"

"Why did you have him killed?"

"Because it pleased my sensibilities. Because I could. As I told you, I am a Vestossi lord. If you're looking for a better reason, you won't find it."

"He might have changed the world. Were you afraid of him? Or did you do it to hurt Sera?"

"Afraid? Of a common Raentzman? No. I detested him. If you must know the truth, I loathed the very thought of his filthy common blood mingling with my family's purity."

"And what of your family? Now you've abducted Sera, and you mean to kill her come morning."

Blake raised his eyebrows in surprise. "Forget about the admiralty; I'll make you master of my spies."

"Why?" Corin snapped. "Why would you go after Sera?"

Blake shook his head, baffled. "She is in line to be the queen of all Ithale. And she meant to marry that farmer."

"He went to the Wildlands to earn himself a name."

"A name cannot be earned! A common man cannot become noble."

Corin scoffed. "You can't believe that. There's nothing noble in your house. But Auric was a good man."

"He's better dead and so is she! All Ithale will be better off for it."

"Those are treacherous words, Blake. You should be ashamed."

"Ashamed? I speak them proudly! They're the decisions of a statesman."

"You're proud of all your sins. You're proud you played the pirate Ethan Blake."

"I was a better pirate pretending than you ever were while giving it your all."

"You're proud you conspired against Princess Sera?"

"Who does not conspire against her?'

"You're proud you murdered a justicar aboard the *Diavahl*?"

"A master stroke. It was perhaps my finest hour."

"And you killed Ezio in his loyal service to you, just to tie up your loose ends."

"It is the way of kings. At the rate I'm going—"

"You aspire so high?"

"I do. And that aspiration could benefit from a clever right-hand man. If you want the part."

"I'd rather nail you to the wall," Corin said. "But I will not. I will refrain."

"Oh?"

"Indeed."

"But you won't take me on my offer?"

Corin shook his head. "No chance."

"Then you leave me no other choice—"

"But to call the guards?"

He shrugged, disappointed. "It seems such a common end for such a storied rogue."

"And one I think you would regret."

"Only a little."

"You misunderstand me," Corin said. "You would not regret what they did to me, but what they did to you."

"Me? How?"

"Because I am not alone."

Blake blinked at him, and Corin let his grin escape. "It's true." He sheathed his sword. "While you stood here prattling on about all the wretched things you've done,"—Corin went to the window and caught the heavy curtains in one hand—"confessing *proudly* heinous acts unfitting of a noble lord, you didn't know you were in the presence of a most charming eavesdropper."

He ripped the curtain aside to reveal Aemilia, seated on the window ledge. Her eyes shot wide, her hands went white-knuckled where she gripped the windowsill, but Blake could not have seen that from across the room. Corin stepped aside and revealed her with a flourish.

"Don Giuliano de Vestossi, may I introduce Her Royal Highness, Sera de Vestossi. I am afraid she is no longer in your gentle custody. And she *may* have heard your every word."

(31)

"D-P-Princess Sera," Blake sputtered.

For a moment, Corin's heart hung in his throat. He wasn't sure the druid would be up to the task. But then Aemilia uncurled herself from her place on the window ledge. She came forward with all the haughty grandeur of a queen, raised one eyebrow at Blake, and spoke with icy disdain. "Giuliano."

"Y-y-you heard—"

"Everything."

His gaze went reflexively to the lockbox once again, and Aemilia gave him a theatric sigh. "I understand you lost some important papers there. Such a shame."

"Y-you don't understand. I never meant any harm."

"You conspired to kill the man I love."

"Ah . . . yes . . . but it was . . . politics. I'm not the only one. . . ."

"You may discover that you are. I suspect the others will be rethinking their positions soon."

"But you ha-have always—"

"I have been understanding. But no one else has left my lover to his death. And none has *dared* to act against me directly."

"I-I-I beg your mercy!" He flung himself on the floor, groveling, and inched toward her, clutching at her hem. "Please, Princess. Forgive me! I thought it was for the best."

"You dare—" she began, all puffed up with rage, but Corin stopped her with a hand on her arm. Out of Blake's sight, he made a calming gesture.

Aemilia looked at him a moment, trying to comprehend his intention, and then she shrugged and prodded Blake's head with the tip of her shoe. "You waste your time treating with me. My heart is hard against you, but perhaps if you can win some mercy from this noble vagabond ..."

Blake sank back on his heels. He stared up at her, baffled, then transferred the same look to Corin. "You can't be serious. Him?"

"He has served me well this day."

Blake heaved a huge sigh. "He has at that." He climbed to his feet and turned to Corin. "Very well," he said, with no real hope in his voice. "I beg my mercy of *you*."

"It's granted," Corin said. "Princess, show him mercy."

Blake's head snapped up, and his eyes narrowed. "What? Why would you ... what?"

Corin met his eyes. "Not for you. Nothing for you. I do it for the sake of your good lady."

"My lady? You can't mean Iryana?"

"Aye. I shared a glass of wine with her this evening. She seemed most distracted by the party. Perhaps that's why she forgot to mention it to you."

Blake snarled something vile against her, but Corin knocked the words from his mouth with a vicious backhand. "Watch your tongue. She is a Vestossi lady, after all."

"She is desert trash."

"I would not discount her so quickly. I think you'll find her skills most useful when you are a country farmer."

Blake spat. "I'll die before I tend a farm."

"Those are indeed your options."

The lordling narrowed his eyes, but he gave no reply.

Corin nodded. "Ah, you're learning. Yes. These are the terms I'd recommend to Princess Sera. Don Giuliano de Vestossi is no more. You'd meant to make her disappear, so I find it fitting to make you do the same. If you leave Ithale forever and renounce your family name throughout Hurope—you'll take no money, take no power, take nothing but your clothes and your dear Iryana if she wants to go—if you will do these things, the princess will not testify against you."

"I might prefer my chance at trial."

Corin chuckled. "There's no trial. Think of the precedent. No one wants the commoners believing Vestossis can be brought to trial. No. The princess will have supper with the king and relate the history of tonight's events—gods' blood, Blake, she doesn't even need to embellish them—and when that dinner's over, you'll be disappeared."

"My father—"

"Will disown you in an instant when the princess testifies concerning the things you've done."

"Were *proud* to have done," Aemilia corrected.

"Ah, indeed," Corin said. "Such a shame that she was here to hear all that."

"I won't go down like this!" Blake snarled.

"You will," Corin said. "You killed a good man because he was a commoner, and tonight you tried to rob a princess of her family and her life. The only justice I can find within the world is for you to replace them."

"I will not live like that!"

"Then you will die like that," Corin said. "That's my promise to you. The princess ... she only threatens to testify. But I am not so subtle. If I find you have betrayed the terms of this agreement—ever, anywhere—then I will hunt you down and kill you."

"You wouldn't."

"I would. I should really do it now, but the princess has inspired in me a new faith in humanity. I'll give you a chance. One chance. Don't test me."

Blake hung his head in mock repentance, though Corin didn't buy it for a moment. "I thank you, then, for this small mercy. I do accept your terms. And cousin ..." He turned to Aemilia. She straightened her spine and stared down her nose at him, playing her part beautifully. Corin had to admire it.

But that distracted him a heartbeat too long. Blake moved like a serpent, darting forward, and in the blink of an eye he held a dagger in one hand and Aemilia's slender throat in the other. Corin drew as well, *Godslayer* in his hand like lightning, but Blake pulled Aemilia tight against him, shielding his body with hers, and backed slowly toward the other wall.

"I'll kill her, Corin. I'll kill her and then blame you. Who would doubt my word? Oh, it's almost perfect that you brought her here!" A madness flashed in Blake's eyes, and Corin saw his knuckles go white around the dagger's hilt. Blake meant to kill her, here and now. He was already past considering it and ready to commit the act.

Then time froze around him. It was not the strange gray mist of Oberon's magic, but that simple, sharp clarity that sometimes arrives like inspiration. He met the druid's eyes and showed her a little smile for courage and shouted, "Dart him and duck away."

Blake heard the words, but he couldn't comprehend. Aemilia did. She didn't hesitate. She pressed the muzzles of both dartguns against his abdomen behind her, and pulled the triggers. His eyes went wide. He convulsed, though it might as likely have been from surprise at the tiny stab of the darts as from any action of the druids' poison.

It didn't matter. It bought her time enough to wrench away from him, and even as she fell, Corin lunged. The legendary sword pierced Ethan Blake between the ribs. He stood a moment, stunned, then toppled slowly back.

And out the open window.

He landed with a crunch.

A moment later, Aemilia joined Corin at the window. For a while, they both stared down in silence. It was Aemilia who broke it.

"You killed him," she said, stunned.

"I'd do it again."

She turned to Corin, eyes wide. "What will we do?"

Before Corin could answer her, a startled gasp from by the doorway caught his attention. He spun around, sword lashing out, but he stopped it short when he recognized the new arrival.

Iryana. She stood there in her ball gown, draped in gold, lovely as a sunset. "Corin," she said, strangely calm. "I see you found your princess."

Corin had to bite back a curse. For a moment he wished the druid had thought to drop her glamour. Or better, to resume the appearance of the serving girl. Instead, her disguise only placed the princess in greater danger.

Iryana could not have mistaken what had happened here. It was Blake's own office, and Corin's blade still dripped with the man's blood. But Iryana contained whatever grief she felt at Blake's demise. She stood tall, shoulders straight, eyes hard.

"I did not believe you'd succeed here, Corin."

"Aye."

"You are … something more than a man." She shook her head. "You are something … extraordinary."

He grinned. "You're not the first to say that."

She came a step closer, no seduction in her expression, but a simple plea. "I find myself again in need of a protector." She cast a glance toward the princess and instantly dismissed her. "And you will need some aid to escape this situation. Perhaps … perhaps *we* might …"

He shook his head. "Alas. I have been made a better offer. But you can tell them it was me who killed him."

Her jaw dropped. "They'll come after you with everything they have."

Corin shrugged. "I'm looking forward to the reputation. But … if you don't want them suspecting you, you should probably start screaming now."

She was never short on wits. He had to give her that. She raised a fearsome cry, and in a moment there were guards outside the door. Corin heard more coming from far off, stomping up the stairs or shouting out on the wide, lovely lawn. Those who had patrolled the halls up here were already crowding into the room, already lowering their crossbows.

Corin spun, cloak flaring, and caught Aemilia in his arms. Then he closed his eyes and stepped through dream, and they were gone.

(32)

They appeared together in Corin's rooms at the tavern. Corin opened his eyes, and his gaze went to the window. It was night outside, but which night?

Corin's heart still hammered in his chest. Blake was dead. Corin had seen the man dead on his father's lawn. He'd expected the sight to bring relief, but his jaw still clenched tight. His breath felt too thin. Too short.

"I won," Corin said, his voice weak. "Didn't I?"

Aemilia still clutched him, eyes squeezed shut, but when he spoke, she finally looked. Then she gasped and pulled away. "Corin Hugh! You can't just tear a path through causality like that!"

Her misplaced outrage pushed his fear aside for a moment. He smiled at her. "I saved our lives. You realize that, don't you?"

"Well ... yes ..." she said, flustered for a moment, but then she shook her head. "You still should show some care."

She dug some strange druid device from an inner pocket—something like a silvered hand-mirror, but foreign glyphs danced across its surface, ever changing. She stared for a moment, tapped the device's face with one finger, and then stared some more. At last, she shook her head. "The damage seems fairly benign.

Something like ninety minutes at the epicenter with a falloff of six to eight minutes per mile."

Most of it sounded like gibberish to Corin, but one phrase stuck out at him. "Per mile? From Blake's house? That would cover most of the city."

She nodded a little fiercely. "I've been trying to tell you: this thing you do is dangerous."

"I know it cost *me* time. But ... what really happened?"

"Time skipped. Just as it does for you."

He rushed to the window again, staring out. He listened for a moment, then shook his head. "I'd expect an uproar. Riots in the streets. A whole city full of people just lost an hour of their lives—" He cut off short when he saw Aemilia shaking her head.

"It's not like that. Not for them. They didn't step through dream. The dream rolled right on for them, filling in the gaps. Most of them will feel like they've been operating on autopilot, like they've been walking in a daze. Their memories of the affected time period will be hazy, especially their specific decisions, but they'll put it all down to distraction, forgetfulness."

He sank down on the edge of the bed. "Gods' blood. What have I been doing?"

She came to him, settling beside him. Her voice was gentle. "This is what I've been trying to tell you. You've been meddling in people's lives. Tonight ... it's not so bad. Half an hour here or there, especially when it's late enough that most decent folk are sleeping. They'll never know."

He sighed. "I've been reckless with a lot of lives, Aemilia."

"You have. And you've been lucky. You left a righteous mess behind you in Khera."

He groaned and fell backward on the bed.

She laughed. "I'm pleased to see you're taking this seriously at last, but it's not so bad as that. The dream has fixed everything you've broken so far. If you will just restrain yourself in future—"

He shook his head. Bile burned in his gut as he remembered the fear he'd pressed aside before. "I've done worse than stretching time."

She did not deny it. She swallowed hard, and still a stammer touched her voice. "O-only what you had to do."

"I don't mean Blake. That man deserved to die. I mean the innocent people I roped into my schemes. Ben Strunk—"

"Ben Strunk is fine! He's probably still drinking and seducing serving girls."

She was probably right, but Ben was not the one who would hurt the worst. Corin continued as though she hadn't interrupted. "Princess Sera too."

"You did destroy the letter."

"I did, but she might still be in the grasp of Blake's people. Will they wait for his order or kill her at dawn? How will they react when they hear she is dead?"

"Don't you trust the Nimble Fingers? They were going after her."

Corin sighed. "Even if they rescued her, Iryana and a dozen guards think they saw her at the scene of Blake's execution. They saw her leave with me."

He heaved himself up so he could meet her eyes. "And Princess Sera isn't the last. There's also you."

She shook her head, trying to dismiss his concern, but she put no words to it. He bit his lip and tried to slow the hammering of his heart. What would he do if some harm came to her over this? To either of the women? How could he possibly protect them? Worry clawed at the back of his breastbone, and he heaved a weary sigh. "What will I do?"

Aemilia took his hand in hers. "You've done so well so far. You'll think of something."

"No. This ... this is beyond me. I don't believe I've ever used an innocent person in my schemes before. If she pays for my sins ..." He squeezed the druid's hand, feeling wretched. "If you do ..."

"Would you have done anything different?" she asked. "You went after Blake to *protect* the innocent people he could have hurt. Surely you—"

She cut off short as the door burst open. In the blink of an eye, Corin leaped to his feet and drew the sword, *Godslayer*, blade flashing out to stop this new intruder.

But the sword's tip flew two hands too high. The intruder was a dwarf.

Ben Strunk blinked in surprise. He held a fat, unstoppered wine bottle in one hand and led a pretty young serving maid in Vestossi colors by the other. He hesitated a moment, swaying slightly, then lifted the bottle and used it to push Corin's blade aside. He licked his lips, thinking, and a long moment passed in total silence. The serving girl just stared with eyes wide.

Then Ben Strunk's face lit up. He threw his arms wide. "Corin! I knew that you were still alive! I had this *feeling*, see, and thought, 'We ought to check on Corin's rooms.' And *that's* why ... that's the only reason we're ..." He trailed off in the face of Corin's smirk.

Corin nodded to the serving girl. "I can guess what you were feeling, Ben."

"Ah, well ..."

"Forget it," Corin said, sheathing his sword. "In truth, I'm glad to see you escaped the Vestossis' grasp. It does somewhat complicate things that you brought one of their attendants to my hiding place."

"She'll never tell," Ben said, tossing the girl an adoring smile. "She's seen their villainy. All her sympathies are with the princess."

Corin quirked an eyebrow. "Are they?"

"Oh, aye! Once I told her how poor Sera had been misused, and all the secret, heroic things I've done … well, her heart was won."

Corin felt a flash of irritation at the dwarf, but it came closely paired with amusement. He hid it all in a polite bow of his head toward the girl. "Your loyalty does you great honor. Will you serve your queen now? I have a favor to ask on her behalf."

The girl's eyes shot wider still, and she bobbed a frantic nod. "Oh, certainly, Lord Hugh! However I can help."

Lord Hugh. Corin bit his tongue for a moment, before he could trust himself to speak. Then he tried for an air of authority. "Slip downstairs and search out the inn's proprietor. Tell him I have need of him and then return here straightaway. Do you understand?"

She nodded once.

"Good. Then go."

She slipped off down the hall, and Ben watched her leave with a wistful look in his eyes. "Such a brave lass …"

Corin shook his head. "You're three times a fool, Ben Strunk. But I spoke true before. It does my heart good to see you alive and well. Thank you for your aid tonight."

Ben grinned. "I've found reward enough—and scant risk, really. They never suspected *me*. I'm just some drunken dwarf. But you? They want you with a passion, Corin."

Corin licked his lips, trying hard not to look at Aemilia. "*Just me?*"

"Hah! Not a chance." The dwarf's expression turned grim. "They want the princess too. Your druid played her part; no one doubts that it was Sera in the room."

Corin cursed, though he felt a guilty spark of relief too. At least Aemilia was safe. But Sera ... He'd used her well, and now she'd pay the price unless he found some way out. It had seemed so easy back in Blake's study, when he'd wrapped one arm around Aemilia and escaped through the dream, but now ...

He hesitated, the memory strong in his mind. With all the Vestossis' guards crowding into the room, Corin had grabbed the princess and disappeared. He considered how that must have looked to all the witnesses, and some of the tension left his shoulders. He grinned. "I have a plan."

Ben's eyebrows lifted. "Oh? It had better be a good one."

"It depends entirely on your wit and charm, my friend."

Ben barked a laugh. "Then it's a sure thing. Speak! What's on your mind?"

"A rumor," Corin said. "They saw the princess in the room, but she made no admissions. She had no blood on her hands. What else did they see? A pirate, a wanted man, who grabbed the princess and whisked her away."

"Aye. Some say you are a wizard now. Wiser heads suspect you must have stolen some major artifact—"

"That's good," Corin said. "Do what you can to strengthen that belief. But I'm more concerned with Sera. What reason do they have to think she was at fault? We must convince them she was a bystander. I stole her as a hostage."

Ben whistled softly. "You'll have to send them some demands, pretend to negotiate a bit."

"That's not so hard. And it will throw them off my trail, confuse them while I put my true plans in motion."

"Clever. Clever. If you can spin it out a week or two, keep the princess hidden, then give her back—"

Corin clapped his hands together at a flash of inspiration. "No! I'll drop some hint, pretend to make a slip, and let *them* discover where I've hidden her. It'll look like I just barely escaped, and they can throw themselves a feast to celebrate their victory."

Ben chuckled. "You're a conniving devil, Corin Hugh. Shift their focus to the girl—to *rescuing* the girl—and in one move you'll clear her name *and* make them forget your greater crime."

"Perhaps," Corin said, but already his elation began to fade. "There is one problem."

"Just one?" Aemilia asked, incredulous.

Corin shrugged. "One at a time, then. The first is quite a large one. I don't *have* the princess. Last I heard, the best of the Nimble Fingers were setting out to rescue her, but—"

Ben cut him off with a wave. "That one's not so hard at all. They found her, Corin. Thanks to you. And where do you think they brought her?"

Corin licked his lips. Ben's grin suggested she was here, but he couldn't make himself believe it. He offered the more likely answer. "To the palace?"

"What? With family still set against her? She knew about Blake's plan, about the letter. Old della Porta wanted to hide her somewhere *safe* until he could discover all the details."

"Here?" Corin asked, his heart beating faster. "She's here at the tavern?"

"Just down the hall."

"Then get her! Bring her to me. We'll need her aid to pull it off. Fortune favor, we might just get away with this."

Ben nodded, beaming, then slipped off down the corridor, opposite the way the serving girl had gone. Corin watched a moment, biting his lip, and then at last he turned back to Aemilia. His heart felt almost light, but a cloud of worry still darkened her eyes.

He went to her. "We'll go away. We'll take Sera and hide among the druids. We're going to escape. We've done it."

But Aemilia shook her head. "It's not that simple. You killed a Vestossi."

Corin sighed. "I know, I know. A thousand men have warned me already, and Blake among them. The Vestossis won't let this go unpunished. But *that* is where I can succeed. Trust in me. I've spent my whole life staying out of their grip."

She stared into his eyes a moment. Then she sighed. "If only that were all you had to fear."

He blinked. "What else is there?"

"Ephitel."

The name alone brought all his fear crashing back. It wrapped around his gut like a fist and squeezed. Corin swallowed hard and only managed to answer, "Oh."

She nodded. "Your ruse with the princess might distract her family, but Ephitel will not forget you've wronged him. You slaughtered one of his protected and defied his power."

Corin summoned up his courage. When he found it lacking, he summoned up some false bravado to fill the gaps. "I've not forgotten Ephitel. He's the next one on my list."

She clenched her jaw. "This is no joke. It's not some grand adventure. You murdered a Vestossi in his house!"

"I call it a good start."

"You'll have the gods set against you, Corin. Not just the Vestossis. Not just Ephitel. All the gods and all their armies. What will you do? What will *we* do?"

He held her gaze a moment, then quirked one eyebrow. "You made me a promise once before. You said you'd go wherever I had to go. Whatever I endured, you'd be there with me."

"I remember."

He licked his lips. "I'll release you from that promise if you ask it of me."

"I wouldn't let you."

He found his courage, then. It was hiding somewhere deep in her dark eyes, but as he stared into them, he knew what must be done. He showed her a grin. "Then we'll do what the princess and the farmboy wanted to. We'll run away. We'll find someplace our own, where the Vestossis cannot reach us. And then we'll do what they never could have done."

"We will?"

"Aye. We'll change the world."

"But how?"

"We know the villains' deepest secrets. We wield the power of King Oberon. We have connections to the Council of Druids, to the Nimble Fingers, to a crew or two of pirates I would trust."

"A lot of scofflaws and skulkers."

"A lot of men well trained in defying the Godlanders' power structures. Do you think we can find some elves?"

She gasped. "You mean it?"

"Aye. If there are any left who'd fight for the memory of Oberon ..."

"There must be at least a few."

He waved a hand. "You see? We have an army in the making."

"That's it? We go to war? An open war against the gods?"

Corin turned to stare out the window, toward the manor where he'd left Blake's corpse on the lawn. "We'll call this our declaration. Or is it too subtle?"

A little laugh escaped her. "No. No, I think it's good enough."

"Then let them come. We'll slay the tyrant gods and save the world." He licked his lips, and despite himself, he grinned. "It is begun."

About the Author

Aaron Pogue is a husband and a father of two who lives in Oklahoma City, Oklahoma. He started writing at the age of ten, and has written novels, short stories, scripts, and videogame storylines. His first novels were high fantasy set in the rich world of the FirstKing, including the bestselling fantasy novel *Taming Fire*, but he has explored mainstream thrillers, urban fantasy, and several kinds of science fiction, including a long-running sci-fi cop drama series focused on the Ghost Targets task force.

Aaron has been a Technical Writer with the Federal Aviation Administration and a writing professor at the university level. He holds a Master of Professional Writing degree from the University of Oklahoma. He also serves as the user experience consultant for Draft2Digital.com, a digital publishing service.

Aaron maintains a personal website for his friends and fans at AaronPogue.com, and he runs a writing advice blog at UnstressedSyllables.com.